DOUBLE DOWN

By the Author

Strictly Need to Know

Running Off Radar

Double Down

Visit us at www.boldstrokesbooks.com

DOUBLE DOWN

by

MB Austin

2019

DOUBLE DOWN

ISBN 13: 978-1-63555-423-6

THIS TRADE PAPERBACK ORIGINAL IS PUBLISHED BY
BOLD STROKES BOOKS, INC.
P.O. BOX 249
VALLEY FALLS, NY 12185

FIRST EDITION: AUGUST 2019

CREDITS
EDITOR: RUTH STERNGLANTZ
PRODUCTION DESIGN: STACIA SEAMAN
COVER DESIGN BY TAMMY SEIDICK

Acknowledgments

This story turned out to be even harder to write than I expected. For Maji, *Double Down* functions as a prequel, occurring in her lifeline very shortly after a devastating combat-related trauma. When we met her in *Strictly Need to Know*, she had already put significant work into her recovery. That allowed me to leave the hardest parts of that process out. But now I had to tackle that.

Concern for getting the interior world right for Maji, Erlea, and Celeste led me on a deep research dive into trauma recovery and resilience. Are the experiences of soldiers and civilians fundamentally different, or can they understand each other well enough to help one another? Surviving combat is not the same as surviving political violence or intimate partner violence or the loss of a loved one to suicide. Yet the body and mind have common responses, and similar resources and techniques can help survivors move from merely coping with aftereffects to rebuilding a healthy sense of self to fully thriving as they tackle new challenges in life. Three awesome professionals in this arena gave generously of their time and expertise to help me more realistically convey the thoughts and feelings of Erlea, Celeste, and Maji as they supported one another: Julie Graham, Lauren Osinski, and Dr. Shannon M. Baird (Mental Performance Specialist). They deserve credit for any detail that rings true.

Regardless of the challenges in a specific story, writing about badass women in love and danger remains a joy, and I always want the reader to share that. Julie's early feedback and Basha's careful beta-reading helped keep me on track. Ruth's clear, compassionate, and meticulous editing ensured that the final version will please readers who want both an exciting thriller with a satisfying romance. And many thanks as well to the production team at Bold Strokes, whose work on every book makes it as shiny as possible. Finally, to my partner in life and travel, thanks for making every day (at home or in Spain) a great adventure.

For the survivors.
And for those who support them.

CHAPTER ONE

"I am packing right now, as we speak," Erlea assured her manager.

Nigel's constant harping on image wore on her. On tour, jeans and sweatshirts were fine for rehearsals and on the bus. Costuming conveyed her carefully crafted rock star image during performances. Nigel insisted she live up to that image for the occasional party or night of clubbing as well. But a two-month residency show on the Mediterranean island of Majorca would give the media a chance to see her outside those controlled settings. "I can get a swimsuit there, right? And something for the VIP reception?"

"No one is going to see you in a bikini, unless you've made more progress than your trainer tells me," Nigel replied. "And I'll select an appropriate outfit for the reception. For now, just make sure you don't look like a street urchin tomorrow morning. The car will pick you up at seven."

Erlea rolled her eyes at the reference to the fantastical narrative he created for her backstory, the rough-edged waif plucked from the gutter and catapulted from Barcelona's bar scene to fan-packed arenas across Europe and Asia. She let her cat in from the balcony and closed the doors, shutting out the perpetual hum of traffic below. The plaques and instruments adorning the walls of the spacious living room bore testament to both her years of formal training and her grandparents' support. This apartment was hers now, swapped with them for the quiet house they enjoyed in the countryside; but the paparazzi didn't know that. Which made it the perfect haven in the city.

Erlea stared down at the Barcelona street dark with late afternoon drizzle. Why did she have to leave when it was so lovely and quiet, the beaches and markets nearly free of tourists? She could record a few more tracks, maybe even pen another song if she could just relax. No one had warned her how much the stress of having to be likable to the whole fucking world, fans and industry alike, would impede her ability to pull the words and melodies together. Not so long ago, music was her passion. "Seven?"

"Seven sharp. You know how traffic is. Please refrain from staying out late tonight."

"Don't worry, I'll be ready." Nigel's view of her as a party animal fit his narrative, and it was nearly as fantastical as his rags-to-riches story. At least here at home. "It's just, does that make me the last stop? Earlier is fine if it lets the others sleep in."

"I need you rested when we land, looking every inch the rock star. Try as I might to keep your arrival a secret, you know how word leaks out." Nigel paused. "Besides, the others will find their own way to the airport."

Erlea didn't try to keep the bitterness from her voice. "Oh, so it's just me and my minder." The new assistant hired for the residency was a nice enough young woman, but she resented Nigel's thinly veiled attempts to keep tabs on her.

"Ah, the girl. Did I forget to mention? Nico let her go."

"What? When?" Erlea might not want a minder, but her assistant was outside the production director's arena.

"Yesterday. She gave notice by text." Nigel sighed loudly. "Youth. No manners."

"She wouldn't quit on a whim. What the hell did Nico do to drive her off so quickly?" Erlea fumed. "No—never mind. Are we insured for homicide? Because if I don't kill him first, one of the crew is bound to."

Athena wound her lithe, silky frame around Erlea's calves, a welcome distraction. Erlea scooped her up and cradled her in one arm, rubbing a thumb along her chin and cheekbones just the way she liked it. A little massage to the ears and the lanky cat pressed her nose into Erlea's jaw, purring.

"Don't even joke like that," Nigel said. "Once you two get settled at the Gran Balearico and start setting up the show, I'm sure you'll work together like the professionals you both are. Remember, you're the one who asked for an alternative to another tour."

Erlea's shoulders sagged. "I remember." It was a compromise, making audiences travel to her, with the added draw of the resort setting. But even there they would lock her in the hotel to shield her from the paparazzi. At home she knew how to dodge them when she didn't want to be seen. Erlea knew Barcelona intimately, every back street and shop of her favorite neighborhoods. She could sit in a café with friends, anonymously buzz down the streets on her moto, even ride the metro most days. Like a real person. "I'll do my best. But he'd better meet me halfway."

Erlea hung up on Nigel and followed the cat to the open suitcase on the bed. "If I put you down, will you help me pick what to take? Or will you curl up in there again? You know I'd go naked, if I could take you with me instead."

Athena springboarded onto the floor and off to her bowl of crunchies in the kitchen. The telltale tinkle of her tags on the bowl told Erlea she was eating again, feeding another growth spurt. By the time the residency was over, the lanky kitten would be a cat. Would she still want to play, batting at everything and maniacally chasing the red dot? Or follow Erlea from room to room, wanting to be with her while awake and curl up next to her to sleep? "You'll forget me and adopt Jordi and Maria, won't you?"

Well, it would serve her right. Getting a kitten had been selfish. She knew Nigel wanted her on the road again, not in the studio or at home composing. Erlea could get by just fine on song royalties alone, but her career wasn't just about her. The band and crew and all the bit players on the production side needed jobs. Now she was Erlea, Inc., an industry supporting at least a hundred people with homes and families. And if she fell off the public's radar, her next album would tank. Assuming she ever wrote enough decent songs to fill another.

Stop it, already. Erlea paced from the bedroom out to the living room, finding Athena by the balcony door, washing her silver-gray face with one paw. If only cats liked to travel. It would be so comforting to have her there, but caging her wildness in a hotel room would be cruel. Erlea let her out, then watched Athena leap in an agile arc toward the balcony next door. Thank goodness she loved the neighbors, and they her. The cat was like all of Erlea's lovers, providing temporary comfort and then finding better homes than she could offer. With her life on this trajectory it was foolish to wish for more.

"*Bona tarda*, Athena," the neighbor said, scooping her up.

"*Bona*, Maria. I think she's changed alliances already. Are you sure about this?"

Maria beamed at Erlea. "You know we've wanted a cat for years. And she's the perfect cushion for my retirement. Maybe when you get home again we'll get a kitten and they can both go back and forth together."

"Who knows when that will be? I may have to tour after." Erlea cut the complaint off. She chose this life, and she didn't need pity from anyone, even herself. "If she gets hurt, take her to my vet and they will bill me. I can't stop her from climbing up to the roof, so don't feel bad if you can't either."

"I wouldn't try to tame her wild nature," Maria replied with a wink. "She takes after you, no? We will keep her as safe as we can, but love her as she is."

Erlea felt her spirits lift. "Good advice from the happiest married woman I know. You must have trained Jordi well."

Maria set the cat down with a humble shrug. "We have had years to learn how to trust each other." She gave Erlea a look of real concern. "I only wish you had someone on the road with you, Beatriz." Like family, Maria was allowed to use her given name—and to meddle in her love life. "But not that drummer. You don't have to see him again?"

Erlea loved Maria for taking her side without ever asking the details. "No. I hired a new drummer. A gay one this time. I'm swearing off cigarettes and dating the men I work with." Dating was too genteel a word for her last romantic disaster, but she moderated her language around Maria. Some days she envied Jordi his life in the symphony, getting to come home every night to the woman he loved.

"All the bad tour habits, eh?" Maria asked. "What about the parties, the clubs? I know you don't do drugs but…still, I worry for you."

Erlea looked at the tiles beneath her bare feet. She only drank hard when she was miserable, when she had no place to run home to. But would a residency really be better than touring? "I can't make any promises."

Maria reached across the divide for her hand. "Just remember we are here for you, in the same time zone and only a short flight away. You are not alone out there."

"Thank you," Erlea replied, keeping hold of Maria's hand. She leaned over the rail and gave Maria a parting kiss on both cheeks. "I'll do my best."

❖

"Split and double," Maji instructed the dealer in Spanish. Just to be clear, she made the hand gesture, too—without touching the cards in front of her. Touching the cards was forbidden, forgivable only once and only if they really believed you didn't know better. Otherwise the Gran Balearico would ban you from the premises just as surely as any Vegas casino. And while Majorca offered white sand beaches surrounded by the Mediterranean, it did not offer any other places to play blackjack. So Maji couldn't afford to wear out her welcome.

Reimi, looking as attractive as she had every day that week in her dealer's uniform, quirked an eyebrow but made no comment as she reached across the table to separate the aces on the felt in front of Maji. Any experienced dealer could tell who the counters were, and Maji made sure neither Reimi nor the floor manager minded. She tipped well, acted pleasantly surprised by her wins, chatted with the other players, and—most importantly—kept her betting spread modest. Playing the tourist meant fewer euros won per hour but more hands available to reach her goal to afford Dr. Lyttleton's expensive services.

The minute she hit that magic euro mark, she'd be out the door. Well, maybe she'd ask Reimi for a date first. Casinos had a hands-off-the-players rule for dealers, a firing offense. And although she didn't expect Reimi to gamble with her livelihood, Maji wondered what other games she might enjoy. Maji smiled as she pushed her second stack of chips out to double the original bet. "Hit me."

"Stop. You'll regret that, trust me," the player to her right said, speaking in English as if of course it should be the island's lingua franca. The clipped authority in his tone matched his upper-crust British accent and expensive leisure clothes.

Maji spared him a sideways glance. "I only regret having to share the table," she said in Spanish.

"Miss, I implore you." He'd switched to Spanish. "At this game, I am something of an—"

"Interloper," Maji said in English, looking him squarely in the eye. "And too late. The bet is placed. So kindly sod off."

He recoiled. "I beg your pardon. If you want to throw away your chips, be my guest."

Maji turned her attention back to Reimi, who dealt two more cards onto the split aces. A ten on one, a nine on the other. Maji waited to watch the house break, which it certainly would. No magic involved. You simply had to maintain perfect play while watching several other players and keeping the count on what the dealer held in a two-pack shoe.

Magic was starting with a banged-up brain barely able to add two cards for a saintly occupational therapist, with no stressors or distractions, and after only a few months of rehab being able to stay in the zone even with real money at stake and an asshat pestering you. Talking back was a slip, but sleep had been rough again lately. Better watch that.

Reimi congratulated her on the double win and laid a final card on the asshat's hand. Maji felt no sympathy when the ten pushed him over twenty-one and he forfeited the foolishly large bet in front of him. Then Reimi dealt the final card onto the house's hand, breaking at twenty-five. No magic, just simple math that dictated when to risk and when to pull back.

Reimi paid out and began shuffling the two decks of cards, resetting the odds. Maji indulged herself by staring at the Brit, giving him a look that dared him to try mansplaining again. He began to stack his chips, grumbling about needing a fresh start.

A wave of fatigue rolled over Maji, the hours of concentration catching up. "At last we agree on something," she said to him in Spanish. "I'm out."

Maji gathered up her chips and tipped Reimi generously. As she turned to go, a clammy hand on her elbow sent her to high alert. She twisted free and stepped back, glaring at the handsy jerk. "Hands off."

"I do hope I didn't scare you away," he said, apparently oblivious to her climbing adrenaline. "Clearly you know what you're about here. May I buy you a drink?"

Maji forced herself to breathe. Not a threat. Just an idiot. "No. You may leave me alone."

"Of course—I see it now." He looked delighted rather than put off. "Wait until I tell my wife I played at the same table with Erlea. She'll never believe it. Wait—" He reached for a napkin, adding, "Do you have a pen?"

Maji shook her head in confusion and stepped farther away.

"I'm not with the media," the Brit assured her, holding the napkin out like an offering. "Just here for a nicer place to work, like you. Good to get away from the spotlight, eh?" And then he winked.

What the actual fuck? "Whatever you think is going on here," she told him, "you are mistaken."

"Right, of course. You're not officially here yet. And I hate to impose, but my wife is smitten with you," he said, reaching for her. "If you could just…"

Maji didn't wait to hear what nonsense followed. Before his hand could latch on to her arm, she took control of it and twisted. His body responded predictably, turning and yielding to avoid damage. He stumbled toward the nearest table, and Maji's instinct to protect kicked in. With another simple move she redirected him toward the floor boss, whose late arrival to the party spiked her pulse anew.

"Here," she said to the startled floor boss. "You deal with him."

As she strode off, Maji's left hand began to throb. Must have smacked it against a table. *That's what being rusty gets you, Rios. At least you only hurt yourself this time.* She cradled the hand against her center, thinking about where to find ice in a warm-drink town. Any tourist bar by the marina would do.

"Wait," called out a deep voice behind her. A native Spanish speaker, not angry but insistent nonetheless.

Maji tamped down the urge to flee. She could get out to the street easily enough, but then what? She had no plan B if they banned her. *Don't borrow trouble. Just breathe.* She stopped, took a deep breath, and turned back.

A uniformed security guard headed toward her. By habit she sized him up in less than a second, taking in his soft belly, the pristine uniform, the neatly trimmed salt-and-pepper mustache along with erect posture and a slight hitch in his step. *Injured vet.*

With a solicitous smile, he held her chips out. "You dropped your winnings."

When? Without even noticing. *Off your game, Rios.* "Wow. Thanks." She reached out with her good right hand.

The guard's expression shifted to genuine concern. "You are hurt. We must see to that. Please."

❖

Celeste scrolled through the online tabloid articles, reliving the night Adrienne picked a fight with Erlea. The worst of them, salaciously titled "Catfight at the Kitten Club," made it sound as if the rock star and the soccer player tried to claw one another's eyes out in a drunken scuffle. Well, perhaps Erlea was drunk, but Adrienne was merely possessive and cruel, with enough whiskey in her to let her mask slip off in public. Even a year later, Celeste shuddered at the memory. Her scalp tingled where Adrienne had used her hair to jerk her about, hissing in fury about Celeste's behavior. When Adrienne abruptly released her, Celeste fell. By the time she picked herself up off the club floor, bruised and humiliated, Erlea had Adrienne pinned to the ground several feet away. The crowd turned their phone cameras toward the two celebrities, ignoring Celeste.

And now Erlea would arrive here tomorrow, living in the same hotel with her for months. If Celeste ran into her, would the singer even recognize her? And what would Celeste say to her? *Thank you for rescuing me from my hateful girlfriend. Sorry she tried to sue you* sounded terrible. No; she would avoid the star and her crew altogether, unless they called for the house doctor.

A knock at her office door announced someone here, today, in need of her services. A welcome reprieve from dark memories. "Doctor?" a deep voice asked before a second knock. "I have a patient for you."

Ah, Santxo, head of security. A friendly man, willing to be a friend if she let him. "One moment." Celeste blacked out the screen on her computer and put on her professional face before opening the door. "Yes, Mr. Quintana?"

Santxo's broad form in the doorway nearly blocked the guest from view. "I really don't need a medic," the woman said, peeking around him.

"Wonderful," Celeste replied. "A miracle cure."

Moving aside at last, Santxo volunteered, "This lady was accosted by another patron and defended herself ably. You do have an X-ray machine in there, don't you?"

Celeste blocked his effort to step inside. "Thank you, Mr. Quintana. I will interview our guest and determine what she needs." She met the gaze of the woman who quite disconcertingly seemed to have given her a full examination in the few seconds Celeste had stood within her view. "If you wouldn't mind coming in for a moment?"

"Not at all," the woman replied with a smile. "Thank you," she added to a puzzled-looking Santxo as she stepped inside. "I can take it from here."

"Yes, thank you," Celeste reinforced, moving to close the door on him.

He hesitated. "But shouldn't I tell you what happened?"

Celeste looked at her new patient. "Did you strike your head? Are you capable of speaking for yourself?"

"I think I can manage," the woman said, a mischievous smile playing on her lips. She turned to Santxo and addressed him in Spanish. "If you'll take my chips to the cashier, I promise to stay until you return with my winnings."

With relief Celeste closed the door behind the well-meaning head of security. He was nosy by nature, which might have been an asset in his work but sometimes put him at cross-purposes with hers. And this time he seemed particularly interested in the guest, who looked familiar somehow. Intriguing.

"You must be someone famous for our head of security to be so concerned when you seem fine," Celeste said. "If I should recognize you, I apologize. Now, how can I help?"

"No apology needed." The guest lifted her cradled hand a little. "And this barely counts as an injury, Doctor. A little ice for the swelling and I'll be good to go."

"Please, call me Celeste. And you are?"

"Maji," the woman said, not offering a last name. She snugged her left hand back to her belly, protected like her identity.

A pretty name, Middle Eastern sounding. Celeste thought she looked more Spanish, but then she had always been bad at guessing ethnicity. In her sports practice, her clients often played for teams outside their home countries. Without her notes on their biographies, she would be hopeless. "Maji," she repeated. "Ice, of course."

"If it's no bother. I can hit a bar for some, otherwise." Maji seemed restless. "I should get out of your hair." Then she laughed when Celeste self-consciously brushed the pesky new bangs from her eyes. "Your hair's fine. I just don't want to keep you from any real patients."

Celeste laughed. "No need. You are the most real of my day. In fact, it would be a great favor if I could please examine your injury."

"Well, when you put it that way, how can I refuse?" Maji hopped up onto the exam table and pushed her left arm forward, supported by the right.

Rotating the hand gently, Celeste noted that Maji's pinkie was swelling, with a redness that would become a nasty bruise. She palpated, listening and watching for any sign of discomfort. None. This woman either had a high pain threshold or was trained to not betray an injury. Testing that theory, Celeste wiggled the finger. Not a twitch. "Does this not pain you?"

"A little. Maybe some tape after the ice."

Celeste gave her a hard look, but Maji did not flinch at that either. "I see. And in what sport do you compete?"

"I don't do competition." A smile, finally—somewhat sheepish. "Martial arts. And yes, we self-diagnose and self-treat. Bad habits."

For that smile, Celeste thought she might forgive a number of peccadillos. "And how did you sustain this mortal wound?"

The smile vanished. "An annoying guy interrupted my winning streak. I should have let it go. But then when I tried to leave, he grabbed for me, and...I overreacted."

"Well, no one has a right to touch you if you don't want them to," Celeste insisted, then worried how that might sound. "What I mean is—"

"No, you're right, of course. And if he'd been a real threat... whatever." Maji sighed and frowned. "But I need to do better. Plus, the casino could ban me."

A client more concerned with the impact of events on her future performance than with the injury itself: familiar ground. Celeste smiled at her. "I'll tell you what. While you ice, I shall investigate. If you are in any danger of a reprimand, I will warn you so that you may prepare your defense."

"I don't have a defense. I'm a black belt."

That reminded Celeste of Adrienne's lawsuit. Her ex had tried to use Erlea's martial arts background against her. "No need to worry. Santxo seems concerned for you, not about you."

"I hope you're right. If the casino wants to ban me, it's a done deal. But I meant it more…morally. Ethically?"

"Like a code of behavior," Celeste confirmed. "Admirable. Explain?"

Maji looked relieved. "Thanks. But I'm more wiped out than I realized. Can we just say that I should know better?"

"Really you don't owe me an explanation at all," Celeste reassured her. "Why don't you rest now?" She left Maji reclining with the cold pack and stepped outside to speak with Santxo.

"Well?" he said, his bushy mustache twitching with worry or excitement. Or both.

"She'll be fine with rest and ice," Celeste reported. "A bruise, nothing more. No lawsuit…*Tranquilo.*" Chill out, she translated mentally to American slang.

Santxo looked disappointed. "So it really isn't Erlea? I thought maybe she would tell you."

Seriously? Well, the VIP treatment made sense now. "I am quite convinced she is just an average tourist. Besides, don't you have your crew scheduled for Erlea's arrival tomorrow?"

He winced at her look. "She could have arrived here early…and incognito."

Celeste smiled at the dramatic notion. Santxo had confided that the media had been seen inside the complex already, sniffing about. He seemed to relish kicking them out. Perhaps this mystery woman was a reporter.

"Wishful thinking, my friend. But aren't you trained to observe? I admit there is a resemblance, but that is all." Maji was nice looking, with a definite charm. But Erlea? Unforgettable. Despite how the evening had ended, Celeste held on to the way she'd felt when Erlea had turned her charm on her.

Santxo's eyes sparkled with intrigue below bushy brows that rose with excitement. "Indeed, I am trained. And you are the mistaken one. I have seen all the music videos and behind-the-scenes clips on the web. Erlea is not always so glamorous. Sometimes she looks quite like the woman in there." He pointed to her office. "And she has kept a very low profile, not like most gamblers. If not for the tidy sum she has earned these past days, we would have taken no notice of her at all," Santxo explained. "No trouble until today, when this Brit sits down and tries to talk with her at the blackjack table. She discourages him from interrupting her game, but he persists. Then he puts a hand on her arm, calling her *Erlea* like it is their little secret."

"You saw all this yourself?" Celeste wondered exactly what security was for then.

"Well, I was just keeping an eye out for her. I would have helped if she needed it."

"And yet she was injured, no?"

"Yes, and he's very lucky. She handled him like a pro. Or a black belt, I should say." He looked smug. "Did you know that?"

Celeste mustered a blank look in response. "So I have heard. In Aikido, right?"

Santxo's exuberance deflated. "Correct. The man she handled so adroitly told me so, too. He is a bit obsessed with Erlea, I think. And you know who he is?"

Celeste opened her mouth to cut this line of gossip short, but too late.

"Dr. Lyttleton! You know, the famous one. He does all the nip and tuck on the celebrities. And now he is mortified, afraid she will ban him from the VIP reception."

Celeste smiled. "Santxo, my friend, what an opportunity to use your diplomatic skills. You know I cannot give you information about my patients. But you could comp this mystery woman a room. Then she would have to give her passport to the front desk, and you could assure the doctor that he has not offended the great and mighty Erlea."

"Genius. You are as brilliant as you are beautiful. How are we so blessed to have you?"

Celeste only smiled and waved him away. If he knew the answer, he would not think so highly of her.

CHAPTER TWO

M aji jolted awake when the door opened. "I should get going."
        "Don't forget your winnings," Celeste said with a smile, handing her a stack of euros. She took Maji's chilled hand and confirmed that all the joints moved freely with the swelling reduced. "Let me get that tape."

While Celeste lightly splinted and wrapped the pinkie with practiced ease, Maji asked, "So…I'm not in trouble?"

"Definitely not. However, Santxo—Mr. Quintana—is quite curious about your identity. He thinks your attacker may be right, that you are Erlea traveling incognito." Celeste's wry smile showed what she thought of the idea.

Maji laughed, looking down at her tan slacks and boat shoes. "I look like a pop diva? That's a first." Could be worse. "I haven't seen her photos or videos. Do I look like her? You tell me."

Maji watched the Frenchwoman tuck her stylishly bobbed hair behind an ear, an odd mix of diffident and professional in her unbuttoned white coat over pressed slacks and an aqua blouse that went with the shifting blue-green of her eyes. Dressed for the indoor climate, not for the bright sun outside. And to impress whom? Perhaps she was always neatly put together, by habit and culture.

"From a distance," Celeste replied at last, "you do resemble her. But anyone who saw you both up close would not be confused."

"Have you seen us both up close?" Maji enjoyed Celeste's blush in response. "You have. And she made quite an impression."

"It was a fleeting introduction. She would not remember me."

Celeste looked studiously nonchalant. "It was a dark and crowed club, and she was drunk, living up to the stories about her wild behavior."

Maji wondered about the story behind that story but didn't prod. "Do you like her music? She must be very popular, to sell out arenas."

"Oh yes—her concerts are spectacles of a large scale. So much, she is bringing a show here to try onstage before taking it on tour. Wait, I will show you…" Celeste twirled her rolling chair back to the desktop computer. She woke the screen, closed a news article, and clicked on a paused video. In it, a woman in an outrageous outfit curled around a pole onstage while belting out a song. Quite athletic, and the tune was catchy.

Maji laughed. "Seriously? I should have just sung something. That would have shut him up."

Celeste smiled and clicked on another video. "This is Erlea live, performing her most recent hit, 'Salvaje.'"

Maji squinted at the little image of the star dancing in sync with a bevy of muscled men, all of them in animal-print bodysuits. "Untamed, huh? Somebody could get hurt in a show like that and need care from a fan with an MD." She raised a brow. "Good thing you're doing your research."

Celeste blushed. "She will be staying here. I like to be prepared." While Maji let the air-conditioned hum of the room call bullshit for her, Celeste straightened up her pristine coat self-consciously. "Anyway, Santxo wants to offer you a free room here to get a look at your passport. A pretext, you understand?"

"I do. Nonetheless, I prefer to sleep on my boat. But I would show it to him for a dinner at Cuina Mallorquina. If you'll agree to join me."

Celeste blushed again. Too much teasing for one day?

"Sorry. That's not fair. Never mind," Maji backpedaled. "I didn't mean to embarrass you."

"I am not embarrassed. I am…*on rougirait à l'idée*. You know this expression?"

"I think we'd say tickled. Tickled pink. You are, huh?" Maji felt herself grin.

"My girlfriend always said that women did not hit on me because I looked too straight. As if I should wear a leather jacket and moto boots to express myself. No, to…proclaim myself."

Maji's tiny bubble of hope burst. "I see. Does she?"

"Not that I have seen. But I would not know. She is in Marseilles and I am here."

"Finished or just on holiday from each other?" Maji asked.

"For me there is no going back. For her…"

Maji reached out and touched Celeste's arm lightly. "It's complicated?"

"Close enough." The cloud over Celeste's demeanor cleared. "But dinner is simple. I hear the restaurant is worth its exorbitant prices, and your company I know I will enjoy very much."

Maji exited the casino feeling almost giddy in the afternoon sun, winnings in her pocket and a dinner date in hand. But as the reality sank in, her joy ebbed like the outgoing tide and a familiar feeling of dread flowed back in. What if Celeste wanted more than dinner? Like a whole night—or more. Maji did a quick calculation of the time difference between Majorca and New York. *As if there's ever a good time to call home and whine.* But she had promised Ava she would reach out if she started to spiral down. And this definitely counted.

Maji closed the sailboat's cabin hatchway, shutting out both light and cooling breeze. She pressed speed dial, then nearly hung up at the second ring. It was selfish to pester Ava when she needed all her energy to fight that stupid fucking recurrence. Anyone who won two rounds with cancer should be off the hook for the rest of their life.

Neither of her godmothers needed more to worry about. *You should be there, helping them for a change.* On the fourth ring, she reached out to close her laptop.

"Maji?" Hannah answered, looking concerned. And tired.

"I'm sorry," Maji began. "Bad time, huh? I can just—"

"No, hang on," Hannah said, turning away to speak quietly in Hebrew. She returned with a weary smile. "She wants to see you for herself. I'll go make tea, and you will keep it brief."

"Thanks."

Ava's face appeared, pale but calm. "The doctor is in. And so happy to see you, darling."

"Hey." Had Ava lost more weight? Was that hair wrap a bad sign? Maji was afraid to ask. "How's chemo?"

"A lot like having the flu for a few days every other week. Not so bad, really."

"You know I know you're lying, right?"

Ava laughed. "Yes, but you're supposed to humor me because I feel like shit and you feel sorry for me." The humor in her eyes took some of the sting from that bitter truth. "Now, Hannah will be back soon to fuss. So spit it out."

"I have a date tonight," Maji confessed. "I don't know what I was thinking."

"That you are allowed a little joy?" Ava scrutinized her in the silence that followed. "Do you like her?"

"Yeah. She's cute, and nice, and smart, and...nice."

"Nice is bad?"

Maji groaned in frustration. "She's not a hookup kind of woman, I can tell. And we're both in town for a while, so..."

"Oh no. She might want to get to know you? She might really see you?"

"You know that's not an option. And lying isn't fair to her." *And it's fucked up every relationship you've tried since enlisting.*

"There is more to you than your work," Ava reminded her. "She doesn't have to know what you do to see who you are."

"Who I am would send her running." At least Celeste had that option. *You, Rios, are stuck with you.* Ava sighed and Maji wanted to sign off, let her off the hook. "Sorry. I know, I'm not a bad person, just human, I did my best, yadda yadda. Really, I get it intellectually. I'm just...not there yet."

"No, darling. You have to earn back your own trust. And that takes time." Ava smiled sympathetically. They both knew patience wasn't Maji's forte.

Hard to picture that future, but Ava had faith enough for the two of them. "And until then? Dinner's tonight."

"Perhaps you need a friend right now, more than a lover. There is nothing wrong with keeping your physical and emotional needs separate while you heal. What are you doing for exercise these days?"

"A little running, the usual. I need to bump it up."

"Perhaps Hannah could help you find a dojo or someone on the island for real workouts. You need some physical outlets now that you are stronger."

"Guess I'd better, if I'm going to be a nun."

Ava laughed. "Oh, to be twenty-four again. I never said you should avoid sex. If you can enjoy some, by all means do. Just not with the drama."

Maji heard Hannah's voice in the background, announcing the arrival of the tea. "I should go." And not talk about sex anymore. "You need to rest."

"Not so fast, darling. Give me my closure." Ava smiled faintly at the old joke. "I know you are not ready to stop punishing yourself yet. But it does not help you, and it does not help anyone else. You need to allow yourself some joy, some human connection again. Making a friend is a good start."

"I'll try. But I'm pretty crappy company."

"Child of mine, you are never terrible except to yourself." Ava yawned and sipped the tea. Maji waited for her final word, feeling stripped bare. Finally Ava delivered the advice, simple and clear as always. "Just don't spit at kindness. And do what you do naturally—be a friend to one who needs you."

"Okay. Ava...I love you." Tears blurred Maji's view of her godmother. "Sleep tight."

Ava blew her a kiss. "Be well, darling. I look forward to an update."

Resolved to not let Celeste down, Maji stopped into the security office. She watched as Santxo—head of security, as it turned out—perused her passport. Back at Fort Bragg, where her unit trained for missions and Joint Special Operations Command was headquartered, a variety of passports with her picture lived in a file along with other documents needed for any particular mission's cover identity. This one did not match her military ID, which tagged her as Sergeant Ariela Rios of the US Army. This one only included the first and last of her legal names, Majida Ariela Kamiri Rios, all of which appeared on the passport her parents held for her at home in Brooklyn. But it would register as valid at any border, hotel, or casino.

"Well, Ms. Rios," Santxo said at last, handing the blue folder back, "we again sincerely apologize for the incident this morning. Please enjoy your supper, to include any food items. The bar and wine menu are, unfortunately, not included. I did my best, but…management."

"You've been more than generous. Thank you, Mr. Quintana."

"Santxo, please. We are friends now. I will see to it that no more patrons get strange ideas about you."

Maji smiled politely. The key to saving lives was her ability to be mistaken for someone else. Never a famous someone, though. That would be as stupid as tossing old men around the casino floor. "And I'll try to be more restrained if they do. Have a good night."

"Ms. Rios." His voice stopped her just as she reached the door.

What now? She turned and gave him her relaxed-interested expression.

"Your Spanish is excellent. Where did you learn it?"

What a nice way of saying she had effectively erased most traces of Brooklyn and the many sounds of Central and Latin America that she grew up with. "At home, from my father. He is a Latino American, while I am an American Latina."

Santxo laughed good-naturedly. "But your first name. It sounds Middle Eastern."

"Lebanese," she lied with practiced ease. "My mother's parents loved Majida El Roumi. You know of her?"

He shook his head. "Sorry, no."

"A famous singer. Ironically, I can't carry a tune. Erlea would be insulted if she heard about today."

"Then let's keep it among ourselves, hmm?"

Roger that, amigo.

Celeste waited in the lobby for Maji, shifting nervously from foot to foot. First she'd agonized over her paltry wardrobe choices, nothing seeming quite nice enough. Then she'd stressed about makeup, finally erring on the side of understated. Ridiculous to be so wound up over a simple dinner.

It wasn't as though she'd had no dates these past few months since leaving Marseilles—and Adrienne. She'd said yes to a mechanic on the cruise ship; and here at the Gran Balearico, she'd spent a nice enough evening with Reimi. But those encounters were shallow, out of character.

Celeste jumped at Maji's touch. "Where did you come from?"

"Sorry to startle you," Maji said. "Deep thoughts?"

Celeste nodded, taking in her date. A bit casual for fine dining. But the sporty look suited her, the sun-highlighted thick brown hair pulled into a simple ponytail and her slacks and tailored shirt pressed. No makeup but a bit of shine on her lips, and…eyes too puffy and red for eyeliner and mascara to hold. Allergies or crying. "Are you quite fine, yourself?"

"Finer by the minute." Maji's charming smile dimpled her cheeks, then faded. "I was on the phone with a friend who's fighting cancer. I'm just worried for her, and feeling useless so far away."

Celeste found her honesty refreshing. "That is always hard. I do not know if my heart could handle oncology. The clients I see all have robust health and merely seek to perform their best. Sometimes it seems trivial by comparison."

"You prescribe a lot of Viagra?"

Celeste laughed. "No, hardly. I work with athletes, dancers, and… sporting people."

"Cool. I want to hear all about that over supper. And I'm starving. You?"

"Famished. I want to try everything on the menu."

Maji grinned. "Poor Santxo. I hope he's still a good sport when he sees the bill."

When Celeste saw the prices on the menu, she hoped so, too. "The food might be marvelous, but I think this place is charging for atmosphere."

Maji looked around the dimly lit and tastefully designed restaurant from the overlook their cozy leather-backed enclave in the corner afforded. "It is romantic. But mostly I like that it's quiet. I hate going out to eat and having to yell across the table."

"Well, it is very early yet, hardly dinnertime." Celeste looked at her watch. "Later the loud tourists—the Americans and British and Germans—will go away and the Spaniards will lean in close to hold private conversations, like we French do." She leaned toward Maji, feeling bolder than she had in months.

"Are you flirting with me?" Maji's expression didn't give anything away.

Celeste smiled. "That depends. Do you want me to?"

"I wouldn't dream of stopping you. You have a natural talent."

"Thank you. I thought I had lost the knack, for a while."

Maji looked thoughtful, like she was gauging the meaning behind Celeste's words. "Out of practice?"

"I stopped for a bit," Celeste admitted. Not being pushed to talk about it made her want to, for the first time. Something about Maji's manner elicited her trust. "Another issue with my ex. She was easily threatened. At first I thought her jealousy was sweet, but in time I realized it was just another way to try and control me."

"Here's to freedom," Maji said with a wry smile, lifting her water glass to toast.

Celeste clinked it with her wineglass. "And respect. Are you sure I can't buy you a drink?"

"Nope. My budget could handle a cocktail here, if I really wanted one. But it's never a great idea for me. We'll both like me better sober."

Why did everything remind her of Adrienne tonight? "Your honesty is very refreshing. And your self-knowledge and consideration for others."

"Your ex must have set the bar for good behavior very low." Maji didn't ask, but she did look concerned.

"I learned a lot of hard lessons—many about myself." How to make such a long story short? "I will never again be with someone who thinks everything is about them, that their feelings count more, that they should not be held accountable for their actions. Drinking was only one of many excuses, none of which I should have listened to."

The first of a series of delectable tapas and small plates shifted their attention to happier topics, tales of favorite meals and travels and their hometowns. When they compared musical tastes, Maji shook her head. "I still can't believe two strangers mistook me for Erlea in one day."

Celeste shrugged, feeling unusually content with her fully belly and second glass of wine. "Side by side you don't look alike. But they've never seen her up close."

"So you mentioned." Maji grinned her encouragement. "Spill."

"It was at a nightclub. Adrienne's football team was celebrating making it to the semifinals, and she was ignoring me, so I started to dance by myself. When I went to get a drink, Erlea was at the bar getting a whole tray of shots for her band. She offered me one and complimented my free spirit."

"Nice."

Celeste shook her head. "Adrienne did not think so. After paying me no mind all night, she barged in and accused Erlea of trying to steal her girlfriend."

"Like you were her property?" Maji's voice had become very flat.

Celeste smiled at the contrast. "That's what Erlea said." Only she had sounded amused. "Well, she said, *You cannot steal what no one owns. But if you won't treat her right, someone else will.* She was pretty buzzed, I think. They both were."

"Maybe so," Maji replied. "But alcohol can't make someone do or say things they don't mean. It just takes away the inhibition."

"Then they also both share a violent nature. For a fight followed."

Maji looked skeptical. "Really? Who hit who?"

"Actually, I left them at the bar and Adrienne followed me." Celeste wasn't sure she wanted to say the rest out loud. "She was… hurting me, and Erlea stopped her."

Maji reached over and took her hand. "Hey, you don't have to relive it. We can talk about something else if you want."

"It's okay," Celeste said. And it was. "That was the only time she hurt me in public. But you are right, the alcohol only makes you feel free to do things you would like to do if you weren't held back by what other people might think."

"Or having to live with the harm you've done, after you sober up." Maji smiled crookedly and lifted her water glass.

Celeste squeezed Maji's comforting hand. "See, that is what makes you different from those celebrity types. You don't think you can do whatever you want and get away with it."

Maji chuckled. "So you're not planning to offer Erlea a second chance to treat you right, while she's here?" Seeing Celeste's deep blush, she nodded knowingly. "I'm just teasing. That's my natural talent."

"I will forgive you, in exchange for dessert."

"Well, that's easy. Done." Maji waved for their server.

Celeste withdrew her hand. "Are you calling me easy?"

"I wouldn't dare. But now I see how the flirting works. I'm going to study you until I get to be a natural, too."

And with that, they were back on safe ground. After coffee, Celeste glanced at her watch for the first time that evening. "Oh my God. I had no idea it was so late."

"You're not on vacation. I should see you home." Maji sounded penitent, not flirtatious.

"It's not a home. It's a place for workers to sleep, those of us just here for the season." Celeste thought of the hostel-like accommodations. The best she could offer this sweet woman was tea in the lounge. "Why don't I walk you home, instead?"

"Oh. I'm flattered, but…"

Celeste felt a mix of relief and disappointment. "Not interested?"

"I may kick myself later, but I think I need a friend as much as you do."

Celeste nodded. "You make an excellent friend. How about I walk you home and then take a cab back? I would love to see this yacht of yours."

Maji smiled at last, that delightful playfulness reemerging. "Prepare to be underwhelmed. She's a pretty little sloop, but no yacht."

"I see. But do not worry yourself, we French are very stoic. I shall hide my disappointment at your lack of wealth and fame."

Maji signaled for the check. "Let's waddle out, then."

Celeste laughed at Maji's impersonation of a duck, and they walked arm in arm toward the waterfront. "Thanks for scoring us a great free meal," Maji said. "And for real conversation."

"Thank you for listening and not judging me," Celeste said. "I hid my troubles from my friends in Marseilles, never even told them when I ran away." When Maji just gave her arm a friendly squeeze, she continued, "I tried once to tell my mother, but Adrienne had charmed her the way she did everyone. My mother just said that relationships take work, and I should try harder."

Maji snorted. "Bullshit. Sorry. I just hate it when people don't believe the women in their lives. You deserve better."

Celeste stopped and pulled her into a hug, too emotional to speak. When they walked on again, she said, "I'm starting to know that again. It's hard to blame others when even I didn't want to believe it. How could that be me? I'm a doctor, for God's sake. Educated, from a good family. A person who makes healthy decisions. At least, I used to be."

"She's still in there, I'm sure," Maji said. "Do you miss Marseilles?"

Spotting the harbor, Celeste noted, "When I took the cruise ship job, I thought I would love life on the water. But it turns out I prefer life *near* the water." They stopped and leaned on the rail by the water, watching the boats rock gently in their slips. A picture of peace and safety. "This job at the Balearico will do for now. Until I know who I am again, and where I want to be."

Maji put a comforting arm around her waist. She was small, but clearly strong and very warm as well. "I haven't been through what you have, but everybody's got their demons. My godmother is a therapist, and I don't know if I'd be standing here today without her support."

Celeste pressed a kiss to Maji's cheek. "Then I am very thankful to her."

Chapter Three

"Get off," a woman cried, struggling to break free.

Maji held on tight, keeping her eyes shut against the smoke and dust. She had to get them all out, ignore the panic, the noise.

"Maji. Let me go," the woman insisted. "You're hurting me."

Maji opened her eyes, recognized the boat, a woman's face. No camp, no gunfire, no... She opened both hands and let Celeste's sweaty skin slide from her grasp. In the little bit of moonlight from the V-berth hatch, she saw the glint of Celeste's eyes.

"I'm sorry," Maji stuttered. "How did...?"

"You were yelling and banging yourself on the walls." Celeste's expression held a too familiar mix of fear and pity.

"Why are you here?" Maji asked. "Didn't you go home?"

"Yes. But I realized I left my keycard behind, so I called you. You were slurring your words, and I was worried. You wouldn't tell me what you took, but your vitals were steady. So I helped you to lie down and took the little bunk to stay nearby."

And now you want me to thank you. "Oh. Sorry."

"I am happy to help." Celeste looked so earnest. Ugh. "But now tell me, please, what did you take?"

Not enough. Florence Nightingale should have left her alone. She was too fucking tired for this shit.

"I said, what did you take?" Celeste's hand forced Maji's chin toward the sound of her voice.

Too loud. Too bright. "Shh." Maji tried to brush Celeste's hand away. Stronger than she looked. Damn.

"Fine. Stay put. There is daylight now." Celeste rummaged through the main cabin, swearing softly. *Nosy.*

Maji curled into a ball and pulled the pillow over her head. Ah, darkness. Someone grabbed her ankle and tugged. She reared up, trying to grab her attacker, and smacked her head on the low ceiling. "Fuck!"

"Please, stop. You are hurting yourself."

Oh, Celeste again. Looking worried and angry. "Sorry."

"Get out here." She held the pill bottle in her hand. "How many did you take?"

"Two. One stopped working."

"Working to do what? Kill you?" Celeste swore quietly in French and forced Maji's face toward her again. "Open your eyes."

"Hurts."

"Too bad. I must look. Let me examine you, dammit."

Maji took a deep breath and tried to find her center. It kept moving. She took another slow breath and opened her eyes. "I'm sorry. Did I hurt you?"

"Shh. Just breathe." Celeste shone a penlight in each eye, then checked her pulse. While Maji drank the water from the glass she pressed into her hand, Celeste delivered the verdict. "With your weight and metabolism, one-half is a proper dose. And they are not for everyday use, either. There are better options."

"I already ruled out a bullet. And liquor makes me puke." Maji pulled herself to standing. "Let me walk you home. I'll run back, sweat out what's left."

"The sun is up," Celeste said. "I'll be fine. And so will you, if you stop with these. Come see me at the office."

Maji just nodded. *As if.*

"Promise me, my friend."

"Fine."

"I have your phone number. Don't make me call you."

"I said yes. Don't worry."

Celeste stroked her face so tenderly Maji couldn't bring herself to move away. "Too late. Arrive before one in the afternoon."

Or what? You'll call me? Only Ava's voice reminding her not to spit at kindness held the snark back. "Yeah. Got it."

As soon as she was alone, Maji checked the time in New York: still night there. What would she tell Ava anyway? Made a friend, freaked her out? No, that would require explanation, and Ava only knew about the nightmares. She thought Maji had tossed the sedatives when she left Landstuhl. Along with the counseling referrals.

No needed to worry her. Maji opened her laptop, logged into Hannah's private chat line, and started typing. This form of conversation offered a delete button.

MR: *Tell Ava I made a new friend, as advised. On related note for you, C has a volatile ex in France and is keeping out of range for now but career break getting old. I offered support. And then scared her w my own fucked-upness.*

Maji deleted the last sentence. She started typing again, looking for a way that wouldn't worry Ava. Finding none, she hit send and went to shower. Hannah should be asleep, but with her, who knew?

A protein bar with cold leftover coffee stood in for breakfast. She should start cooking real food again, but that meant shopping. And giving a fuck. It was just fuel, after all. As she laced up her running shoes and located her sunglasses, the laptop pinged.

HC: *Happy to help any friend of yours. Send specifics at your convenience. How are you?*

MR: *Tan. :) On wait list for appt.*

HC: *Very funny. Let me know when you need funds wired.*

MR: *No need. Earning locally.*

HC: *Explain.*

MR: *21 ways. Call it occ therapy, next level. Blew a fuse with asshole tourist yesterday, but no blowback.*

In the pause that followed, Maji sensed a reprimand coming. Maybe she should have been clearer. No harm to civilian, no police involvement—that kind of thing. Maybe she should finally learn to not rat herself out.

HC: *Stay below radar at all costs. $ available here, no limit. Your face is priceless.*

Oh, fuck. The Gran Balearico might be big enough to have a facial recognition program running to filter out cheats and grifters and egregious counters, like the Vegas casinos. Of course they wouldn't tag her as Sgt. Rios, famous female Iran hostage. But getting a rep under her civilian identity wasn't a great idea, either. She needed to finesse Santxo and find out if they'd already profiled her or had the means to. Damage control.

MR: *Copy that. How is Ava?*

HC: *Good. Sleeping. Sends love.*

MR: *Back atcha both. Signing off.*

HC: *Be careful. Out.*

Stupid, stupid, stupid. The sunglasses popped apart when Maji threw them across the cabin. She didn't check to see if they could be fixed. Why bother? The fairy godmothers would get her another pair. Bail her out of trouble, just like they always had. And how did she thank them? Mangling old men in casinos while on video. Fucking brilliant.

Maybe she should give up on Dr. Lyttleton, get her ass on a plane home and help. Ha. Be underfoot and an extra project, more like. They didn't need her lying around brooding about her shoulder. The doctors at Landstuhl had done a decent job, taken the scar down from a recognizable brand that announced she had survived capture by Tarik al-Mashriki to just some ugly lumps. Maji wondered what the rest of the team's survivors had done with their scars. Removal? Or maybe tattoos, like the flowering vines over Ava's mastectomy scar, a triumphant reminder of life beating death. Well, not her. She had neither the pride nor the discretion to add a distinguishing mark to her body. Better that every trace be scraped away.

Ava wouldn't want her to give up so easily. She had suggested plastic surgery during those early days in the hospital when Maji was so fucked up. Stoned on pain meds, but never enough to forget. Just enough to ramble on about getting a tattoo with an AK-47 and the names of everyone she'd hit with it. Why wouldn't they tell her the names? Not that the list would fit on one arm. So she'd tried notches, until they took the knife away and put her under surveillance.

The thought of getting out of that damned hospital and finally erasing the mark for good had kept Maji going for months. The doctors and rehab crew thought she had grit, the will to recover and get back to the field. But really she just wanted to get the hell away from all those people looking at her every day, knowing what she'd done.

❖

Erlea followed Nigel, Nico, and the roadies up from the parking garage and into the hotel, shepherded by Alejandro. She put her earbud in and dialed Imane. "When are you coming in?" she asked her closest friend and choreographer.

"A week or so. What's it like?"

"Like the inside of every other hotel," Erlea said. When Imane joked about touring the world and seeing only the inside of hotels, she made it sound charming. "Wait, here's the lobby. It's…Oh, hell."

"I can hear them," Imane replied. The crowd noise reverberated in the tall-ceilinged room. "Mr. Bait-and-Switch set you up again?"

That shit. "Yes." So much for a quiet arrival and time to get settled in before any public appearances. No wonder Nigel had badgered her about her traveling clothes.

"You should have signed with Claudia Sandoval, habibi."

Erlea glanced toward Nigel and caught the smug look on his horsey face. Didn't all managers feed their clients the same bullshit about image and artistry, puffing them up while poking at their egos to deflate them enough to make them take direction? "Too late."

"Your loss." Imane didn't sound sympathetic. "Then could you at least fire Nico?"

Until he'd hired Nico to manage the new show, Erlea had been able to let Nigel's attitude roll off her back. "I'm starting to wish I could." Nigel kept taking Nico's side in planning meetings.

"Nico had better be as good as everyone says," Imane grumbled.

"That's why he gets away with being such a prick. Hey, I'm going deaf in here. Later."

Between the lights, the din, and the hangover, Erlea felt her vision begin to narrow. But now was the absolute wrong time to collapse. Days like this made her miss being an unknown in the clubs, jamming with her friends. Real people, who liked her as well as her songs. They'd all dreamed of reaching this point, with paparazzi chasing them and fans clamoring for a smile or a selfie. If only she'd known then what it actually felt like.

A man called her name, broke through the line of hotel staff holding the throng back. He started yelling in Euskara, which her Basque grandparents had always wished she would learn.

Erlea stopped and turned to greet him. But then she recognized the shouted slogan—*Bietan jarrai*—and the wild look in his eye. She started to back away just as he reached into his jacket.

❖

With Reimi pressed close to her, Maji enjoyed watching the scene below. Being led by the hand through the back halls of the hotel hadn't sucked either. Points for Reimi. From the balcony that overlooked the casino entrance and its grand stairway, Maji took in the aggressive media angling to get photos and the equally enthusiastic fans pressing forward against the flimsy human barricade of hotel staff.

And there was the entourage, right on cue. Eight people flowed through the front doors into the marble-floored lobby, looking far too scruffily hip for the stately room with its frescoed ceilings.

"Who's who?" Maji whispered in Reimi's ear. A faint hint of smoke mingled with an outdoorsy scent from Reimi's hair. The first was no surprise, the second intriguing.

"Erlea is the one in heels," Reimi answered, not bothering with the star's companions.

Erlea seemed smaller than she appeared onstage. Not just her height but her body language. *She hates this.* And yet she'd dressed the part in tight jeans, big sunglasses, and a leather jacket that Celeste's ex would covet.

As Erlea's group reached the base of the stairway, cameras whirred and clicked, the crowd encroaching further. A man all in black but for a blue beret broke free from the group and sprinted toward Erlea, yelling. Maji couldn't make out his words, but Erlea's reaction spoke volumes. First she perked up and turned toward him; then she started backing away.

Maji registered the object in his hand. "Gun!" She mentally mapped the quickest route down to the shooter, shouting the warning again, this time in Spanish.

Maji flipped herself over the rail, aiming for the banister. Using it as a pivot point, she turned and launched herself at the man. She collided with him before he could take aim. He cushioned her fall, crumpling beneath her as the crowd's collective gasp gave way to screams and shouts.

Above the jumble of voices, a familiar deep voice rang out in Spanish. "Make way. Security. Make way."

The shooter struggled to regain his feet and she put a choke hold on him, knocking out the back of his knee to bring him lower in front of her, a human shield between her and the cameras. Maji checked the crowd for an accomplice, saw none, but spotted the fallen gun and flicked it away with her foot. As security pushed forward, shoving tourists aside, Maji fisted the gunman's collar and belt and rolled him in their direction. He landed in a heap at their feet, facedown. They should have him cuffed in seconds.

Get out. Go go go. Maji turned toward the base of the stairs, spotted the Employees Only door, and slipped back into the maze of service corridors.

CHAPTER FOUR

As soon as the local police left his suite, Nigel poured a glass of whiskey and handed it to Erlea. "What a troublesome business. How are you holding up?"

Nigel's avuncular act always put Erlea on alert. She sipped the drink casually, trying to project a calm she didn't feel. "I'm fine. I just want to go unpack."

"Soon. Let me just see if your new room is ready." He opened the door and spoke to the hotel security guard standing sentry in the hall.

"Very soon, sir," the guard reported. "She is on a different floor now, and only a select few have the number. May the house doctor come here in the meantime?"

"Certainly." Nigel closed the door and turned back to Erlea.

"Nigel. I'm fine. I'm not letting some strange man examine me."

Nigel set his own whiskey tumbler aside. "Just answer a few questions for him so he can check off the right boxes for the insurer."

Of course. The insurance. Nigel needed her in top shape to get the rest of the show's backers on board. No wonder he was being so solicitous. "Fine. Just give me some privacy."

"Naturally. I'll be in the bedroom, making some calls," Nigel assured her. "Help yourself," he added, gesturing to the tall bottle on top of the minibar.

A moment later, Erlea opened the door at the first knock, ready to dispatch the house doctor as quickly as possible. The terse words she had prepared for him vanished from her mind at the sight of a lovely blond woman in a white coat. "Hello?" she said instead, feeling stupid for being tongue-tied.

"Hello," the woman said, her hand extended. "I am Dr. Guillot. Were you not expecting me? If this is a bad time…"

"No, sorry," Erlea managed. "I mean, come in." She stepped aside, as much to break the hold of those oceanic eyes as to make room. "Can I get you something?"

The doctor eyed the bar skeptically. "I don't drink on duty. But thank you."

"Right, of course. Water? Or there might be soda, or—" Erlea's phone rang and she moved to silence it. But it was Imane calling, and Erlea didn't want her hearing about this from someone else. "I'm sorry, I have to take this. Please have anything you like."

Erlea turned her back on the distractingly attractive stranger and took the call. Before she could even say hello, Imane asked, "Are you all right?"

Too late. "I'm fine. Not even a scratch. It's on the news already?"

"Some guy shot at you—how can you be fine? He shot at you."

Erlea sighed. "Calm down. He only tried to. And it was a stunt, with a paint gun."

"Really? Twitter said you were attacked by Basque separatists." Imane sounded calmer but still anxious.

"Yelling a slogan and wearing the blue beret do not make you a real politico. It was just stupid, that's all."

Imane was silent briefly, then asked, "Did Nigel stage it?"

"Well, he wanted an entrance," Erlea conceded. "But this is not the kind of publicity he likes. Anyway, now I have to answer some dumb insurance questions. I should go. I wish you were here already."

"I'll try to shave a few days off the wrap-up here," Imane said. "You know I love you."

Erlea smiled. "I love you, too. See you soon." She turned back to the doctor, who had found herself an Orangina from the minibar. "Sorry about that. Let's get this done and not waste any more of your time."

"Don't worry. Dumb insurance questions are very quick." The doctor's voice and expression didn't give away her feelings, but Erlea swore her eyes looked stormy now. "Let's start with your physical well-being. You were not injured?"

"Well, I got pushed out of the way when the asshole with the gun pointed it at me." She wasn't hurt, but Erlea couldn't just let this woman walk out, insulted. "My arm is kind of sore, from trying to catch myself."

"Okay, let's take a look. Would you mind sitting?"

Erlea grabbed the chair from the nearby desk, then zipped off her leather jacket. She felt a bit exposed in just a tank top. Didn't matter that this woman was a physician. Just knowing she was watching made Erlea feel buzzed. "Sure."

"The other direction, please," the doctor said, her French accent coming through her precise Spanish. "Your chest to the chair's back."

So Erlea straddled the chair, her hands draped over the top of the leather upholstery. "The left arm," she said, deciding on the spot.

"Just let it hang, please. I am going to check your spine first."

Warm fingers pressed firmly on either side of her neck, walking down the tight cords along the bone. Erlea stifled a hum.

"Let me know the instant anything hurts. Yes?"

"Mm-hmm." Erlea breathed as slowly as she could, allowing her head to be tilted down, up, and side to side. The fingers gliding down her back, gentle and smooth, felt like a caress. When they reached her belt line and withdrew, she asked, "Nothing out of place?"

"No structural issues. May I manipulate your arm? Do not assist with your muscles."

"Whatever helps, Doctor," Erlea replied. Imane would tease her mercilessly if she could see her now, faking an injury to get a woman to touch her.

After an equally pleasant examination of her arm, interspersed with questions in a caring, professional tone, the doctor stepped away. "I can sign off that you have sustained no lasting injury." She took a seat on the couch facing Erlea and sipped on her soda. "And you do not appear to be in shock. So the usual antidote is working."

Erlea followed her gaze to the whiskey glass. "It doesn't hurt. I will admit the guy scared me and the cops pissed me off. But your bedside manner is better than liquor. I'm sorry if I was rude."

"No matter." Above the white coat, pink bloomed on the doctor's throat and cheeks. "I am happy to assist. And relieved that you are well."

She's blushing. Erlea felt her own face begin to heat and stood, seeking out her jacket. Feeling more composed with it on, she said, "You seem so familiar. Have we met?"

"That is a terrible line. Surely you can do better." The teasing look turned sardonic. "You did the night we met. And you offered me a drink then, too."

"Was I a total jackass?" A vision of herself plastered and hitting on this woman made her cringe. "I had to have been really drunk to not remember you."

"You see? That is a much better line." The Mona Lisa smile suggested forgiveness, the sparkle in her eyes the possibility of more.

Erlea stared back at her, all the clever comebacks fleeing when she needed them most. Why were the women she liked best the hardest to talk to?

A knock from Nigel's bedroom broke their connection. "Everyone decent out there?"

"Enter," the doctor replied, sounding again like the woman in charge. It suited her.

Nigel stepped out and gave them a quick scan. "Thank you for your prompt service, Doctor." He shifted his attention to Erlea. "And speaking of which, security called. Your room is ready. You needn't stay for the paperwork—we'll handle it from here."

"Right. Good." Erlea zipped her jacket, scrambling for words that didn't sound sleazy. "If I need anything...medical, can I call you?" *Dork.*

"Of course. Dial my office from any hotel phone. Good day."

That was it, then. Erlea headed for the door, done embarrassing herself. She stopped, struck by an idea that had fled the moment she looked into those aquamarine eyes. "Nigel, I want to talk to that woman. The one who leaped off the balcony to protect me. Maybe she knows what this was really about."

"I can't imagine how," Nigel replied. "But fine, yes. Give her a thank-you and an autograph. Have Alejandro video you being gracious."

"That's not making-of footage," Erlea protested. "And I don't want him lurking around with that camera, taping every fucking minute of my day."

"Just the highlights," Nigel promised. "Now go unwind. Tomorrow work begins."

❖

Celeste opened her office door to find Maji waiting inside, her smile strained.

"Sorry to sneak in. I needed a place to hide out again."

Unsettled as she was by her office's lack of security, Celeste was more concerned with Maji's welfare. "How badly did you hurt yourself, jumping like that?"

"You heard already? That it was me?" Maji frowned, moving without her usual catlike grace to the exam table, her gait thrown off as she resisted putting weight on the right foot.

"It is normal to call in a physician after incidents like that."

Maji settled herself on the raised bench, crinkling the paper coverlet. "Of course. Is the guy I jumped okay? I didn't stay to check."

"I don't know. The police took him away before I was called." Celeste unlaced Maji's sneaker, thinking about her encounter with Erlea. Had the star found her as awkward as she felt? Had Erlea noticed the effect she had on her? And who was that on the other end of her phone, the one she said *I love you* to—a parent, a sibling, a boyfriend?

"Oh," Maji said slowly, drawing the sound out. "Right. The star. Is she okay? I'm pretty sure she didn't get hit in the confusion."

Celeste gave her a stern look. "You know I cannot discuss my clients, even to confirm who they are. At any rate, you have nothing to feel bad about. Word is you were quite the hero."

Maji didn't respond, didn't even flinch or make a noise as Celeste palpated the ankle, then the heel and arch of the foot, and finally the toes.

Celeste looked up at her, frowning. "It would be helpful to have an indication of which parts hurt. Before the swelling interferes with an accurate diagnosis."

"Nothing feels broken," Maji offered. "There's just a sharp pain when I flex it. You want me to show you?" She made a move to sit up.

"No. Just stop being so damn stoic." Celeste flexed Maji's toes up and down, watching her face.

Maji shrugged. "Maybe I'm more French than you."

"A smart-ass is what you are. Be serious for a bit." Celeste rolled the foot gently clockwise, then counterclockwise, putting the ankle through its full range of motion. "Anything?"

Maji frowned. "Yeah. Go slow and I'll say when it hits."

"Very good," Celeste said. "Do speak up." She put her palm on the ball of Maji's foot, cupping the heel with her other hand, and pressed the whole foot slowly and steadily toward her shin.

"There."

Celeste eased the pressure off and repeated. "Here?"

Maji nodded, swallowing.

"If you are as stoic about pleasure as you are about pain, then I am glad we decided to be friends."

Maji colored at the reminder. "So nothing's broken, right?"

"In my opinion, no. But if you want an X-ray, I will refer you to the local hospital."

Maji shook her head. "No offense, but I'm sick of doctors."

Celeste rolled the chair back, giving her friend some space. "Then let's talk about those pills. There are alternatives you should consider."

Maji sighed. She'd been composing the story in her head all morning, trying to find the balance between truth and divulging classified information. "Yeah. I...thanks. Do you have anything to drink?"

Celeste left her with an ice pack and disappeared into the adjacent room. After a few minutes, she wheeled a metal instrument cart out with a full spread—teapot, real cups, cookies, and even a sandwich. "*Et voilà*. I cook here more than in the staff housing. My supplies there are not secure, even with my name on them."

"Living with strangers can suck. No rooms in town?"

Celeste narrowed her eyes in suspicion. "Oh no. You are too good at moving the light off of yourself. Now you begin your story wherever you like. Wait." She removed the white coat. "Two friends talking, yes?"

"Sure." Oddly, that did help. Maji reminded herself that Celeste had no connection to the Army, couldn't get her in trouble no matter how much or little she told her. Still, less was better, and a little fabrication was warranted. "I have a high-risk job in personal security. Jumping toward jerks with guns is like instinct after years of protecting clients." All true, if she thought of the high value targets, or HVTs, as clients. "A few months back, a job went sideways."

"It went wrong?"

"It went very wrong. My team was hired to get a kidnapped woman back from some people known to kill their hostages even when ransom was paid. We had a good plan, but...we became hostages ourselves."

Celeste waited quietly. *Not letting me off the hook, huh?* Maji picked a focus point on the wall before continuing.

"One of my team was killed, and all of us were beaten, deprived of food and water. The usual." *Except for the brandings. And roasting Palmer's headless body like an animal.* "We didn't know if anyone would come to help, so we tried to escape." Maji shifted her gaze to the second hand on the wall clock, watching it tick inexorably forward. She wished she could remember more—and less. "I lost control during the fight and hurt some people." *Killed, Rios. Killed people.* Her throat closed on the words that wouldn't come out.

Celeste took her hand, but Maji didn't look to see the pity or fear or condemnation in her face. "You have seen someone for this? A counselor?"

Maji nodded. An Army captain had assured her she had followed the rules of engagement, according to the official debrief. That whatever memories came back as her brain rewired itself back into fighting shape were unreliable bits of information. That she'd acted like a good soldier and should let the rest go. Maji was pretty sure he really believed that. The chaplain they sent in was more interested in listening, but Maji had nothing to say to him. And the neuro rehab folks really just focused on function, so sleep mattered for the critical role it played giving the brain a chance to mend itself. Like maintenance cycles between sessions with the speech therapist, occupational therapist, and physical therapist. Too damn many therapists, and none of them called her on acting like a zombie. Maybe they didn't care if she was dead inside. But Ava did. "Yes. Ava, Hannah's wife."

"Good. Did she give you the pills?"

"No. She doesn't prescribe." *Unless you count forgiveness.* They worked on baby steps, two forward and one back. "She would disapprove as much as you do."

Celeste sighed. "I am not opposed to pharmaceuticals when they are needed. I disapprove only of you becoming dead or damaged in the brain from drugs administered without proper safeguards. Whatever you did, killing yourself will not help anyone."

That sounded so much like Ava. She should go home already, try to be of use. Maji slumped over, exhausted at the very thought.

Celeste joined her on the examining table, one arm around her shoulders. "I am very sorry for what happened to you and your friends.

Although this situation is outside of my experience, my practice is very mind-body oriented and quite successful with athletes. If you will let me, I can help you with the sleep and also calming while awake. Yes?"

If she were back at Fort Bragg instead of on leave, Maji would surely work with a performance consultant. All of Special Forces used them to help the soldiers literally keep their heads in the game. As long as Celeste stuck to helping her be able to sleep again and didn't try to put her on a therapist's couch, why not? "Sure. Thanks."

An insistent tap came on the office door. "Doctor?" Sanxto's unmistakable baritone.

"One moment." Celeste leaned back and looked at Maji sympathetically. "Shall I hide you?"

Maji shook her head and blinked back the tears that often threatened but rarely fell. "Let him in." She leaned back and elevated her leg, pushing the last of her emotions down and sealing them off.

"I knew it was you." Santxo shouldered his way past Celeste. "How badly are you hurt?"

"Just a twisted ankle. What did you tell the press?"

Santxo smiled almost mischievously, his mustache and eyebrows lifting in unison. "That we have excellent plainclothes security. And that the police would confiscate their cameras for evidence if they hung around to learn more."

"How did he even get a gun in here?" Celeste asked.

Reasonable question, Maji thought. *Also, is my face on camera now? Will it be in the news?*

"It was a paint gun," Santxo replied. "Plastic."

Maji groaned. "So I saved a celebrity from a trip to the dry cleaner?"

Santxo shrugged. "And now the police wish to speak with you." He turned to Celeste. "In private. You will be so kind as to loan us your office?"

Celeste looked unsure.

"I'm fine. Really." Maji thought of Reimi. "But if you could give a note to a friend of mine? She may be worried about me." She scribbled: *Reimi, blackjack dealer. Maji fine.*

An odd look flitted across Celeste's face as she deciphered Maji's scrawl. "I'm sure she will be very relieved."

Before he let the police investigator in, Santxo said, "Now, don't let this guy intimidate you. We served together in the military, and I know him well. Our wives are friends, but he...well. Always knows better than everyone else, like that Brit who manages Erlea. He contacted me last week, wanted to make sure we had security for a celebrity of her caliber. As if she's our first. Tried to tell me how to do my job. Is it my fault some fans send her terrible messages? No. And they are not the ones who we must watch out for, anyway. No, it is the quiet ones like this man pretending to have a political cause."

Maji held up a hand to pause him. "Pretending?"

Celeste led Maji through the back hallways to a service entrance. Like Reimi's tour in reverse, minus the hand-holding. Maji was beginning to build a map of the non-public parts of the building in her mind—training become habit, turned to distraction. *So what are you avoiding?*

Oh, right. She'd sell a kidney for a good night's sleep. "Thanks for your help. Last night and today."

"Happy to help, my friend."

"Yeah, well." Maji paused. "I won't take anything tonight. What do you recommend instead?"

Celeste stopped before a set of doors, glancing through the windowpanes before speaking quietly. "I can teach you a number of techniques for quieting the mind. And there are supplements—they need to be ordered online but in a few days can be here. Tonight, do you have anything you can hold? Preferably with a scent that comforts you."

What am I, four years old? "No, I don't really have a blankie." Maji followed Celeste's gaze through the door to Reimi smoking by the exit. Maji raised one eyebrow suggestively. "But our mutual friend smells nice."

Celeste scowled at her. "And I'm sure she would...accommodate... you. But a kick in the night would not be a suitable thank-you."

"No. No it wouldn't." Maji stared at her shoes. "I didn't mean to hurt you. I try to sleep alone."

"Hey," Celeste said, touching her arm. "You didn't know I was there. Don't beat yourself up. Besides, I don't think Reimi is the staying-over type."

Maji searched Celeste's face for judgment, but found none. "I'll look for something on the boat that might work. And take a run in the evening."

"Yes, good. A full exercise an hour or two before you lie down. And do not expect sleep to come right away. Just rest and direct your mind to something pleasant. A place you like, a joyful time. Plan to visit there while you sleep. But don't force it—relax yourself."

"Without drugs or whiskey."

"Of course. But if exercise does not release enough endorphins, try self-pleasure." Celeste nodded toward the door. "You can have Reimi all night in your imagination."

Maji fished for an appropriate comeback. "You follow your own prescription, Doctor? With, let me guess, someone *salvaje*."

Celeste blushed. "The advice is medically sound, and my fantasies are off-limits. Now I should go back to the office. Stop by tomorrow?"

"Right after my command appearance with the queen bee." Maji smiled at Celeste's bafflement. "Erlea means *bee* in Euskara, the Basque language. I looked it up. Anyway, it's some thank-you thing. Want an autograph?"

"No, no. Not I. Enjoy the brush with greatness, yes? You earned her gratitude, paint gun or no." Celeste left her at the exit with a kiss on each cheek.

When she spotted Maji, Reimi's face lit up. "Thank goodness. I heard you were well, but I hoped to see for myself."

"The doctor promises I'll live to tell the story. Thank you for the behind-the-scenes tour."

"I couldn't leave you out there on the sidewalk with such excitement inside. I would gladly show you more, if it were not against the house rules." Reimi gave her a kiss on both cheeks, casual as female friends all over Spain. But she only stepped back a fraction, keeping close eye contact.

Maji felt herself flush and caught a hint of satisfaction in Reimi's eyes. "Well, I wouldn't want to get you into any trouble."

"You are capable of handling trouble." Reimi ran a fingernail lightly down Maji's bicep and smiled enticingly. "Are you sure you won't change to a game I don't deal?"

"I can't. I'm playing for money, not for fun."

Reimi stroked Maji's forearm lightly. "Myself, fun is all I seek. No harm in that, is there?"

"Not if that's all two consenting adults both want."

Reimi smiled and continued caressing her arm, creating a pleasant tingle. "There are so many other pleasures to enjoy here. The beaches, the ocean, the sun on your skin."

Hannah's offer popped into Maji's head. "As soon as I can afford to give up the game, I'll definitely let you know."

Reimi drew her in, someplace between a slow dance and a hug. The softness of her breasts and hips pressing against Maji's own lit up all the nerves in her body at once. It was hard to hold back the urge to claim the lips so close to hers. But if Maji broke the house rules, one of them would pay. And she wasn't that kind of player.

"Promise?" Reimi whispered against Maji's neck, her warm breath a caress.

Maji sighed. "Promise."

Reimi chuckled and pushed herself away.

Chapter Five

Maji found her way to the backstage door in the dim morning by the utility lights mounted near the CCTV cameras. She put her sweatshirt's hood up, shielding her face. With the hoodie, old jeans, and running shoes, she might be mistaken for crew, but not for the star of the show. If she met Erlea in person, Celeste would enjoy the story. If not, she'd at least get to see the inside of the theater. Assuming she got in.

Maji knocked on the heavy door, watching the roadies moving equipment in through the nearby loading dock. They paid her no mind.

"Morning," she said to a man in a long-sleeved T-shirt as he passed her. He grunted a greeting in return, not looking up from his path to the loading dock. She left the unattended stage door and followed him in, skirting around a man and woman rolling gear in heavy black cases off the large truck.

Maji scanned the backstage area and picked a direction to wander. Curious to see the fancy theater from a performer's point of view, she passed between the two sets of curtains in the wings and walked to center stage. A runway extended out into the middle of the high-roller seats.

Out past the orchestra level, near the doors leading to the audience lobby, Maji expected to spot a control booth. Nope. She scanned the box seats to the sides, then the upper and lower balcony seats in the middle. An impressive place, with more than two thousand seats for sure. Plenty of ticket revenue with a more controllable crowd than in a stadium. Sweeping her view up to the ceiling, Maji finally found the control center, a glass-fronted pod suspended over the upper balcony. Space-age. The electronics probably were, too.

"Coffee stage right, love," someone said in English with a British accent. "Pour me a tall one and find me in the do shop."

Maji turned to see who had spoken to her and watched a lanky frame in fashionably distressed denim, with a shock of platinum fauxhawk, disappear into the wings without looking back. Intrigued, Maji bypassed the coffee table and looked for movement beyond the curtains. A door clicked shut down the hallway and she headed for it. The handwritten sign *Do Shop* below the permanent *Hair and Makeup* stenciled on the door in Spanish made her smile. She knocked.

"Door's open," came the familiar voice.

Maji pushed through and surveyed the chaos. "How do you like your coffee? Other than tall."

Fauxhawk looked up from unloading cases of cosmetics and his jaw dropped. A narrow jaw on an aquiline face with a fluorescent green goatee, which Maji noted matched his nails.

She gave him her open, nonthreatening look. "I'm not press, I promise. Erlea asked to see me this morning, but nobody seems to be around. Is it still too early?"

He straightened up and looked down at her. "Not too early for working folk. But you might as well get a cuppa and put your feet up in here."

"Okay, thanks." Maji backed out and the door swung shut behind her. Maybe one of the croissants on the coffee table was chocolate. Or ham and cheese. The Spanish put ham in everything, with cheese as an extra bonus. Maybe she should grab one of each.

Returning to the do shop juggling two mugs and a plate with three croissants, Maji pushed the door open with her shoulder. "Where can I stay out of your way?"

"Take any seat," he answered, not pausing his progress in organizing an impressive array of containers on the counter.

Maji turned one of the padded pedestal chairs to face him and sat with the plate balanced on her knees. She sipped the coffee and savored the chocolate croissant quietly, watching him efficiently create order.

"You're easy company," he said, glancing over at her. "What do you think of our new house and home, then?"

"For such a swanky place, security sucks."

He puffed a laugh out through his nose. "There'll be a guard out by the lobby. Fans don't tend to come around back."

"And the paparazzi?"

"Oh, they know the tricks. But nobody sells shots of the crew to the papers, do they?"

"Will the back at least get locked up after load in?"

"Sure. The equipment's worth a fortune. Nico would shitcan someone if so much as a synthesizer walked off."

Maji let that sink in. "So the equipment's worth keeping safe. Just not the talent."

"Not my department, love. Believe me, I'm as fussed by yesterday's dustup as the next bloke, but..." He paused, recognition lifting his tweezed brows. "You're her, aren't you? The flying wonder."

Maji quirked a smile. "I prefer leaping lizard."

❖

A bright stream of daylight hit Erlea and she cursed. Must have left the blackout curtains open. Oh, fuck—morning call. Nico would shred her in front of her crew if she arrived late to call on the very first day. And he'd be right for once. A prick you couldn't argue with was the worst kind.

The bathroom door opened and a tall, stout guy with a beard walked out, buttoning his fly. "Oh, hey. Good morning." The eyes she must have found attractive last night smiled at her.

Great. She'd brought him back. Perfect. Name? Her memory search came up empty. "Morning. Uh-oh."

Erlea stumble-ran into the bathroom, slamming the door and making loud retching noises. That usually got rid of them. Except for the sweet ones. They were the worst.

He knocked on the door. "You okay?"

"I'll be fine. Don't wait for me."

The pause was long enough to worry her. Finally he said, "Okay. Can I call you?"

"Sure." *No. Of course not.*

"What's your number?"

Oh, thank God. At least she hadn't given him that last night. She called out her usual made-up string of digits.

"Thanks. Ciao."

Erlea stood, pulled her jeans up, and sighed with relief. If she was fully clothed, maybe she hadn't given him anything else last night, either. Probably a hand job, a few hours' sleep, and as many stories as he wanted to fabricate for his friends. Could be worse.

❖

Fauxhawk circled around Maji, studying her head and face from multiple angles.

"What?" Maji asked.

"I could make you twins in ten minutes. You and herself."

"Bullshit."

"Fancy a wager?"

No harm there. "Dinner for two at Cuina Mallorquina."

"Can I bring anyone I want, or are you angling for a date with me?"

Maji wiped her hands on her jeans and set the plate on the counter behind her. "In your dreams, fauxhawk."

He looked at her uncertainly.

"No offense, you're just not my type. And you're *fauxhawk* until you tell me your name."

He laughed. "Right then. I'm Roger. And you, leaping lizard?"

"Maji."

He pulled up a work stool and stared intensely at her features. "Plate," he said, waving his hand without taking his eyes off her face.

Maji reached behind her, making sure to not let the remaining croissants slide off. "Tick-tock."

"Shh," he said and bit into the almond one. "Hmm."

And then Roger got down to work, wielding sponges and eyeliner, mascara, and finally lipstick in a surprisingly rapid succession. He leaned back and looked at Maji, a slow smile spreading across his face, and turned her chair to face the mirror. "Ha. Now all I need is a date."

Maji studied herself in the mirror. It was a subtle transformation, less than she'd undergone for some missions where her cover required heavy makeup. She looked at his smug reflection. "That's it? I've never seen this face in the tabloids."

"They like the glam shots, love. Anyone can put on a costume and do an Erlea send-up, but this—"

The door swung open. "Rog, have you seen..." A fortyish man with a sprinkle of gray in his wavy black hair looked at Maji's reflection and paused, clearly surprised. "Oh, good. Why are you dressed like a grunge puppy? Well, it's just blocking. And at least your shoes are sensible. Now stop stuffing your face and get your ample ass out on stage, *Erlita.*" He snapped and pointed down the hall while pivoting away.

"Nice move," Maji muttered. "*He's* really, really not my type."

Roger smiled as the door swung shut. "Just one more thing you and Erlea have in common. Nico's always charming like that. You can guess how well they get on."

Maji sighed. "You're an expensive fellow to underestimate."

❖

On her way to the stage, Maji passed two of the roadies and made a point to make eye contact before nodding at them. They simply nodded back. Did only Nico see the resemblance? Or was the big rock star no big deal backstage? *All dressed up and nobody to impress.*

Usually Maji took pains to not be noticed while using a cover identity, but today she had thought it might actually be fun. If not, why be a rock star? Maji paused by the coffee table. Nico didn't notice her arrival, busy pointing up into the rafters, heatedly discussing lighting options with someone on the other end of his headset, presumably up in the control booth.

Maji was about to give up and head back to the do shop when she spotted a woman emerge from the far wings and saunter toward the coffee. She was Maji's height, similarly dressed except for the flip-flops, and damned if she didn't look just like her. Or did *she* look like Erlea?

The star paused and stared back at Maji, looking puzzled. A mild reaction. But maybe people impersonated her all the time and she was just deciding whether to call the police or write an autograph. Either way, Maji put one finger to her lips and gestured for Erlea to sneak over to her.

Up close Erlea muttered in Spanish, "What the fuck?"

"I'm your stand-in," Maji whispered back. "You know, a double. Roger did my face."

Erlea scrutinized his work. "Sorry he couldn't make you prettier than me. Is this another one of Nigel's bright ideas?"

Maji rolled with it, nodding and pouring Erlea a cup of coffee. "But could I really fool the paparazzi?"

"You don't sound like me." Erlea gestured toward Nico. "Does he know yet?"

Maji shook her head. "Called me Erlita and told me to get my ass out here." She left the *face-stuffing* and *ample* digs out, but mimed the snap-and-point move.

Erlea rolled her eyes. "Prick. I say we fuck with him. Go out and show some attitude."

Maji smiled and strode quietly out to center stage as if she had every right to be there. Erlea stepped a little deeper into the wings, into shadow. "Pick on someone your own size, Nico."

Nico turned and spotted Maji, who waved at him. He frowned and pointed Maji to a mark on the marley. "Stand there." Then into his headset he said, "Spot."

Maji flinched at the sudden glare and turned her head away.

"Christ, how late did you stay out?"

Maji just shrugged, her face still averted from the full force of the light.

"I will put a minder on you if I have to," Nico warned. "Take three steps back and strike a pose."

Pose? Maji walked backward three steps, one arm over her eyes, and thrust the other fist into the air.

"Don't take your hangover out on me, princess." Nico grabbed the pen from his shirt pocket and tossed it at Maji. It bounced off her chest and plunked onto the stage floor. "Strike a goddamn Erlea pose."

Maji lowered both arms and glared at him. Then she gave him the pose his behavior warranted: one fist thrust up like an uppercut, the other fist over that arm's elbow. So much more satisfying than just flipping a middle finger.

Erlea's laugh rang out from the wings, followed by a slow clap. She strolled out and slapped Maji on the shoulder. "You can be me every day before noon—then I will take over."

Nico looked at Maji and back at Erlea. "Who the fuck is that?"

"The stand-in," Erlea answered. "More me than me, eh? Not Nigel's worst idea."

Nico looked between the two Erleas, even less pleased with two than one. "Well, he didn't clear it with me. Just another distraction." He squinted at Maji. "Where did he even find you?"

"I fell out of the sky," Maji said. "Onto an idiot with a paintball gun and a stupid hat."

"You," Erlea said, lighting up. "That's almost as good as saving myself."

Nico snorted. "Now if she could just save you *from* yourself. At least she shows up on time. Can she sing and dance, too?"

Erlea looked expectantly at Maji. "Can you?"

"Lead or follow?" Maji joked, holding her arms in partner frame.

Erlea stepped in. "You lead."

Maji swayed in time to the first salsa tune that popped into her head, humming "Vivir Mi Vida." When she started singing the refrain as they danced, Erlea laughed and jumped in.

"Stop," Nico yelled. "Worst duet ever. Do not ever sing in public, no matter what Nigel tells you."

"Harsh," Erlea commented, dropping her hands to her hips.

"But fair," Maji said. "I'd ruin your reputation."

"Very funny," Nico said with no sign of amusement. "Now get out." He pointed with a snap toward the loading dock.

"Gladly," Maji said. "But don't you want all this back first?" She gestured to Roger's Vivir Mi Vida makeup job.

Erlea snorted. "Yeah. Otherwise she might be nice to the press and ruin my reputation as Queen Bitch."

"Fine," Nico said. "Just get out of my sight." He looked at Erlea's flip-flops with distaste. "And you, put on some sensible shoes before you trip and delay rehearsals."

❖

An hour later and barefoot, Erlea eyed the table's offerings. She should stick with black coffee and a little fruit. But dammit, she deserved a reward for managing to not cry, yell, or give in to the urge to hit Nico. She piled both fruit and pastry on the plate, poured coffee from the carafe, and added cream. Fuck his snide comments. If Nico wanted someone to lose weight, he could start with himself. She added another croissant to the plate, looked at it, put it back.

Erlea carried the full plate down the back hall to the do shop. Maybe Roger would share. If not, he'd at least appreciate the thought. You could never be too good to the person in charge of making you look great. And that man could work magic. She'd met impersonators at events and on the street but never before had that weird sensation of meeting herself. Maybe Maji would still be there. Erlea sped up.

"Ack." She dodged the swinging door but couldn't stop the coffee sloshing or a pastry falling onto the corridor floor.

Roger gaped at her, then the fallen treat. He picked it up, took a bite, and began talking around it. "Thanks. I prefer my coffee in a cup, though. Come in, love."

"I should clean this up. Don't you have towels?"

"I do. But don't you have an assistant fawning around somewhere? Let her do it."

Erlea scowled at him. She would never be like that, no matter who Nigel threw at her. "No. She quit, I think."

"Nico got to her that fast? Maybe she wasn't cut out for the industry."

Erlea sighed. "Putting up with abuse shouldn't come with the job. Speaking of which"—she peeked around the empty shop—"is she gone already?"

"Back to her old self and out the door in two winks. Couldn't get a word out of her, either. How bad did I bodge things this time?"

"You? Never. If Nico gives you trouble, tell him to go fuck himself."

Roger snorted. "Wouldn't it be nice for all of us if he could? Specially…never mind."

"Who? Someone here, already?" Please not one of the crew. "I suppose I'll find out who it is when they quit. Such a waste." Roger's pointed look and deliberate silence called out her hypocrisy better than any comeback could have. "Fine. But he wasn't working out, musically. He didn't mesh with the band as a drummer must."

"Hard to relax with your mates when you're worried they'll poach your woman."

"I was not *his* woman," Erlea snapped. "He knew the rules."

"They all say that, love. But even the macho ones have hearts. *Especially* the macho ones. And you know hearts don't listen to rules."

"Oh, please. It wasn't his heart I bruised—it was his ego. First they just want to fuck, then they want to sleep over. Then, bam, they think they own you."

"Okay, he was a bit of a wanker. But pretty. Very pretty. What makes you think the replacement will be better?"

She shook her head. "*Alvaro*, Roger. He has a name and it is safe to learn it—I promise. He's got excellent rhythm, plus actual social skills. Oh, and he's gay."

The look on Roger's face was so satisfying. "Should have led with that tidbit. When do I get to meet him?"

"A couple days. And if you like him, Roger, be nice."

"Me? I'm the sweetest bloke on this crew. A regular gentleman. Is he single?"

Now it was her turn to make him squirm with a look. "It matters to you, doesn't it? You're adorable."

"Don't you dare ruin my reputation."

Erlea laughed, letting the last of the darkness dissipate. If only they all got along so well. The band, the crew, the dancers—on the road they were the only family available. Sometimes dysfunctional and never without some drama, but she really did want all of them to be happy. They gave up time at home and other opportunities to help her chase her own success. Roger could work for anyone he wanted to, and his choosing to be here meant more than she could put into words. "Your secret is safe with me. And if Alvaro hurts you, I'll do more than fire him."

"Slow down, woman. Don't get me married off and divorced before you even introduce us."

She sipped her coffee. "I can't help it. I am a songwriter. I see a glimpse of the authentic you and a whole story unfolds in my head. Maybe it's a happy story."

"Maybe you're a romantic at heart, deep down where nobody can see it." He must have seen the flash in her eyes, for he latched on to the idea. "That Maji lass. Was it love at first sight? She's not really your twin, you know. All fine there, nothing smarmy."

Erlea shook her head at his fancies, savoring a bite of croissant.

Tomorrow the diet would begin. "No lightning bolts from the sky. Just a wild idea."

"Wilder than me finding Mr. Right with a drummer?"

"Definitely. What if Maji could fool the paparazzi? She could keep them occupied, and I—"

"Could enjoy a little peace?"

Erlea nodded. Roger might indulge in an occasional prowl of the clubs with her, but they were kindred souls when it came to work and quiet downtime. "If I could just focus for a few weeks, it might actually be a very good show."

"It'll be the best, love. Even with that tosser at the helm. And the idea's brilliant."

"You think Nigel would go for it?"

Roger looked skeptical and her heart sank. He'd worked on Nigel's productions off and on for years. "It's always the bottom line with him, love. And your run-ins with the journos do feed the marketing machine. More press, more bums in seats, and who cares if the show's as good as you want it to be? It just has to sell out."

"But…if I'm afraid to go out, then there are no photos and no stories." She gave him a sly look. "Surely a morose, drinking alone, hiding in her hotel room Erlea would be terrible for marketing."

"Not bad. Just don't actually hurt yourself to sell it. Don't want to make him a fortune the Santiago way."

Erlea shuddered at the thought. "He wasn't even good." Nigel's most lucrative client of all time had been a midlister until his suspicious death. The endless news articles, the conspiracy theories, and the lawsuits over his estate drove album sales like his concerts never had. Even today, some gossip show would find an angle to bring the mystery back to public attention. Erlea waved one hand in the air, an imaginary headline banner. "Santiago: Still dead! Fans demand to know how this can be! Details at eleven."

They laughed ruefully together.

"Try the frightened little girl angle," Roger advised. "Nigel's old-fashioned enough to buy it, and he doesn't know the stuff you're made of. God help him, neither does Nico."

Chapter Six

Maji turned her back to Erlea and her asshat manager, pretending to admire the view of Alcúdia's waterfront while she mulled his offer. Nigel Winterbottom's posh suite exuded the kind of luxury expected of a music industry mogul. Nigel and his pontificating about art and image fit the plastic-fake classiness perfectly. Did he actually care about Erlea, or even the quality of her music?

Which was not classy or fake but good, really good—especially the early years. Erlea's sound reminded Maji of Ani DiFranco in tone, a bit more like Pink in oomph, plus something else. Something in the instrumentals—wild fiddles and exuberant horns, not the straight up guitars and drums of most American rock. Almost like zydeco. If Erlea were a guy, the press would ask her about her craft, not just clothes and boyfriends. It wouldn't be that hard to fool the paparazzi, as Nigel proposed, but then the press wasn't a real threat to her safety.

"Well?" Nigel prompted her.

Maji took in his imperious figure reflected in the glass. She should just walk out, but she owed Erlea politeness at least. "Not interested." She gave Erlea an apologetic look. "Playing dress-up was fun, but I've got other business here."

"Like playing blackjack," Nigel said, looking satisfied with himself. "That gullible security chief may think highly of you, but I could have you barred from the game room."

"Nigel," Erlea protested. "There's no need to threaten Maji. She put herself in harm's way for me."

"Oh, please. A political stunt. It was bound to happen, what with the peace talks looming on the horizon. We should go over your talking points for the press."

Erlea acknowledged Maji's evident confusion and curiosity. "My father is Arturo Echeverra. A rather famous Basque separatist."

"Was, dear," Nigel corrected in a tone that made Maji cringe.

"If you have proof he's dead, Nigel, I'd love to see it," Erlea retorted.

Nigel sniffed. "Apparently those ETA types have doubts, too, if they're trying to get his attention through you."

"That idiot was not ETA," Erlea said.

"And you would know this how?" Nigel countered.

Erlea looked incredulous. "Because I grew up with them. I may have been a kid, but I know how they act, how they talk, even how they think."

"Then you should be more concerned with your safety than with the paparazzi," Nigel replied.

"He's right," Maji said, hating to agree with him. "The Gran Balearico's security is not adequate for you. You need a professional review by a third party to tell the resort what to upgrade."

Erlea looked intrigued.

But Nigel's nostrils flared. "And you would know this how?"

"Mr. Winterbottom, personal security for high-profile individuals is my field." Maji suppressed a smile. It was true. She wondered if Hannah's agreement to help one friend would extend to two, plus using her for a tidy little job like this. Hopefully. "If you're interested, I can give you references, a quote, whatever you need."

"That sounds like an unnecessary expense. The hotel is providing security, after all."

Erlea coughed pointedly. "Like they did in the lobby? Thank God it wasn't a real gun."

"I'm not trying to undermine Mr. Quintana or his staff, Mr. Winterbottom," Maji said. How had she gotten so invested, so fast? *Hero complex, Rios.* "But the truth is, practically anyone can get into the theater, the rooms, the kitchen, or the parking area here. Security staff follow normal protocols for a casino resort of this caliber, but they're concerned mainly with normal economic threats—gamblers who beat the house, dealers who collude, guests missing their jewelry, rooms missing their fluffy towels. Sure, they use CCTV like everyone in the EU. But all the closed-circuit cameras in the world won't keep an intruder at a safe distance. And keeping Erlea in one place for months means you should take the threats she receives more seriously, not less."

The color draining from Nigel's face told Maji her guess had hit home. He glared at Erlea. "What have you told her?"

"I didn't say a word," Erlea replied. "But I will, if you don't take her seriously."

Nigel breathed slowly, his aquiline nose flaring again with the effort. "Have your proposal ready for my review tomorrow."

❖

Celeste jumped when the phone on her desk rang. She paused the music video on the large desktop monitor. "Dr. Guillot. How may I help you?"

"Doctor, are you in your office?"

"Yes, Santxo. That is where the office phone rings." Celeste blinked at the frozen image of Erlea on the screen. Maybe it was time to stop hiding out here. She could forward the phone to her mobile, wear her pager, and get out more.

"Of course, of course. What I meant was, do you have a patient in there?"

"No. I am alone. What can I help you with?"

"I have great news," he said. And the office door opened, the frame filling with his beaming figure. He spotted the monitor before Celeste could black it out. "Oh, good, you are doing your research."

"Pardon?"

"Learning about the prior tours, getting prepared for any medical issues that might arise," Santxo explained. "Like watching the training tapes and competitions for your athletes."

Celeste fiddled with the computer to cover her shock. What had management told security about her troubles? She didn't want to discuss them with Santxo, but she was done hiding them. Calling in sick after Adrienne hit her, covering the bruises with makeup, fabricating excuses to decline social invitations—old behaviors. But her work... "My athletes, yes. What about them?"

Santxo looked sheepish. "I am sorry. You are on sabbatical, I shouldn't have brought it up. But with the dancers and all, this just seems so perfect for your expertise."

"*This* what? What is this great news?"

"Oh. Yes." He pulled himself to his full height to make the announcement. "They want medical supplies backstage."

"I see. And they should have first aid materials on hand. Wraps, ice, the usual. So?"

"So perhaps they will need you." His smile vanished. "Unless that is what you are on vacation from, dealing with sports injuries."

"I think, my friend, you have the wrong idea about my normal practice."

"But you are a physician. And you work with athletes. Your website says so." He looked puzzled. "And the testimonials, from Olympians and prima ballerinas and—"

"Yes. All that is true. I did start in traditional sport medicine, sending injured athletes to proper rehabilitation. But the interesting part was how they dealt with their recovery. I got additional training and now specialize in the mental aspects of performance."

"You mean all that visualization business? See the ski slope, feel yourself making all the slalom turns, win the gold?"

She chuckled. "Close enough. But I can help them stock bandages and splints, for now."

"They will be pleased. And if you told them about your success with famous athletes…"

"Santxo. I am on sabbatical from dealing with the rich and famous, remember?"

His posture drooped. "Of course. Are they very demanding, the big name players?"

"Some are very self-absorbed. Some are humble and just driven, hard on themselves. Like everyone, I guess. A mixed bag."

"Hmm. I wonder which type Erlea is." Santxo brightened. "Perhaps you will find out. And then tell me."

❖

Erlea cleared a corner of the stage-side coffee table and sat to review Alejandro's spreadsheet of tasks and timelines. The kid was turning out to be an ideal production assistant, super organized and the polar opposite of Nico in personality. Fresh out of school, he deferred to everyone on the crew. In time he'd learn to draw clearer lines, say no when appropriate. But on the technical side he was nearly as meticulous as his boss, asking all the right questions and taking thorough notes. This one about her doing aerials in one number, though…whatever he had in mind, some other dancer could fill that role. And where was he this morning?

Erlea dialed his mobile.

"At your service," Alejandro answered. Perky as always. Did he say that to everyone, or just her? If he started fawning, she'd have to nip that in the bud.

"Where are you? I want to run through the set list again."

"Of course. I went to the airport. We'll be at the theater in three minutes—no, two. Make that—"

The door by the loading dock banged open and Imane appeared seconds later. "Erlea, darling. Always the worker bee. Put that thing down and hug me already."

Erlea grinned, closed the laptop, and ran to her old friend. Imane's long arms enveloped her, and Erlea squeezed back. "God, I've missed you."

"Not as much as I've missed you," Imane said. "How long since we've been on the same continent, much less the same city?"

Erlea stepped back to meet her gaze. "Too long." The beads in Imane's hair clinked together as they touched cheeks, and Erlea swatted at them, thinking of her cat. "Love these. Nico will probably say something hateful though. Ignore him or punch him, I don't care."

Imane squinted down at her. "Oh, seriously? His reputation is earned then."

"On the best-shows-ever side, we'll see. But for Asshole of the Year, no competition. I swear he's driving me to drink."

"As if you needed anyone's help with that." Imane smiled to take the sting from her words and slung an arm over Erlea's shoulders. "We'll show him. Don't you worry."

"What do you think of the theater?" Erlea asked, hoping Imane would find the space suitable for her signature choreography, a blend of modern dance and Cirque-style acrobatics. That Imane had put other projects on hold to finally work with her meant the world.

"It'll do."

"Staying here for an extended run, we can do things with the set and rigging that a concert tour would not permit," Alejandro piped in. "Within limits, of course—bearing in mind the risks of repetitive stress and sheer physical fatigue for the performers." He caught himself, coloring. "But why am I telling you this?"

Because you want to impress her, silly boy, Erlea thought. "Perhaps you've caught the mansplaining bug from Nico. I hear it can be cured, if you catch it early."

Imane just shook her head at Erlea. "Really, I've missed you more."

"Not possible," Erlea countered. "Alejandro, show her the set list. I want to know what will really work here. And after the residency, what we should scale back for touring."

Alejandro fished a folder from his shoulder bag and handed it over, blushing. "I made you a welcome packet."

Imane scanned the notes in the color-coded information packet. "Mostly your top hits, eh? Playing it safe. I wish you'd include those two I love from your first album. I have some ideas for them."

"Ready to hear them any time." Alejandro held his tablet in both hands.

Imane glanced over the sheaf at him, a little smile playing on her purpled lips. "Soon. What cities do you have lined up?" she asked Erlea.

"Nigel has a list, but he hasn't locked in any venues. Says we might extend our run here, give us more time to engineer the live album from the new show."

Imane raised one skeptical brow. Erlea knew how her friend felt about Mr. Bait and Switch and hoped she knew better than to say it in front of Alejandro. Sweet as he was, he still reported to both Nico and Nigel.

"And the making-of video," Alejandro added. "I'll be filming bits of rehearsals, that sort of thing. But I promise you'll never even know I'm—"

"There you are," Nico bellowed from the wings, sounding aggrieved as usual.

All three of them turned to face him.

Alejandro put on a face that showed he was used to placating difficult people. "Yes, we made good time from the airport, and I already have some notes—"

"You don't take notes from them," Nico interrupted.

Imane extended a hand. "You must be the legendary Nico. I'm—"

"I know who you are. When we've got lights and sets ready, you can bring your dancing boys out to play. For now, you two get off my stage."

"Your stage?" Erlea felt Imane's hand on her arm, a gentle reminder to curb her temper.

"My boys arrive in three days," Imane said without a trace of irritation showing. "And when will the aerialists get here?"

"Who the fuck knows? They are pleading some business with visa issues. Like always, they want to work here but don't want to follow the rules to get here."

Erlea bristled at his tone and insinuation. Barcelona might be an official refuge city, but that didn't stop the prejudice toward outsiders. She'd lost her tolerance years ago for the micro-aggressions Imane faced every day. Erlea took a deep breath, ready to crucify him.

But her friend jumped in first, with her usual aplomb. "I'm sure it will work out soon. If you give me their contact information, perhaps I could help."

Nico snorted. "Of course. Who understands a *harraga* better than another—"

"That's enough," Erlea spat at him, stepping between her friend and Nico, her face so close to his that he instinctively took a step back. The distance only gave her room to charge up.

"Cool down," Imane cautioned her. "He's not worth it."

"Damn right," Erlea agreed, still glaring at Nico. "You're not worth it, you ignorant asshole. You know how many people wouldn't work this show when they heard you were stage-managing? And I've already lost two, not counting my assistant."

"She hardly counts," he replied. "Replaceable as your precious roadies."

"Everybody on my crew counts," Erlea snapped back. "It's my name on the show, and they rise or fall with me. They trust me and I need people I can trust in return. You drive any more off, and we'll do the show without you."

Nico crossed his arms over his chest. "Then you'll all fall together. I'd like to see you pull off a show this ambitious with anyone else in the industry today. I'm irreplaceable. Nigel can see that, even if you're too blinded by love and stardust to see anything in the real world."

"This is my real world, you arrogant prick. And my people. Either you treat them with respect or you go. Try me, Nico. Just try me."

❖

Celeste watched from the wings, frozen by the ferocity in Erlea's tone. Despite having excellent Spanish, the heated exchange was a bit too fast for Celeste to follow completely. She caught the word *harraga*, a slur for Algerian immigrants. Was the woman Erlea shielded with her body North African? Perhaps. And gorgeous. Did Erlea stand up for all of her crew this way, or was this woman special?

Either way, Erlea in protector mode was electric. Celeste let herself soak in the details of Erlea's physique, aware even as she did so that her assessment was not clinical. Where Maji was all hard angles and wiry muscle, Erlea had a bit more softness, a curviness that Celeste found quite alluring. Plus that sultry voice.

Nico turned away from Erlea and noticed Celeste witnessing the charged interaction. "You." All eyes shifted to her. "Are you the medic? About time you showed up."

Apparently the lecture on respect hadn't sunk in. "I am Dr. Guillot, the house *physician*. I understand you requested assistance with medical supplies."

"Talk to the boy," he said, then literally snapped his fingers. "Alejandro."

The young man stepped forward, offering Celeste a handshake and looking apologetic. "Thank you for coming, Dr. Guillot."

Nico strode off, and seconds later a slammed door reverberated through the stage floor. Celeste smiled uncertainly at the trio. "If this is a bad time…"

"With Nico, every minute is a bad time." Erlea sighed and looked to the tall graceful woman. "I'm sorry. You know me."

The woman gave her a wink. "Don't ever change, love." To Celeste she added, "*Erlea* means *bee*, you know. And she can sting."

"Yes," Celeste said. "So I hear. And I thought your singing voice was powerful."

"Thanks," Erlea said, shifting uncomfortably. "This is Imane, our choreographer, and you've met Alejandro." When Imane winked at the young man and snapped her fingers, Erlea scowled. "It's not funny."

"Laugh or cry, my dear Doña Quixote," Imane replied with obvious affection. "If your words were lances…"

"He'd be dead. But if I started with him, where would I ever stop?" Erlea shook her head. "And I shouldn't admit this to a physician, but now I really need a smoke."

Celeste laughed, charmed despite the tension still roiling in the pit of her stomach. "Understandable. But if you decide to quit, remember I am here to assist."

"Can you find me a stage manager who isn't a racist or a misogynist? One must exist."

"That's outside my realm, I'm afraid. I have only nicotine patches to offer." *Courage, Celeste. That's not all you have.* "And some well-tested techniques for dealing with stress and anxiety." Damn—that wasn't supposed to sound flirty. Why was it so hard to act professional? She was a doctor, not a hormone-addled adolescent.

Imane smirked. "I bet you do. Do you make house calls?"

Erlea blushed, and Celeste felt herself color as well, gratified to see her reaction and embarrassed by how much it pleased her. "I have an office here."

"May I come see you? Or others on the crew?" Alejandro asked. Bless him.

"Of course," Celeste responded. "All resort guests are welcome, although my resources are limited. I should give you local hospital information, in addition to advice on supplies."

"Excellent." Alejandro gave Erlea and Imane a little nod, as if totally at home with the power couple. Were they a couple? There were rumors about Erlea and women, but the media always photographed her with men. Not that Celeste should care. She wasn't in the market for a celebrity of any stripe.

"We won't forget you're available," Imane said, nudging Erlea.

"Yes, thanks," Erlea said, shifting again from one foot to another.

As they walked away, Celeste couldn't help but grin. *She's bashful.* Not from a thousand videos would Celeste ever have gleaned that insight. And now, just like that, Erlea was a person. Brave for others. But also shy. *Surprising—and sweet.*

❖

"Your boat is so charming," Celeste said as she laid her silverware aside, full of fresh fish and salad. A crisp white wine would have made the meal perfect. But with the sedatives issue, perhaps it was best that Maji had no alcohol on board her little boat. "And the days finally feel longer. I love spring. And your magnificent yacht."

"I'm glad you like her." Maji gathered up the plates with a nod to the sunset. "Can't take credit for that. But I have an offer for you. Tea?"

"How can I resist?"

Down in the cozy cabin, Maji put the kettle on and leaned back against the cabinets that stored everything away so neatly. "I may be off the boat for a few days. If you like, you're welcome to use it."

"Oh, but I love the dorms so. My cheese never spoils. At least not the expensive kind—the mice are very discerning." Seeing Maji's uncertainty, Celeste abandoned the attempt at humor. "Yes, I'd love the privacy. Thank you. Starting when?"

"Probably tomorrow. I'll let you know as soon as I hear."

"That's very generous of you. Would you like me to stay here tonight?"

"No strings." Maji pinked up beneath her deep tan. "That's not why I offered."

"No, not like that. I meant only to watch over you. You are trying to sleep without the sedative, yes?"

"Right, of course. That's sweet, but I'll be okay. I ran your suggestions by Ava and she approved."

"What a handy friend to have. Does she help with your work?"

Maji shook her head. "Not officially. Ava has her own practice, but she's also married to my boss. I spent a lot of time with them growing up and saw what they both did to help people. They inspired me to channel my teenage angst into doing some good instead of just raising hell."

"Well, they sound like excellent role models."

Maji gave her a self-deprecating smile. "At least I picked up the jumping on bad guys part."

"Another similarity you and Erlea seem to share. You really should have seen her today."

"The way you told it, I feel like I was there. And you do a great Nico the Horrible impression."

"How do you know?"

"I had the pleasure of meeting him when I went to collect my celebrity thank-you note."

"I'm sorry, then. He is so aggressive. Frankly, I'm surprised Erlea showed such restraint." Surprised and impressed. A star like her could get away with terrible behavior, and even Celeste would have been tempted to strike him. But Erlea had made her body a shield, and then used words. And her threats sounded appropriate, protective of her friends and business interests. Just the kind of person you would want on your side.

"Well, she's a black belt, right?"

Celeste sensed a theme. "You said something about that the other day. But you never explained."

Maji paused, gathering her thoughts. "Well, don't use me as an example, but martial arts train discipline—restraint. At best, to master the lizard brain. At the least, to never start a fight or use force for punishment. If Erlea really earned a belt in Aikido, then she's had years to learn to hold her own without resorting to violence."

"Ah. I had not thought of it that way."

Maji gave her a rueful smile. "Yeah, well, it's not what you see in the movies. Fight scenes look a lot cooler than walking away does. And in real life, hurting people is easier, too."

"Hey, don't be so rough on yourself," Celeste said, slipping out from the little dinette table to give Maji a hug.

Maji held on tightly a moment, then sighed and spoke into Celeste's shoulder. "Thanks."

Celeste loosened her hold and started to step back. As she turned her head to reply, her lips brushed Maji's cheek, the unintentional contact tantalizing. Why was she hung up on an unobtainable celebrity, when this attractive woman was right in front of her? Celeste grasped Maji's jacket and leaned in.

Maji tensed all over and stepped to the side, scraping the cabinets at her back. "I'm sorry." She blinked rapidly, staring past Celeste.

The clear signs of trauma kicked Celeste into doctor mode. She backed up, put her hands in plain view. "You are safe. Are you all right?"

"No." Maji thumped the back of her head against the cabinets, twice. "Clearly not." Maji squeezed her eyes shut. "Damn fucking lizard brain. What good does it do to understand the limbic system if you can't stop yourself from freaking out when something perfectly normal and nonthreatening happens?"

"It was unexpected contact. And a natural reaction, after an incident like the one you described for me."

Maji laughed bitterly. "My whole life's been a series of *incidents*. And I've been training since I was five. Got fight-or-flight under control years ago. Not that you can tell. If I can't even handle a kiss, how am I supposed to work again?"

Celeste hated to see Maji pressed up against the edge of the little space like that, so on edge. "I'm going to sit. Over here. Okay?"

Maji stayed put as Celeste slid back behind the dinette. Then she started to pace. "Great. Now I've got you scared of me. Not that I blame you."

"No. I just want to give you room to breathe. I don't think you would hurt me."

Maji put both palms on the little table and leaned toward her. "Really? In the hospital, I hit a guy who tried to hug me. Knocked him out. And now I'm tossing around any jerk who touches me. But I'm glad one of us isn't afraid."

"Were your captors all male?" Celeste asked. She wished Maji would back up again, or sit down. Though she trusted her, being loomed over brought Adrienne to mind.

Maji spun around and started pacing. "No. And before you ask, I was not raped. Okay?" Apparently, Celeste's carefully composed expression did not satisfy as an answer. "Though every shrink assumes so. And letting them think they were right got them off my back, at least."

Celeste waited for more. Maji so clearly wanted to talk. But instead she perched on the bench seat and started unbraiding the cord acting as a bumper on the edge of the table. Finally, Celeste prompted, "Did you ever talk through what really happened?"

Maji shook her head, eyes on her fidgeting fingers. "They had the incident reports."

"Those don't tell how you experienced the incidents. You know, trauma does not come from the events so much as how you respond to them, what you feel in the moment. Do you want to talk about that?"

Maji met Celeste's gaze, but her expression was shuttered. "No. I know what I did, and I have to live with it. Talking won't change that." She closed her eyes. "And I'm just so fucking tired. Like, all the time."

"Good sleep is vital to the nervous system," Celeste noted. "Did you try—"

"Not yet." Maji popped up and started searching for something, closing and opening all the little compartments around the galley. She pulled out a plastic squeeze bottle, popped the lid, and inhaled deeply. "Bingo."

Celeste caught the scent of peppermint. "Good. This aroma calms you?"

"It's worth a try. Even asleep, I can't confuse this with…anything else." Maji visibly relaxed, even gave Celeste a ghost of a smile. "It's Ava in a bottle."

"How so?"

"She uses this kind of liquid soap for everything." Maji looked wistful. "Even shampoo. Ava used to tuck in me and Bubbles—my best friend, more like a sister. We thought we were too cool and grown up, but she'd do it anyway. And when she'd lean in to kiss us on the forehead, her hair smelled like this. I never had nightmares at Ava's house."

"Definitely worth a try, then."

CHAPTER SEVEN

Maji woke to the gentle clanging of the spars. She stretched luxuriantly and looked at her watch. *Holy shit*. Had she really slept through? No, she remembered waking a few times, orienting herself. And then snugging up to the minty pillow. *Rios one, lizard brain zero.*

She should call Ava. And go running. Then a big American breakfast before that diner got too busy with tourists. Yes. She rolled out of the V-berth and spotted her laptop on the dinette. Oh, right, she had a contract to deliver. To help Erlea. Hannah had said yes so quickly that Maji wondered if Ava had sold the idea to her as a safe form of occupational therapy.

Maybe Hannah had sold it to JSOC the same way. Since Command had approved Maji's return as a Select Reserve, technically she could hold a job wherever she wanted to. But working for their top consultant's firm was pushing the envelope. But then so was being one of the US Army's first female operators. This assignment might be small, but failure was never an option. Maybe she'd luck out and Nigel would balk at the price tag, reject the contract outright.

No. *Wrong day to give up, Rios*. Maji dressed herself carefully in one of her tourist-gambler outfits, slacks and deck shoes with a button-down shirt. If Nigel said no, back to the tables. She'd work for the money, one way or another. If Nigel signed off, Hannah could fund her bankroll for Dr. Lyttleton with a paycheck instead of a bailout. And Maji would double down on keeping her shit together and putting the mission objective first: keep Erlea safe.

❖

Maji stepped away from the desk in her hotel room, leaving the building's schematics open across it. She flopped onto the bed and twisted, right leg to outstretched left hand. Her low back gave a satisfying pop. So much room and no one to play with. *Fuck you, lizard brain*. But it felt good to be working again. Maji reversed the twist, got a series of little pops. And damn, it felt good to move freely again—a minor miracle, considering her injuries.

Getting this far took four months' intensive rehab. *And two more on your own, Rios*. Maji thought about the check-ins with Ava, the solo exercises, the workouts. Plenty to feel good about, if she needed to hunt the good. Or whatever the mental fitness trainers were calling it these days. What she really needed was to complete this job without fucking up.

Time to get rolling. The Gran Balearico was a huge site, counting the hotel, casino, theater, and grounds. Maji grabbed her laptop and scanned through Hannah's protocols for her Paragon Security contractors, which varied slightly from what Special Forces followed. She checked the time in New York and called Hannah.

"You have questions on the specs?" Hannah answered by way of greeting.

Maji chuckled. "Just a couple. Is this a good time?"

"For you, always."

"Aw. You say that to all your contractors?"

"On their first assignments, yes."

"This is hardly my first mission."

"It is your first time with Paragon, and it is not a mission," Hannah corrected. "Otherwise, we would not be speaking."

Maji sighed. She hated the Army's firewall, cutting all communications between them. But she'd do whatever JSOC demanded to keep them both working for the unit. "Point taken. Okay, question one: You really want me to inspect the whole facility before starting background checks on any of the crew?"

"Yes. You only have the all-access key card for forty-eight hours. I have others doing the data pull for you."

"Oh. Thanks."

"On my team, Maji, no one works solo." Hannah paused. "Also, we can help with the facility notes if you send photos of obvious deficiencies as you spot them."

"Great." On a Delta team, Maji was never alone either, even when she was the only one to infiltrate. A support system always stood ready to help with exfil. "But I have access to the crew tonight. Just a social gathering. I planned to use it for recon."

"By all means. Send notes afterward, please. Other questions?"

"That's it for now. Thanks for covering me on this." Maji wanted to say more, but the words stuck.

"It's a good simple assignment. And a pleasure to see you working." Hannah paused again. "How would you feel about teaching camp with me this summer?"

"Seriously?" Of all the things Maji missed about home over her years in the unit, Hannah's self-defense camp was near the top. Right after family. "Hell, yes. Could I stay with you and Ava?"

Hannah chuckled softly. "You know Ava will insist. And I wouldn't mind seeing you, myself."

Several hours later, Maji hung the maid uniform back in the closet, next to the parking valet, kitchen worker, and bellhop outfits. Those had given her access to guest rooms, dumbwaiters, heating ducts, maintenance conduits, and more, all without attracting attention. For the next step, she needed the security uniform—trickier.

Like Maji's Army battle dress uniform, the security officer's trousers and jacket were cut for a man, too big and also boxy. Even with her hair tucked up under the hat, she'd get second glances. Looking at herself in the mirror, Maji weighed whether to spend the time going into town for makeup and other supplies against a quick and easy visit to Roger.

Avoiding hotel guests until her look was complete, Maji rode the service elevator down to the theater level. She let herself in through the audience lobby with the all-access key card and took a few minutes to explore the vacant front of house areas: box office, coat check, concessions, restrooms, and VIP lounge. Then she took the theater-goers' ramp to the upper levels, the loges and the box seats.

Maji stopped at different vantage points to assess the line of sight and distance to center stage.

On the orchestra level, Maji spotted all the side exits and made a mental note to try them each from the inside and outside later. Then she skirted the seats on stage right and considered the most direct route to the backstage area. Unlike some theaters, this one had no stairs at either end of the stage and no orchestra pit. The stage itself, including the runway portion, was about seven feet tall. Clearly not meant to encourage enthusiastic crowds to rush the performers or even to reach up and touch them. *One point for safety.*

Maji backed up the aisle about fifty feet, got a running start, and leaped at the wall, catching the top with both hands and levering herself over the edge. She brushed the uniform down before heading to the do shop.

Roger spared her having to lie or explain, delighted to tackle the challenge of completing the disguise. But his idea to turn her into a man seemed like a stretch.

"Lots of women work in security. Can't we just add padding to my hips and bust? You have noticed my height," Maji protested. The idea did tickle her a little, though. Despite having donned the styles, languages, and personas of invented women in over a dozen countries, she'd never tried to pass for a man. How hard could it be? And if she messed up on this experiment, the consequences weren't death or torture. "Tell me how. I'll think about it."

"We'll put you in boots, add an inch and a half," Roger said. "Still short, but not unreasonable. A binder for your breasts, of course."

"Charitable. What else—hair under the hat?"

"Unless you want to cut it. You'd look fierce. And cute."

Longer hair was a pain, but it was a mission-ready style. "No."

"Then yes to the hat, and we tailor that drab suit a wee bit to fit you better. Now are you game?"

Maji ducked behind a cabinet and managed the binder on her own, tight enough to compress her breasts but not to inhibit her breathing. Running trumped looking perfect. "Shirt ready?"

"Come and get it." When she stepped out, he gaped.

She stared him down, daring him to say anything about her scar. "What?"

"Put you in a leather vest and chaps, and you could pick up a sugar daddy in any bar in London. Where did you get those shoulders? Those delts? I think I'm having a hot flash."

Maji shook her head. "Just one costume at a time, okay?"

With the boots, hat, and uniform pants and jacket on, Maji didn't look half bad, even to herself.

"Wait, just wait." Roger slid a pair of black-framed glasses onto her face and his eyes grew wide. "Almost there." He dug in several cases, finally turning around triumphant. "Come here, lovely lass."

Maji rolled her eyes but submitted to having a small mustache applied to her upper lip. She hoped it didn't turn her into a mini Santxo. Surveying herself in the full-length mirror, she shifted from foot to foot, feeling her way into character. "You win."

"Ooh, try that again, lower," Roger coached her, deepening his voice on the word *lower*.

After a few tries, they agreed that she should just keep quiet.

The grand stone front of the casino made Maji think of Monte Carlo, unlike most of the buildings on the north shore, built in the post-Franco era. She scanned the neighborhood for buildings that could provide overwatch to the hotel-casino complex. Although the Gran Balearico was the largest hotel in the area, there were two nearby with lines of sight to the balconies. Maji took photos and sent them to Hannah, to advise on room choices for Erlea.

Next she sent off photos showing the lack of barriers to automobile access to the complex. A valet handing the keys to a Jaguar over to a well-dressed guest gave her a friendly wave, and she touched her uniform cap in return. She wondered how often someone famous stayed here and whether they brought their own security details. Although Alcúdia was on an island with limited access by boat and air, Majorca's overinflated sense of its own security and its general lack of precautions bothered her. True, the concentration of victims for an attack was low compared to an urban center like Madrid or Barcelona. But getting close to one high-profile target was entirely too easy.

Celeste slipped into the theater from the lobby, hoping for a peek at Erlea onstage. If Maji hadn't left yet, she might be in here to visit. A shabby excuse, but where was the harm? It wasn't like she was taking photos or spreading gossip. And there was Erlea, in the center of the stage now outfitted with a drum set, piano, and cases for other instruments. Oddly, Erlea wore mirrored sunglasses and seemed to be speaking to someone over that blocky sort of headset that theater techs and sports coaches favored. Celeste smiled at the analogy, Erlea as the coach for her team, directing the players. Even alone on an empty stage, she appeared to be in charge. Celeste hoped the sunglasses with this dim lighting didn't indicate a migraine. If it did, she would offer her services. The thought made Celeste blush. *Medical* services.

A row of bright lights came to life all at once behind Erlea. She took a guitar off its stand and slung the strap over her shoulder, pacing back and forth in front of the band's area. Then she stopped and spoke, listened, and hit a mark center stage. A spotlight illuminated her from head to toe, glinting off the sunglasses. Erlea strutted down the catwalk, bobbing a bit to one side and the other, in a rough approximation of her style during a performance. The light followed her.

Celeste wished she could, too. Instead, she sneezed loudly. Twice. Dammit.

"Hello?" Erlea called from the catwalk, shielding her eyes with one hand. "Who's out there? Lights."

Celeste wanted to slide under her seat. "Didn't mean to scare you. Or interrupt. Sorry."

"No problem. Dr. Guillot, right?"

Now she was glad to have worn her white coat. "Yes. Celeste."

"Right." Erlea looked up to the ceiling, nodded, and said, "Give me three minutes."

"Thank you. But really…"

The house lights dropped again and Erlea resumed walking about in shifting levels and colors of light. Celeste stifled another sneeze.

It would be rude to run off, so Celeste found her way to the third row and took a seat on the aisle, looking slightly up. From this angle Erlea looked taller. And even sexier than usual, so focused and professional. *Sexier?* Oh, dear. At least one of them was acting professional.

The lights onstage clicked off. Erlea removed the sunglasses and Celeste caught the last of her words, spoken with a wave toward the ceiling. "Have some fun for me. And photos, please. God knows, I won't see any sights in person." She shrugged in response to the reply Celeste could not hear. "Okay. Until then. Thanks for today."

Erlea removed the headset and rolled her neck, scanning the seating until she spotted Celeste. "Doctor. I thought you didn't make house calls."

"I never said that." *Stop flirting.* "I mean, your supplies are on order. I just stopped by to look for Maji. Is she here?"

Erlea blinked at that, looking disappointed. "I haven't seen her today. But she could be back with Roger. You know, the makeup and wardrobe guy."

"No," Celeste said. "I don't know who's who, I'm afraid. Except for Alejandro and Imane, and Nico of course."

"Yeah, sorry about him. He's rude to everyone. But I think the coast is clear today."

Celeste stood, wanting to be closer despite having no good excuse. "About that. I wanted to tell you…" She paused, afraid of sounding like a fawning fan. But Erlea dropped to one knee and looked at her with such attentiveness, Celeste couldn't backpedal. "I admired your restraint in dealing with him. Without backing down."

"Oh, that." Erlea blushed and stood back up, looking across the seats as if searching for a response. "You know what it's like, working in a male-dominated field. You've clearly put your share in their place, Doctor."

"Celeste."

"Okay, Celeste. Except when Nico is around." Erlea looked over her shoulder. "Well, let's go see if Maji's with Roger. Come on up."

Maji, right. Her excuse. Thank goodness she had questions about the boat ready, in case they found her. Celeste looked for a set of stairs, but spotted none. "How?"

"I'll give you a hand." Erlea smiled. "Are you wearing sensible shoes?" Another awkward pause, and there was that blush again. "I mean, you know, sturdy. Not…"

"Lesbian? All my shoes are lesbian, even the heels. They cannot help it, and would not if they could. But today I have flat soles and am ready to scale tall stages."

Erlea seemed taken aback by Celeste's attempt at humor. Or perhaps her Spanish wasn't as good as she thought. But then a slow smile crept across the singer's face and she tilted her head to one side. "If you got that from a song, I want to hear it." She reached a hand out over the edge, crouching low.

Celeste spotted a security guard walking quietly across the stage, almost in the shadows. "Señor! A moment, please." With a hand from each of them, Celeste managed to reach the catwalk without tumbling over. The guard gave a little bow and hurried off. "Funny man."

Erlea shrugged. "A hazard of fame. People act weird around you. He's probably perfectly nice."

"Or maybe he was offended by the idea of lesbian shoes."

Erlea laughed. "Could be. Lots of good Catholic boys around these parts."

Celeste followed her into the hallway beyond the wings. "I made it up."

"What? Oh. The shoes. Could be a good lyric, though."

"Well, use it if you want. I promise not to sue you."

"Whew." They stopped outside the do shop and Erlea knocked on the door. "The crew are getting together tomorrow evening. Just drinks and tapas in the bar. If you wanted to meet them, you'd be welcome," she said, then shifted from one foot to the other in that way Celeste now recognized meant she was uncomfortable. "And Maji, too, of course."

Celeste hesitated. "Thank you. I think she'll be out of town, and I—"

"Just walk in, already," a man's voice called through the door.

"Join us if you like," Erlea said, giving Celeste's arm the briefest of touches. "Take care."

Erlea hurried down the corridor. Feeling almost giddy, Celeste watched her go. *She wants to be my friend.* Santxo would be delighted to hear how nice Erlea was, especially considering Celeste wasn't even one of her people.

Celeste pushed the door of the do shop open, her questions for Maji forgotten. Perhaps the wardrobe guy would have advice about what to wear tomorrow evening. Not to try and wow Erlea, even if that were possible. Just to fit in. Although if Celeste happened to make Erlea smile, or laugh, or even blush again, that wouldn't hurt.

❖

Maji cruised past the blackjack tables, amused by the close call with Celeste but disappointed to not find Reimi on duty. Locating her at last, alone in the floor staff's break room, Maji dropped her voice to the lowest register she could manage. "Bona tarda."

"Bona," Reimi replied, not looking up from her phone's screen.

Maji pulled out a chair but didn't sit. In her own voice she asked, "Mind if I join you?"

Reimi laid her phone down and looked Maji over warily. "What are you playing at?"

"I can't play here anymore—I'm working now. I shouldn't have bothered you. But I promised you'd be the first to know if I quit the tables." Maji stepped back, worrying she'd blown both her professionalism and her chance to get lucky. Even if *lucky* was just making out without triggering a panic attack. "I really didn't mean to upset you."

Reimi placed a hand over Maji's, on the table top. "Not so fast, *sir*." The wariness remained, but her eyes had a dancing quality now. "How are you working like that? Are you stripping for guests?"

Maji grinned. "No, never for the guests. You like?" The way Reimi bit her full lower lip said yes. "This is a secret. Just between you and me, yes?"

"Definitely yes." Reimi motioned for Maji to turn around. "Let me see you properly."

Maji rotated slowly, absorbing the heat of Reimi's scrutiny like summer sun. This was absolutely the right outfit.

"And you are really not a player here any longer?" Reimi's eyes lingered on Maji's crotch, then rose to observe her response. "For good?"

"Officially. I informed the management. And I have a room here, just for a day or two."

Reimi bit her lip again, her eyes dropping. "You have anything… extra…in there?"

"Just me under the uniform. Sorry."

"Don't be sorry. If you wear this for me in private, we will certainly play."

Maji grinned, feeling the mustache tickle as it lifted. "Can you stop by my room after your shift?"

"Tonight, no. Tomorrow? But I cannot stay the night with you. You understand?"

"Maybe. Please tell me you're not married."

Reimi crossed herself. "No. I am the youngest. Caring for my mother falls to me. I will make arrangements for her dinner tomorrow, but I must be home when she wakes—too early."

Maji smiled. "Whatever you need." She fingered the mustache. "Leave this on? Or off?"

"Whatever pleases you. Either way, I suspect you are just what I need."

CHAPTER EIGHT

Celeste pulled her robe snug and took a good look through the porthole at the men on the dock pounding on the hull. Irritation turned to alarm. During her residency in the trauma ward she had seen plenty of plainclothes police, always asking questions whether her patients wanted them to or not. Had Maji hurt someone?

"One moment. If you please." She stepped up through the open hatchway into the cockpit. That put her a foot or so taller than them, a comforting vantage point.

The man in the suit looked at Celeste, then at the photo in his hand, then at Celeste again. "You are not Maji Rios."

"How very astute. And you would be?"

He held his credentials toward her. "José Luis Romero, Interpol Spain, Madrid bureau office."

Celeste squinted at the pale blue card bearing the globe and sword. She did not ask who the casually dressed, heavily muscled man by Romero's side was. "What do you want with Maji?"

"So you do know her?" the unidentified man asked in Spanish with an American accent. Could Maji be in trouble with her own government? If so, Interpol would be helping him navigate Spanish legalities.

Celeste tilted her head noncommittally. "She has loaned me her boat."

"Do you know where we can find her?" If the non-answer displeased him, he did not show it.

Celeste shrugged. "Not on her boat."

"For how long is this loan?" Romero asked.

Celeste decided to practice her English. "Until I am done or she wants it back."

The American looked almost amused. "So you can get in touch with her then, ma'am?" His tone was polite, almost earnest. "A phone number would be most helpful."

"But I don't suppose you want to tell me why?"

Romero raised his eyebrows and pursed his lips, in that very Spanish manner.

The American shook his head. "She's not in trouble, but we do need her help. Scout's honor." He held his hand in an odd sort of salute.

"Hold on," Celeste instructed them. Below deck, she reached Maji on the first ring and found her both cheerful in general and curious about the unexpected visitors. At Maji's request, Celeste emerged with her cell phone and handed it to the American.

He gave her a polite nod and took the phone, turning away and walking down the dock.

As Celeste watched him go, she mused aloud, "So this is what international cooperation looks like."

"Adventure and glamor beyond imagination," Romero replied with a dry wit that took her by surprise. "Just like on TV."

❖

Maji waited at an outdoor table of a café, casually dipping a churro into her cup of molten chocolate and watching the tourists pass by. Both men when they approached stood out, Romero by his conservative business suit and Dave Barnett by his buzz cut and rugby player build. Although she hadn't seen Dave in years, he was right that she would recognize him.

Dave was a seasoned operator, the kind who worked in the field and also helped weed out the wannabes. He had played an interrogator in the realistically brutal Survival, Evasion, Resistance, and Escape course. Maji still remembered his taunts when he caught her breaking into the makeshift prison to liberate her teammates. Right before she knocked him out. Back then, both aspects made her think twice about how well she could integrate into the coveted unit. Now she just hoped he wasn't the type to hold a grudge.

Maji stood and grasped both of Dave's hands in hers, touching cheeks as if he was a friend. Romero she gave a handshake and polite smile.

"Say," Dave said, touching Romero's elbow lightly, "why don't you take a table over there, keep an eye out for eavesdroppers for us?"

Romero nodded, appearing unoffended. "Take your time." He turned and headed to the far corner, scooping up the morning paper from an empty table on his way.

As Dave seated himself at her table, Maji turned to the waiter clearing the table next to them. "A cortado, please," she said in Catalan.

The waiter nodded and replied in Catalan.

"Not for me," Dave said. "I'll have a macchiato."

"Very good, sir," the waiter replied in English. "And *un cortado* for the lady."

Dave shook his head. "Why can't they just speak Spanish here? Catalan breaks my brain."

"They will if you do," Maji replied, refraining from telling him they had ordered the exact same drink. "But you've got that American look going. Why not just roll with it?"

"People do tend to say more around you when they think you don't understand," he conceded.

This version of Dave Maji liked right away. Realizing she'd held on to his role-playing persona in her mind all this time, she tried to let it go and find out what kind of a teammate he really was. "So, what are you going by here?"

"Dave Brown. I'm big on the Keep It Simple, Stupid approach."

She broke a smile, feeling the tension leave her shoulders. After Mr. Green and Mr. White, Mr. Brown was the most frequent pseudonym for operators. And a no-brainer for Barnett. "What's Romero think you are? CIA?"

"Nah. He knows I'm like him."

Maji looked across the tables and studied Romero with new interest. She'd bought the Interpol cover, with no suspicion that he was really in Spain's Grupo Especial de Operaciones, GEO. She'd love to talk with him operator-to-operator, but the US Army had yet to tell its counterparts about the women in her pilot program. "And my cover?"

"An asset. An insider planted within Erlea's crew to act as our informant."

"I'm not on her crew."

"But they wanted to hire you to be her body double."

"I said no to that and traded up to a security review." *Plus, I'm supposed to be on leave.* "Erlea's people know me as a consultant not interested in playing dress up."

Dave didn't even blink at that. "We'll find a workaround. Which firm?"

"Paragon."

To his credit, he only blinked a little. "Wow, okay. You got cleared for that, right?"

"Course." Hannah would have cleared it with JSOC. Wouldn't she?

"Well, good on you. If I got to go Reserves, I think I'd play golf or something with my downtime. But I guess it figures, considering."

Don't be that guy, Dave. "Considering what?"

"You're a born operator," he said as if it was obvious. "I could tell that even before you coldcocked me. When you're not working, you're training, right? Working out, picking up Catalan, keeping sharp."

"Not so much recently," she admitted. "I'm barely recertified. Sure you want me on your team?"

He scrunched up his face, an apology written in the features. "God knows you deserve the leave time. But yeah, we need you specifically. And this should be a cakewalk, compared to the ops you're used to. Plus, you need anything, I got your back." He handed her a token, a little plastic-encased toggle the size of a thumb drive with a window displaying a six-digit number that changed every sixty seconds. "Access to the I-24/7."

Interpol's web-based, encrypted communications portal held a wealth of information. But not the specifics of her role in this mission. Even the I-24/7 could be hacked, and as Hannah had reminded her, her identity was priceless. "So you going to read me in already?"

Dave grinned and motioned Romero to join them, then ordered another round of drinks and some ensaimadas. He even called them those spiral pastries with the sugar on top, as a tourist would. Working with Dave was going to be just fine.

When they were settled with food and drink, Romero began, "Ms. Rios, how much do you know about the upcoming peace talks between the ETA—Euskadi Ta Askatasuna—and the Spanish government?"

"Not a lot, I'm afraid," Maji told him, mindful of her cover as an American security consultant. "Isn't the ETA some kind of Basque separatist group, kind of like the IRA in Northern Ireland?"

He pursed his lips. "Yes and no. True, they have taken credit for bombings and other acts of terrorism. Some are in prison, some killed. And the group's political party was banned."

"Cease-fires don't hold without real disarmament. And for that you need concessions on both sides," Dave pitched in.

"The government is ready to do its part. Less certain is the will of the ETA."

Maji looked at Romero. "A dissident group, pushed underground, with no single, unified agenda?"

"Precisely. They had a leader of sorts once, who renounced violence shortly before he disappeared. We believe he is alive and in contact with the factions who support a peace accord."

"And what's this got to do with some idiot with a paint gun yelling slogans at a pop star?" Maji asked.

Dave smiled at Romero. "Told you she was quick. The company she's with only hires the best."

When Romero researched Paragon, he'd understand why his American counterpart considered her an asset, Maji thought. Points to Dave. "So?"

"Someone is trying to draw Arturo Echeverra out of hiding. To help him or stop him, we do not know."

"By targeting Beatriz Echeverra, AKA Erlea?" Maji asked.

Romero nodded somberly. "She is his only daughter."

And he's her only father, Maji thought with a stab of pity. "How long's this guy been missing, presumed dead?"

"Nearly twenty years." Romero registered Maji's skeptical reaction. "We have good reason to believe he is alive. Which is tricky for Spain, since he could be vital to the peace accord but also is still wanted for murder."

"Murder," Maji echoed. "I think you left that part out. Was that before or after he renounced violence?"

"After," Dave said. "Chances are he was set up. He had plenty of enemies back in the day. If Erlea is in touch with Daddy, she may be helping him hide."

"No offense, Brown, but this sounds like Spain's business. What's the US want with him?"

"That's on a strictly need to know basis, Ms. Rios," he deadpanned. Maji fingered the token he'd given her. She'd know soon.

❖

Maji cleared the resort blueprints from her hotel room desk. Her review wasn't complete yet. And Erlea really had gotten threats. But were they about her or drawing out her father? In some ways, it didn't matter. The security review focused on vulnerabilities that might facilitate a kidnapping or murder. Doors without locks, staff with no photo IDs displayed, power and telecomm panels too easy to physically hack.

Her rundown of the property would go into the report to Nigel, and now Dave and Romero would make sure the Gran Balearico's management implemented the list of infrastructure recommendations. Whether they cleared Erlea of suspicion or not, no whacked-out fan was getting to her on their watch.

Maji pulled the RFID token from her pocket, slotted it into the laptop, and logged in. The I-24/7's criminal records databases, red notices, and other resources available to law enforcement of partner countries appeared onscreen. Useful, but not at the moment. She found the nondescript-looking icon, clicked through the back alley JSOC maintained for its operators, and with three security questions answered correctly was rewarded with a single folder labeled *Blue Beret*.

Maji nodded in recognition at the shots of Basque separatists wearing the iconic headgear and studied the ones of Arturo Echeverra. Not that he'd look like himself anymore, if he was resourceful enough to still be alive. The brief biography focused on his involvement in the ETA, the acronym translated from Euskara here to *Basque Country and Freedom*. The backgrounder on ETA provided a nutshell about Basque regional culture and language, oppression under Franco, and political recognition in the restored democracy. She could empathize with the drive to maintain a unique identity and resist being erased. The rest of it—decades of political assassinations and bombings with innocent collaterals, the dirty war waged in response by the national government, the paramilitary death squads, and Spain's secret service, and the terrible tangle of communities and families with opposing positions on the creation of an official Basque homeland living together throughout generations of conflict—that sounded all too familiar. It sounded like the stories that refugees from Central America's civil wars told Maji's father at their kitchen table, while she played nearby with the kids.

Echeverra spent his childhood on a farm in the mountains near the French border during Franco's reign, a bleak period for Spain. At college in Barcelona he had promoted cultural recovery after the ban on speaking the Basque language was lifted. After marrying, he got involved in Batasuna, the movement's political arm, publicly advocating for regional autonomy over secession. With the resurgence of violence, he spoke against the killings and distanced himself from the militarized branch of ETA.

By the time Erlea was born, Echeverra was a recognized figure in the Batasuna's local politics and helped broker one of the first cease-fires. But then the National Police implicated him in a bombing in Barcelona, and he disappeared before they could arrest him. Given the number of ETA who died suspiciously in police custody, who could blame him?

All that history, tragic as it was, belonged to Romero and his GEO team, who handled counterterrorism for the National Police. Neither Delta nor any US counterterrorism agency would wade in without a legit interest of its own. Maji opened the Homeland intel summaries. And there was the Nuvoletta, a branch of the Italian mafia she'd run into on an op in Ciudad del Este, the notorious hub of organized crime in Paraguay. It figured that they were the link to the guns, drugs, and money flowing between Central America and Spain.

The Nuvoletta had helped Echeverra get a new face and identity. A penniless activist, intel suggested he traded services as a logistics man, moving drugs and laundering money. Not as bad as blowing up civilians, but not a guy with clean hands either. Even if he was innocent of the bombing, earning blood money always changed people. Would he even want to make amends by informing on the Nuvoletta?

The file listed out a number of Nuvoletta leaders Echeverra had dealt with. Did they know who they had helped, years ago, and what he looked like now? If they did, the National Police wouldn't be the only threat. Spain might let him broker peace talks before prosecuting him, but the Nuvoletta didn't care about Basque autonomy or peace. They'd kill him the minute they suspected he might turn on them.

Maji read to the end and logged out. Erlea probably had no idea what her father did or didn't do when she was eight. Or what he'd done since abandoning her. If she had memorialized him as a great guy, then the truth would hurt. And she might help him anyway, might even use a public appearance to send him a message. But not with a paintball gun pointed at her. What had the file said? *Not traced to ETA. Not traced to Beatriz Echeverra. Not ruled out as an attempt to draw Arturo Echeverra out of hiding.* In other words, the intel analysts had no idea.

Maji wondered if the analysts had thought to rule out stupid music mogul publicity stunts. She made a note to tell Dave every detail of her observations and interactions with Nigel. That man could become a hazard to the mission if they didn't keep him contained.

CHAPTER NINE

Maji wore a dress with a leather bolero jacket to meet the crew in the lounge.

"You made it," Roger greeted her. "And so femme, too. Not that I'm complaining."

"I borrowed them from wardrobe," she confessed.

Roger winked. "Girls just want to have fun."

She smiled mischievously. Parts of the security review had been fun. Not acting like she couldn't afford to lose a crappy service job when hotel guests were rude to her. But tracing all the ventilation intakes and garbage chutes from their origins to their distribution points wasn't bad. And climbing up the outside of the building to test the breachability of doors and windows was cool. Seeing Reimi's reaction to her in the guard uniform? Now that part *had* been fun. "Well, I owe you one."

"Lucky for you, the beer is cheap, and I'm easy."

She fetched him a pint and a caña for herself, the baby draft glass. Just enough to look sociable while fishing for intel. "Introduce me around. I want to meet everyone."

Erlea watched Maji toast with Roger. Why hadn't Celeste arrived with her? If Celeste was her girlfriend, she'd never leave her alone at home. Unless she asked for the alone time. Or didn't want to hang out with a bunch of musicians and roadies. *Or me. Maybe it's me she*

doesn't like. Did she think I was hitting on her? Erlea grabbed the first of the shots lined up in front of her and tossed it back. Just to take the edge off.

Imane joined her at the corner table. "People-watching as usual, eh? Look, there's your doppelganger, having more fun than you. You should have invited Dr. Sexy Eyes."

"I did." Imane's surprise was gratifying, her delight misplaced. "But it was a mistake. I think she already has a girlfriend, and…" Should she tell her? "Apparently I hit on her once before, at some bar. She must think I'm a creep."

"What do you mean, some bar? You don't remember?" Imane's mouth drew tight with worry. "I thought you swore off clubbing after you got sued by that bitch soccer player."

"Hey," Erlea protested. "You know I hate that word. And anyway, I did. It's been strictly cafés with friends since I got home. So it must have been before that, on the last tour."

"Or maybe she made it up," Imane suggested. "She clearly has a crush on you. Maybe she saw you once but embroidered a little to, you know, make a connection."

Erlea glared at her friend. "Celeste isn't like that. She's a grown-up, with a real job. Strictly polite and professional. No fawning, no pandering."

"Good." Imane gestured for the server. "You don't need any more starfuckers after you. Ah, and there's Dr. Sexy Eyes now. I doubt she wore that to work."

Erlea followed Imane's gaze and spotted Celeste scanning the lounge, looking like the essence of springtime in a floral-print halter dress that made her look young and carefree. She raised a hand and waved in Celeste's direction, catching her eye. When Celeste's face lit up, Erlea felt the shot of whiskey kick in. "And for God's sake stop calling her that."

Imane just chuckled. "Thank God she likes you back. The minute she walked into the theater, looking all Taylor Swift—but hotter, 'cause grown-up and French—I knew she'd push your buttons."

"I don't have buttons," Erlea protested, feeling as adolescent as she must sound. "And stop staring at her."

"I'm not staring, you're staring. I'm just being your wingwoman." Imane waved at Celeste, who gave a polite nod and turned to chat with

Roger rather than heading toward them. "On the other hand, maybe she's straight."

Erlea scowled at her. "She's definitely a lesbian. Just not one who's into me."

Imane blocked Erlea's view of Celeste, capturing her full attention. "What did I miss?"

"Nothing. We just talked about shoes, and it came up."

"Shoes?"

"You know, lesbians and sensible shoes. She made a joke about it, but she was very clear." Erlea shook her head. "Anyway, it doesn't matter. She's taken." If not by Maji, then by some other lucky woman. Had to be.

"Yep. She's definitely your type. Brainy, lovely, and unavailable."

"What does that mean?"

"Oh, come on. Have there been women I don't know about?" Imane stopped teasing and fixed her with that concerned look again. "Have you even asked a woman out, since Laura?"

"I don't have to. I'm a fucking rock star, remember?" Erlea threw back the second shot and sipped her beer to wash away the sting.

"So you do take one home now and then, at least for variety?"

"Hell, no."

"But you take the guys home," Imane pointed out. "Because they don't remind you of Laura."

"Don't start with that," Erlea growled. "Not tonight." She reached for the third shot but jerked her hand back when Imane moved to stop her. "Cut it out. I'm fine."

"Really?" Imane crossed her arms. "Because you're imploding right on schedule. But not this year. I'm not letting you."

"Getting wasted once in a while is not a crime."

"Habibi, assaulting some woman in a club *is* a crime. She fucking sued you." Imane threw her arms open and shook them in frustration. "And you could have been hurt. If you don't face what's eating you, it's going to devour you."

Erlea laughed bitterly and grabbed the shot, downing it with a defiant flair. "Save the lecture. It's a lousy anniversary gift."

"I'm sorry, is this a bad time?" Celeste said.

Erlea swiveled on her stool to face Celeste. Her smile felt forced. "Not at all. Glad you could join us."

"Yes," Imane said, giving Celeste a quick peck on the cheek. "Thanks for coming."

"Did I hear you are celebrating your anniversary?" Celeste asked. Her smile looked wooden. "How nice you could be together for it."

Erlea exchanged a look with Imane. Usually they found it amusing when people assumed they were a couple. Tonight everything was too damn serious. "No, we're not—"

"An old married couple," Imane finished for her. "We just act like it." She glanced at her watch. "And look at the time. My taxi must be here by now." Imane leaned over and kissed Erlea's cheek. "Try to behave, habibi."

Erlea sighed, her anger dissipated. "Give Jordi and Maria a hug for me."

"I will. And spoil Athena rotten." Imane gave Celeste a smile and a squeeze on the arm. "Have fun."

Now that it was just the two of them at the dim corner table, Celeste wasn't sure what to say. She glanced around the lounge, searching for a safe topic. There was an FC Barcelona banner. No—no sports tonight. Celeste spotted Maji. "Look. Maji's here."

"Speaking of girlfriends," Erlea said. "Is it your anniversary? Let me guess…one month. No, two." She signaled for the server. "Doesn't matter. Lemme get you a round to celebrate."

Celeste warily eyed the empty shot glasses in front of Erlea. "Now who's making assumptions," she said. "And no thank you. Excuse me."

Erlea grabbed her wrist as Celeste turned to leave. "I'm sorry." Her eyes were sincere, but also a little shiny. They dropped to Celeste's wrist, and she let go abruptly. "Shit. I didn't mean to offend you. Or grab you." She shook her head as if to clear it. "I need to slow down."

Celeste couldn't argue with that. "An Aperol spritz for me," she told the server, "and a Diet Coke for my friend." At Erlea's bemused look, she added, "Maji."

"A pint for me," Erlea said with evident relief. "Whatever is on tap."

Celeste gestured to Maji across the lounge, hoping she would come provide a little buffer. "So, how long have you and Imane been friends?" A safe enough topic.

"Since high school. Over a decade," Erlea said. "Makes me feel old." The beer and soda appeared promptly, with the spritz promised very soon. Erlea insisted they go on her tab.

"Well, you've done well for yourself as an artist," Celeste said. "Quite an accomplishment, at any age."

Erlea curled a lip. "It's not like I have a real job. I didn't even graduate." She drank deeply on her pint.

"If you could go back ten years and do things differently, would you?" Celeste asked. "Even if it meant giving up all you've gained?"

Erlea looked at her over the top of her beer glass. The server set Celeste's fruity cocktail down by her, but she couldn't look away. She'd never seen eyes so haunted.

"Is that for me?" Maji asked, breaking the spell.

Celeste pushed the soda toward her. "Yes."

Roger hopped onto a stool and reached for the last shot in front of Erlea. "Brilliant. Thanks, boss."

"Next round's on you," Erlea said, without a smile.

"Only fair," he replied and tossed it back. "Ladies? What's your pleasure?"

"I'm good," Maji said, then looked at her watch. "I have to take off in a few." She touched Celeste's arm. "You okay getting back on your own?"

"I'll be fine. Thank you." Celeste turned to Roger. "Some water would nice, thanks."

Maji looked to Celeste. "Nice to see you. Unexpected, but nice."

"Yes, I thought you were out of town," Celeste said. "I am a bit surprised myself."

Erlea grinned. "Yep, lots of surprises. I was surprised as fuck when Nigel hired Maji. I'll be even more surprised if he's willing to spend any euros to take security advice."

"Oh, you're the client," Celeste told her with genuine relief. "I was afraid the job was something dangerous."

"Who says it's not?" Erlea protested, her voice rising. She leaned toward Maji and added, "You could have told her. I wouldn't have minded. It's not like the threats are my fault."

"Of course they're not," Maji replied. "But let's talk about something else, okay?" She gave Roger a polite smile as he returned with water and shots.

Erlea grabbed one, ignoring the water. "It's all so stupid. I should print the garbage those trolls say about me, show them for what they are. But no, we have to *manage the image*."

"I really do have to run," Maji said, glancing at her watch again.

Roger winked. "Hot date. Am I right? Tell me I'm right." He raised one eyebrow. "Or tell me after."

"I'm trained to tell no tales," Maji said. "Live with the suspense." She gave him a playful punch in the arm, Erlea a friendly wave across the table, and Celeste a touch on the cheek. "Have Roger walk her to her room," she whispered before stepping back.

Celeste nodded and smiled. "Have fun."

Erlea waved loosely at Maji's retreating form and swallowed a shot. She coughed.

"Are you all right?" Celeste asked.

Erlea squinted at her and laughed. "Oh, you think I'm drunk. Habibi, you've never seen me drunk. If you think this is drunk."

"I should be going, too," Celeste said, not wanting to witness Erlea like this. "Work tomorrow." She caught Roger's eye. "You will see her safely to her room."

Roger nodded. "Back in a jiff and ready to escort." He slid off his stool and left them alone again.

Erlea eyed the last shot on the table. "I'll stop right now if you'll walk me back."

"I don't go home with anyone who won't remember me in the morning," Celeste said.

"No problem." Erlea grinned. "You're unforgettable." She reached for the shot.

"Apparently not." Celeste slid off her tall stool, ready to go as soon as Roger returned. "You don't even remember the first time we met, do you? You came to my rescue."

"No." Erlea drew the word out, shaking her head. "Impossible. One, you don't need to be rescued—you're fucking awesome. And two, I could never forget you." She threw a third finger out, ready to continue.

Celeste spotted Roger making his way back. She raised a hand to Erlea. "Stop. Just stop. Let Roger take you upstairs."

"But we were having such a good time," Erlea said, slumping back. "I really like you. You're real."

"Sorry, boss," Roger said, rounding the table. "We're all having an early night." He slipped his arm through hers. "Doctor's orders."

"Good night," Celeste said and hurried away. Outside, the cool air refreshed her. But the walk home was lonely. *I'm real?* she wondered. *What does that even mean?*

❖

Maji paced in her room, looking at the security uniform on the bed. Should she wear it? Reimi found it hot, but what did she expect, exactly? And what if she wasn't up for it? Self-doubt was a real libido killer.

"Nothing wrong with keeping your physical and emotional needs separate," Ava had said. And Reimi wasn't looking for a buddy. But Maji couldn't even kiss Celeste. Unexpected contact. From a friend. Oh, hell, she should just call Ava.

Maji picked up the phone, found Ava's number. Was she even allowed to? Technically, she'd been read in to the mission, and Ava lived with Hannah. But Bubbles didn't. And talking with your best friend about sex was better than talking to your aunt, right? Even if she is your therapist. Maji stared at the phone. Fuck it. She dialed Bubbles.

"Maji? You okay? I thought you were working," Bubbles said in a rush. Hello was never her style. "Not that I'm not glad to hear from you. Wait, let me go outside. I'm at work."

"Ooh, sorry. You know what, this was a bad idea. I'll drop you an email."

"No," Bubbles blurted. "Don't go. We've barely talked since Christmas and you're going silent again, aren't you?"

Maji blew out a breath. "Yeah, I'm sorry. It was so great to see you." She didn't need to say the rest out loud. Bubbles had given up her first Christmas with her newlywed husband's family to visit her at Landstuhl. And given Maji the strength to keep going. "But I had a not-safe-for-work kind of question."

Bubbles laughed. "My favorite kind. Don't want to discuss your sex life with Ava, huh? She's doing great, by the way. Chemo sucks, but she's a trouper."

"Thanks, Bubs. For everything. I know I should be there—"

"Can it. Best thing you can do for Ava is get your head back together and come home smiling. Speaking of which…sex, right? You forgot what goes where."

Maji laughed despite herself. "As if. But seriously." Maji swallowed. "I get scared. I mean, I freeze and stuff. I can't just relax and have fun."

"Oh, honey. Are you doing the watching yourself from the ceiling thing?"

"Sort of." Bubbles had told her what that was like, when they were teens and she tried dating after years of sexual abuse. "But also, I get angry. Or something like it. Like if I feel good, it's too intense and it crosses over to…aggression. And God knows, I don't want to hurt this woman."

"You won't, Maj. I know you." Bubbles sighed. "But that does suck. And you're going to hate this, but…it takes time. Why do you think I married Rey? The man's a fucking saint. No pun intended."

"So what do I do tonight? She's expecting a hookup, not a therapy session."

Bubbles laughed. "Tonight? Wait—tell me you're not locked in the bathroom, calling me for advice."

"No. I'm picking out what to wear." Maji opted not to tell Bubbles about the uniform and what Reimi wanted her to wear under it. That was too much, even for her best friend.

"Okeydoke then," Bubbles said. "Just try. Stop when you can't handle the fun anymore. If she's nice, she'll understand. If she's not, you didn't miss anything anyway."

"Right, okay. I can do that. Hey, tell—"

There was a loud knock at Maji's door.

"Ava and Hannah that you love them. Got it. Go let your date in. Love you," Bubbles said and hung up. She was never big on good-byes.

❖

Maji followed Dave down the hall to Romero's room.

"I noticed the uniform on your bed," Dave said. "You haven't given it back?"

Maji shrugged. "Could come in handy."

"I suppose. Better pack it up with the rest of your gear. We're moving to rooms by Erlea's suite tomorrow."

Maji sat at Romero's desk and viewed the security video on his laptop. The guy on the grainy images looked like any member of the hotel's facilities crew, in coveralls with the Gran Balearico logo and a photo ID clipped to his belt. He entered the utility closet with a key card and exited with a toolbox. "If I saw him during my security review, he just blended in," Maji told them. "Who is he?"

"We believe this is Arturo Echeverra."

Daddy. "He doesn't look much like his old self. Not even like the age progressions or other mockups." The digital renderings showed Echeverra with glasses, facial hair, bald, semibald, and all the permutations to help them spot the fugitive. "That's a talented makeover."

"Yes. There is a plastic surgeon here on the island, a Dr. Lyttleton. For a price he will perform facial reconstruction without any official paperwork."

Great. The guy she had picked to erase the last physical reminder of Fallujah was a scumbag. "You want me to get into his office, take a look at his files?"

"Nothing that involved," Dave replied. "We'll hack him if you can get in and set the connection up for us."

Romero assessed her. "Will he buy it if you show up as Erlea? He might be able to tell the difference. And we'd rather not tip him off."

"Well, I'll have to be convincing," Maji said. "Give me a few days to get the hang of the double gig before you send me in." She stood to leave.

"We have one more tape," Romero said, cuing it up as she sank back down.

Maji watched the same guy let himself into a hotel suite, exiting barely a moment later. "Still no. He does a pretty good job of not looking at the cameras." If he had a uniform, badge, and card, surely he knew about those, too.

"Yep." Dave gave her a wry look. "Want to see what he left in Nigel's suite?"

Maji looked at the photocopy of the note and envelope. She assumed the original was being fingerprinted and checked for traces of

DNA. The envelope was addressed to Erlea, with a hand-drawn bee by the name. The note inside contained a few lines of verse.

Your forgiveness is too much to ask.
But to see you again would be a peek at heaven.
If only my tears could wash away my sins like the waves on the shore.

"Doesn't sound like a threat," Maji noted. "But definitely coded. And if it's really from long-lost Daddy, two questions: One, why is it addressed to Erlea, rather than to Beatriz? And two, why is it in Spanish rather than Catalan?"

"It's a famous poem," Romero explained. "Every child in Spain learns it. Echeverra may have helped her memorize it to recite at school."

"And maybe Erlea can help with the name question," Dave said. "Plus a few more."

❖

Maji jogged back to her room and found Reimi standing in the hallway, with her hair down and in a figure-hugging dress.

Reimi gave her an uncharacteristically shy look. "Did you change your mind?"

Maji shook her head. "I had an event, lost track of time. You want a rain check?"

"No. I want you to change. I brought the secret ingredients for our special recipe," Reimi replied, drawing Maji close and giving her a lingering kiss.

The embrace pressed Reimi's bag against Maji's belly, and she felt a telling shape—no, more than one. "Let's go inside." She let Reimi into her room and asked, "You keep your toys here at work?"

"No, silly. I keep them in a locked compartment in my moto, underneath the saddle."

Maji smiled at the idea of Reimi commuting with sex toys literally under her motorcycle seat. "Clever. What kind of bike do you ride?"

"A Capri 150. Looks like a Vespa, but without the price tag."

"Fun. I have a bike at home. It's electric." Maji fished for something else to say. "You want a glass of wine or something?"

"God, yes. And to get out of these." Reimi perched on the edge of the bed and slipped her shoes off with a sigh.

"May I?" Maji asked, reaching for one foot but not touching it.

Reimi smiled up at her. "You are such a gentleman, even in that dress. I like that you ask me. Keep doing that." She spotted the uniform hanging nearby. "Why don't you get changed, and I'll pour the wine?"

"Yes, ma'am." If Reimi was willing to lead, she could at least try to follow. She gathered up the pants and shirt, then thought about the accessories. "Do you want me to wear the binder?"

Reimi eyed Maji's chest. "Can you make it easy to take off?"

"Yes, ma'am. How about the…" Maji brushed one finger over her upper lip.

"No. Mustaches tickle." Reimi held out her bag for Maji to take. "Do you know how to dress yourself with this?"

Maji nodded, swallowing. "I've had a little practice. But if I get it wrong, promise not to laugh."

"Oh no, I will only laugh tonight if you please me very much. And I think you do want to please me."

Damn, but she did. Maji crouched low and brought one foot up to press her lips into the sole. "Yes. Yes, I do."

Closed in the bathroom, Maji peeled off her dress without giving herself time to think. She opened the bag and found a harness, a handful of condoms, and not one but two very colorful dildos. The double-ender she laid by the sink, not ready for that tonight. Baby steps. She laughed at herself. If she managed to show Reimi a good time, surely that counted as some kind of leap.

"Red or white for you?" Reimi asked through the door.

"Just water, please."

In the silence that followed, Maji suited up. She didn't really buy the image in the mirror, despite her hair tucked up under the cap and the visible bulge by the trouser fly. In fact, she felt kind of stupid. *But it's not about you, Rios. Get over yourself.* She stood up taller, gave herself a stern nod, and walked out to greet the woman she meant to please.

Reimi's kisses tasted like red wine, earthy with a hint of cherries, and she moaned as she pressed herself against Maji's groin. So far, so good.

Maji's pulse pounded as the kiss deepened. Maybe too good, too soon. "May I rub your feet?"

"Is that really what you want?" Reimi countered, undulating her hips in a way that moved the strap-on in a most distracting way.

Maji grasped Reimi's hips firmly, holding them still. "I want to make you feel good from one end to the other. Just tell me where to start."

"You mean that, don't you?" Reimi arched back to look her in the eye. She sighed. "You are so sweet." She twisted free and sank onto the bed, pulling Maji by the hand. "Feet."

Maji smiled with relief. She knew how to use her hands, how to give. And she could breathe, stay oriented to this moment in time. "Scoot up and get comfy."

She dimmed the lights and grabbed a bottle of lotion off the bureau, then sipped her water and handed Reimi her wine.

Reimi frowned. "I should not drink too much. I have to drive home all too soon."

"Have what you like. If need be, I'll drive you home and take a cab back."

"If you don't watch out, I won't let you leave this island." Reimi sounded wistful, as if she knew that was a feat she could never pull off.

Maji worked her way up from Reimi's feet to her calves and thighs, pushing her skirt up to reach the full length of her quadriceps, noting that the underwear she'd felt under the skirt earlier was gone. Maji hummed a little but didn't solicit conversation, enjoying the simple contact.

Reimi silently watched Maji's hands glide and knead, patient until her torso came within reach. Then she tugged Maji's shirttails loose and unbuttoned the uniform shirt, sliding her hands over Maji's shoulders. "What strong hands and arms you have. Such power. You could be a brute, if you chose."

"That's not a choice I can make, no." If Reimi wanted to be handled roughly, hurt even, this night was ending with the massage.

"No, not you. You are tender," Reimi concurred as she slid the shirt off Maji and tugged the binder loose. She smiled as Maji shivered under her touch. "Better?"

Maji leaned into the palms cupping her breasts and tried to reach Reimi's lips with her own, to really connect. To leave her brain behind, finally.

But Reimi shook her head and instead bit Maji's neck lightly, her hands sliding down to undo the trouser belt and zipper. Arms bracketing Reimi's shoulders to keep her weight elevated, Maji felt the air cool her bare flesh as the layers of pants and underwear bound her thighs together. As she started to twist to work them off, Reimi stopped her again, turning Maji's face so their gazes locked.

"Wait," Reimi breathed, reaching between them as she lifted her hips, wrapping one leg around Maji's hips to draw her closer. "Come inside now."

Okay then, done with foreplay. Maji tried to shush the internal monologue and just be present. "Tell me what you like," she prompted.

"Slow and deep to start," Reimi whispered, her eyes shining.

Maji moved her hips as slowly as she could until the base of the strap-on butted up against Reimi's public bone. As she did so, Reimi arched her back and looked past Maji, up to the ceiling, humming. Maji lifted Reimi's other leg and helped her wrap it around her hips, pulling them even tighter together. And then she started to make tiny circles, eliciting deeper, louder noises from Reimi as her face flushed and her eyes began to glaze. *This, yes. Right now.* "Yes," she said aloud. "All for you."

"Oh yes. Harder now," Reimi urged, starting to drive her pelvis back into Maji's.

Maji's core tightened and she leaned back, starting to thrust in earnest. An urge swept over her to go fast, to let go and—she froze, feeling her pulse pound at her temples, the sweat prickle her back. The taste of metal filled her mouth and she swallowed hard.

Reimi grasped her chin, looking at Maji with pleading eyes, nearly whining. "Please."

"Fuck." Maji met her gaze, coming back down, finding her breath again. "Hold on to me." In one smooth motion, she gathered Reimi to her and rolled them together until Reimi looked down at her.

Reimi seemed surprised to be still connected, startled but not angry. "Like this?" she asked, as though being on top was novel to her. She moved experimentally, smiled. "Oh."

"You set the pace," Maji assured her. She offered her hands to

Reimi, who laced their fingers together, palms pressing for support. "Take what you want."

As Reimi rode her, gradually increasing the pace until her humming grew into guttural shouts, Maji kept her gaze glued to Reimi's face, all her attention on her expression. Her unbridled pleasure kept Maji anchored. It was almost enough to get out of her head completely, to be nothing but sweat and breath and pulse. By the time Maji realized that Reimi wasn't the only one approaching climax, it was too late to hold back. She reached out and pulled Reimi close, feeling more than hearing the urgent curses uttered near her ear. All the boxed-up fear and anger dissolved in a flood of endorphins. *Hallelujah.*

Chapter Ten

Maji opened the door that connected her new room to Erlea's suite. "Does she know we have access to her?"

"Not until we're sure she's not in league with Daddy," Dave replied, laying the comm devices on the desk in Maji's new room.

"She might trust me more if I tell her."

"Let's see how she reacts to the card first," Dave said.

Maji pointed across the room at the connecting doors between her room and Dave's. "You have access to mine?"

"Yes, ma'am. Ready if you need me." He flipped her a second key. "And mine's all yours, if you need out of here in a hurry."

"Thanks." Should she warn him about the nightmares? "And Dave—if you hear voices, well, just me but loud…"

"Don't come rushing in and sing you a lullaby?" He gave a sympathetic half smile. "I won't, if you don't. I get a rerun now and then, too, of some days I'd rather not relive."

"Got it. Very often?"

"Not anymore." He paused. "Taking anything I should know about?"

Maji thought about Celeste's intervention. "They gave me pills at Landstuhl. But I weaned myself off." *Close enough.*

"Good call. I had to take 'em for a while once, and they really messed me up. What about your snoring?"

"I don't snore."

"Not what I hear."

"From who?"

"Taylor."

Tom. She missed him and the rest of her team, the brothers she'd never wanted growing up but wouldn't trade for anything now. "Taylor's out of date. They fixed that when they put my nose back in place. I was overdue for a good cleanout."

"Alrighty then. I hear snoring, I'll politely pretend I didn't." Her look didn't deter him. "Your voice solo in English, Arabic, Russian, Spanish…and I know there's a bunch more. Anyway, leave you alone, check in next day. Good?"

"Good. Fine."

He put on his extra earnest face. "And if I hear two voices and one sounds very happy, maybe calls out your name, should I rush over then? Hypothetically speaking."

Hypothetical, my ass. "What room were you in last night, Dave?"

"Terrible little room in the old wing. Walls like paper over there. I bet they're much better over here, so long as one uses a little discretion with guests."

She laughed despite herself. "Fuck you. Hypothetically, pretend they're soundproof. And try not to be jealous."

"Of having an in with Paragon, maybe. The single life? Nah, I don't miss it for a second."

"Well, mazel tov. I'm very happy for you."

"Hey, I'm not knocking you. Life's short, right? Maji, oh, Maji." His Reimi imitation sucked. "What kind of cover name is that, anyway?"

"Lebanese. Short for Majida El Roumi."

"The singer?"

"Yeah. My grandparents were huge fans." A consistent lie. "I use it on my traveling ID." Paired with a truth.

Dave shook his head. "Shit. I did three details in Beirut. If I never hear that woman again, it'll be too soon. No offense. You sing?"

"Not even in the shower. Dogs howl, small children cry."

He laughed. "No playing double onstage, then."

Maji closed the door behind him and flopped onto the new bed. No more guests. She twisted her back both directions, calculated the time in New York. It was so great to talk with Bubbles. She should tell her. Not the details, but at least thanks. Could she? Not if the firewall was up, like every mission before Fallujah. But she was a Reserve now. Did that change things?

Maji opened the laptop and the secure portal that she and Hannah shared. In place of her standard screen, a message box blocked her sign in: *Firewall operational. Standard protocols apply.* That was it, then. No Hannah, no Ava, and no more Bubbles, until the mission was complete.

❖

Nigel introduced Erlea to José Luis Romero and Dave Brown. "Ms. Rios you already know, of course." He handed her the card. "Now, if you'll excuse me a moment, I'm expecting a call. Tour business, can't be avoided."

Erlea stared at the card with her father's handwriting, nickname for her, and doodle, afraid to open her mouth. *He's alive.* After all these years, she had finally given up hope, finally accepted her mother's logic. How could he be alive, and never once contact them? He had loved them both too much.

"It's a lot to take in," Maji said, breaking the silence.

"Where did you get this?" Erlea asked.

Romero answered. "Mr. Winterbottom found it here in his suite. We think Arturo Echeverra is alive and trying to reach you."

"You think?" Erlea spat. "My whole life I've listened to other peoples' theories about my father. For all I know, the nationalists killed him." She glared at Romero. "Who are you, again?"

He handed her the blue ID card. "Interpol, Madrid bureau office."

"And what does the American government care about my father?" she asked Dave Brown. "Basque country is Spain's business."

Brown nodded gravely, his face a mask. "Yes, ma'am, it is. We have interests he can help us with, based on his time in hiding."

"But you won't tell me why you think he's alive, or what these interests of yours are."

"Sorry, ma'am," Brown said. "However, I can assure you we will not interfere with the peace process. As soon as we obtain the information we need, we'll get out of the way."

Erlea flinched. If they knew Papa was alive, the nationalists would send him straight to prison. They wouldn't give him a fair trial, much less a seat at the table for the ETA. "Does Spain want peace?"

Brown's blank look gave away nothing.

"Really. I am asking you, since you seem to know everything. If he comes here to find me, will my government let him attend the peace talks?"

"That's our understanding with them," Dave said. "We've promised to deliver Mr. Echeverra to Bilbao safely and on time. After that point, I can't say what his future holds. I understand there are old charges still pending."

"If he's alive, he could be cleared of them," Maji offered. "Can you tell us what the note inside the card means?"

Erlea read the poem and tried not to show her reaction. *He's alive and nearby.* "I'm sorry. It's just a poem. Everyone learns it in school."

"Honestly, I don't care for the risks," Nigel said as he returned from the balcony. They all stared at him. "Erlea could get hurt. And the press will have a field day."

Enough. She might not trust Brown, but if he left, the National Police would surely come instead. She should at least appear to cooperate. "Really, Nigel. Aren't you the one who says all publicity is good publicity?"

Nigel sketched a headline in the air in front of them. "Rock Diva Gunned Down Before Tour Opens." He frowned at her. "That'll stop ticket sales cold, my dear."

"Mr. Winterbottom, Ms. Echeverra, if you agree to help us, we will ensure the safety of your full cast and crew," Dave promised. "If you don't, we'll pursue Arturo Echeverra through other avenues, without the mutual benefits that a partnership with you would provide."

"This doesn't prove anything," Erlea said, waving the card. "But someone's clearly trying to convince me. Next time it might be with a real gun. So yes, we will cooperate."

Nigel cleared his throat but didn't contradict her. "Your government will cover your own expenses, of course."

"Yes, sir. Upgrades to the Gran Balearico's security, according to the recommendations in Ms. Rios's report. Free measures, such as impressing the need for confidentiality on your crew, will be up to you. Some of them already know about the internet threats, correct?"

"They know I get them, like anyone famous," Erlea replied. "Only Alejandro has to read them all, as he manages my communications now."

"We didn't want to scare off good crew," Nigel said. "Some of the emails are really beyond the pale."

"I read them all," Maji attested. She turned to Brown. "I recommended they hire someone in computer forensics to track down the senders on the biggest red flags. Maybe your people could help with that."

He nodded. "We have the resources for that. If you'll give us access, ma'am."

"Stop calling me ma'am," Erlea said. "And yes, sure. Anyone who sends that kind of filth for fun doesn't deserve to hide out in their mother's basement."

"Amen," Maji said.

Nigel looked down at Maji. "And your services, Ms. Rios? We've already compensated you, I believe."

"For the review, yes. And you're welcome. But now my terms are between Paragon and the US government," Maji replied as politely as if he'd thanked her properly.

Erlea reminded herself to watch what she said around Maji. All the men might underestimate her, but they were fools. She signed Brown's nondisclosure agreement and handed it off to Nigel. "That document makes it sound like Paragon is providing a body double just to deal with the media."

"Correct." Maji said. "If the media should catch me out, it provides a paper trail to back up that impression. Nothing on your father." She held eye contact. "That paints you as the wild child, the problem to be managed. You okay with that?"

Erlea shrugged. "It is what they all expect anyway."

"At least you're on the inside now," Romero commented when they reached Dave's room. "But I was sure she would know what the card meant."

"She did," Maji said. "She just doesn't trust you guys."

"Sounds like she needs a new best friend," Dave said. "Lots of bonding opportunities coming up."

Romero shot him a look. "Is it wise to become friends with this woman? Erlea is both protectee and suspect, after all."

"If you don't trust me or my methods, Mr. Romero," Maji replied, "you are welcome to replace me."

Romero's thoughts moved briefly behind his otherwise bland facade. "No, Ms. Rios. You are uniquely suited to this assignment." A whisper of a smile surfaced. "And please, call me José Luis."

"Maji," she reciprocated. "And while I'm out playing Erlea for the media and backstage playing her new BFF, what's your plan? Bugs, video, RFID tracker?"

"Already in place," Dave confirmed. "And some of JL's guys just came on staff at the Balearico, you know, custodial and such."

"Also, we will finish the background checks. Not just on the cast and crew but everyone at the resort," Romero said. "This takes time, of course."

"So get busy building rapport," Dave encouraged her.

Maji nodded. "I'll be like family before you know it." To Romero she added, "And I won't forget she's under suspicion."

❖

Maji looked Erlea in the eye, trying to engage her while guessing whether she was annoyed, bored, or just tired. Erlea stared back and yawned.

At least tired, then. "You, too?" Maji yawned as well. "Don't get me started. I never sleep well in hotels."

Erlea didn't bite.

"Is this better than touring?" Maji asked.

"Don't know yet."

To either side of them, Roger leaned in, stood back, and pointed to various body parts, considering how to transform them into twins, while Alejandro took notes. Erlea just closed her eyes.

"Nobody's going to measure her exact height," Roger said. "They won't notice an inch or two. Still, I think we should put Maji in heels when she goes out."

"You just want to show off those calves of hers," Erlea grumbled.

Roger shrugged and resumed his point-by-point physical comparison, noting in clinical tones that Erlea's bust was a full cup size larger than Maji's and her hips noticeably more rounded, along with a wider ass. Or as he put it, "Not like our Maji's little bubble butt." It was clear he admired a more muscular physique.

"Is he always like this?" Maji asked Erlea. A private comment was one thing; tearing Erlea down by comparison was another. Some friend.

"Oh no." Erlea widened her eyes. "He's on good behavior today. For company."

"What about this then?" Roger touched the scar on Maji's exposed left shoulder. "Should we cover it? Maybe a tattoo?"

"No," Maji said, twisting the shoulder away from his fingertips and glaring at him. "I'm having it removed. I need the doctor to see it as is."

"No worries, love," Roger said. "Neither of you goes out sleeveless. Problem solved."

"Contacts?" Alejandro asked Roger.

"Maybe sunglasses. Easier than matching, yeah?"

Alejandro looked skeptical. "Those photogs have amazing zooms. What if she takes the shades off indoors and one of them gets a shot off?"

Maji knew he meant a photograph but frowned at the specter of a sniper anyway.

"All right then," Roger agreed. "Sunglasses and contacts."

Erlea stretched and yawned. "Coffee break." She reached the door and turned to catch Maji's eye. "C'mon."

Maji grabbed a pullover and scrambled to catch up, tugging the top over her head as she trailed down the corridor.

"Are you cold," Erlea asked as she waited by the coffee table, "or self-conscious? Not that you should be. I'd kill to be built like you."

"I need to eat more. Lack of body fat has its downsides, too." Maji reached for a croissant. "Less of this, though. Simple carbs make me bitchy, plus ache all over." She sighed. "I know better. I just haven't managed to care lately."

"Me, too. It's like I'm one person at home, another on the road." Erlea tilted her head toward a woman building sets. "The stage crew runs on coffee and sugar. Not like the dancers."

"We'll get better catering then?" Maji caught herself. "I mean, you will. I'll be out getting harassed by the paparazzi, right?"

"If Roger's comments got to you, maybe you shouldn't go out there. You have to ignore the press, even when they get in your face. They don't respect boundaries, and you can't go off on them."

"I promise not to get you in trouble. How do you tune them out?" Maji didn't have to feign interest. She was used to being invisible, not in the spotlight. "Meditation? Aikido practice?"

Erlea laughed. "Earbuds. Even if nothing is playing, I can pretend I don't hear them." She smiled wistfully. "Aikido does help at home. Here there is no one to practice with. Going to a dojo on the island is too risky."

"What if the dojo came to you? The stage is huge and marley's not bad for falls and rolls."

Erlea scanned the thin vinyl sheet taped over the sprung wood floor of the stage. "Really? How would you know?"

Maji set her plate and cup aside and crossed the stage with a forward roll followed by a backward roll. She made sure Erlea was watching and returned with a series of diving rolls, coming up to standing only a foot away from her.

"Am I allowed to hate you?"

Maji smiled. "Not if we train together. *Onegai itashimasu.*" Might be an overly humble way to ask permission, but Erlea might be higher ranked.

"Don't butter me up. I'm only first dan." Erlea looked amused nonetheless. "You?"

Maji had been truthful all morning. It seemed to be a winning strategy. "Second. But I've been off the mat several years. And I have to be careful to not injure myself."

"Imane would kill me if I got hurt and screwed up her choreography." Something behind Maji caught her eye. "And so would Nico. Heads-up."

"Morning, Mr. Allarcón," Maji said.

He ignored her and spoke to Erlea as he passed. "Onstage in ten, ready to work."

They watched him disappear down the corridor. "Well, at least he can tell us apart. For now," Maji said. She didn't really care what he called her, if anything.

"After you get a taste of the paparazzi, you'll be grateful somebody ignores you. Of course, with Nico that's always a blessing." Erlea picked up her plate and mug. "Let's go wrap things up with the Beastie Boys."

"There you are," Roger greeted them as they entered the do

shop. "Himself gave us five to wrap up, so tick-tock." He nodded to Alejandro. "Hair."

Alejandro stood by as Roger thought aloud, stroking that silly little green goatee. "It's a little longer than Erlea's and definitely thicker. Nicer brown, too, not mousy," he commented. "What did you put these highlights in with?"

Maji smirked at him. "The sun."

"Well, we could give you both fauxhawks, maybe go platinum blond. No? Okay, fine. It's overdone already. Blue?" Roger frowned as Erlea kept shaking her head. "Work with me here. You've done green, orange, and yellow already." He perked up. "How about a dark red?"

"Not a Basque red," Erlea cautioned. "I get enough shit about being too Basque or not Basque enough already."

"Any color's fine. But I need to keep as much length as possible," Maji said.

Roger smiled. "We've got wigs. You could wear a new one each time, let the media try and keep up."

"No wigs," Maji said. "They could come off in a fight, and then I'd definitely be pegged as an impersonator."

Roger sighed. "Well, how much fun are you?"

Maji gave him a dead serious look. "Trim two inches, take out some volume without making it look like I have mange, and find a nice color that will wash out in a couple weeks. Can you do that?"

Erlea clapped Roger on the shoulder. "It's almost like she's done this before." She gave Maji a wink. "Have fun with it. I'm off to face Nico." She turned back at the door. "Could you order us each a gi?"

Maji nodded. "Sure thing." She gave a little bow. "*Onegaishimasu.*"

CHAPTER ELEVEN

Celeste peeked into the theater from the lobby and couldn't spot Maji anywhere. She started to turn away and head back to her office. Then her phone buzzed.

First tier box seats. Stage right.

Celeste zeroed in on that section and spotted Maji waving to her. Why did they have to talk about the boat here, within sight of rehearsals? She headed up the ramp.

The music stopped and Celeste paused to look at the stage. There was Erlea, now with flaming red hair but just as attractive as ever, damn her. The tabloids made a big deal of the hair, which the paparazzi used to spot Erlea as she played tourist all over the island. Didn't her manager know how exposed she was out there? Erlea's safety should come before his demands for publicity. At least Erlea was back to work now, following Imane's direction like a professional. Watching them create a new show was movie-worthy, she thought, spotting Alejandro in the wings with a video camera.

"Hi," Celeste said, taking a seat near Maji. "I like your hair color. Seems to be very popular all of a sudden."

"Yeah," Maji said. "It's been getting a lot of coverage in the tabloids. Did you know red hair was a Basque thing? Not this shade, but still."

"The internet has been quite educational these past few days," Celeste conceded. "About all things Basque—and Majorca, too. The tourism bureau should pay her for the publicity."

"No. They should pay me. Though it has been fun, taking that little train up to Sóller, touring the nature park, visiting the Miró museum. Turns out I really like Miró."

Celeste looked from Maji's red head to Erlea's on stage. "Oh my God. Why?"

"Misdirection. I play hard so she can be in here ten hours a day, working her tail off."

"Is that safe for you? Overzealous fans are not to be taken lightly."

"I promise to be careful," Maji said. "And you know this is a secret, right? Like the review."

"No need to worry about me." Celeste glanced at Erlea moving sinuously in time with her backup dancers. "But if you don't want her talking, you'll need to keep her sober."

"Ouch." Maji raised an inquiring brow. "Did she get worse after I left the lounge?"

Celeste rubbed her temples. "It's none of my business. I was just put off by her behavior. But I suppose it comes with being a rock star."

"Do I even want to know?"

Celeste thought about it. Compared to what she had told her new friend already, this was nothing. "She made a pass at me. And said I was…real."

"So suave. But sincere. Gotta give her points for that." Maji looked to the stage. In profile, she looked remarkably like Erlea. "About the boat…"

"Of course. I can be out whenever you like."

"Actually, would you mind staying? Maybe a couple weeks."

Celeste laughed with relief. "As long as you like. The peace is delicious. Also my cooking. Come for supper."

"Not looking like this. Think how the press would talk: Erlea and mystery woman dine at love nest on the water." She stopped laughing when she caught Celeste's expression. "What? The thought of being linked to a rock star, or making your ex jealous?"

The whole world could gossip about her love life, for all Celeste cared. But not Adrienne. "She found me once already. Sent me a threat," Celeste confided. "She can't know I'm here."

"You sure I can't set you up with some help on this?"

Celeste looked away. "No. I got myself into this mess. I'll find my own way out."

"Hey." Maji took her hand. "If you're in danger, it's not your mess—it's a crime she's committing. And you deserve safety. It's not on you to shield her from the consequences."

"I know. Intellectually, I know." Celeste squeezed Maji's hand. "And when I'm ready, I'll tell you."

❖

Imane called a halt and the music cut off. "Lunch. Better call your hungry twin."

"She eats enough for both of us," Erlea acknowledged, peering up to the box seats to locate Maji. And there was Celeste, the first Erlea had seen her since the other night. What had she said to scare her off? Whatever she'd done, at least now she could apologize. "Lunch break. Come on down, hollow leg. You, too, Doctor."

"On our way," Maji replied.

But Celeste seemed to resist. Erlea couldn't hear them, but the body language spoke volumes.

"Uh-oh," Imane said from behind her, putting her chin on Erlea's shoulder. "I told you to behave. What did you say to offend her?"

"I'm not sure," Erlea replied. "I did a few more shots after you left."

Imane groaned. "Enough to think you were funny?"

Erlea shook her off. "I am funny. You just don't get me."

"Well, let's hope Dr. Sexy—Celeste—does. Here they come."

Celeste looked very professional in her work clothes, even without the white coat. All business, but not angry. And just as beautiful as always.

"Welcome to our feast, such as it is." Erlea gestured to the table prepared by hotel catering, heavy on bread and processed meats and cheeses, light on fresh local ingredients. A pity, with all Majorca had to offer.

"I asked Alejandro to get us better options," Imane said.

Alejandro appeared, pulling off his headset. "What? Oh, the food. Yeah, working on it."

"Not that you're eating anyway," Imane grumbled at Erlea. To Celeste she said, "The diva is starving herself. Tell her to cut it out before she faints on stage."

"I don't need a doctor to tell me how to eat," Erlea said. *Or anyone.* Celeste put on a brittle smile. "Then I won't."

"Your loss," Alejandro said to Erlea. "Don't you know who Dr. Guillot is?"

Celeste stared at him. "My background really isn't relevant here."

"But you must tell the athletes how to eat," Alejandro insisted. "As a performance coach to the elite. Olympic swimmers, prima ballerinas—"

"Magda Dobrovich?" one of the dancers blurted. "You're that doctor she raves about?"

Celeste paled. "She was an excellent client. But—"

"Can I come see you?" another dancer asked. "On my own time, my own dime," he added, looking to Alejandro.

"What are you doing here?" a third dancer asked. Celeste paled and looked frightened.

"Not giving interviews," Erlea said. "Let her breathe, for Christ's sake."

"Sorry," said the first dancer. "It's exciting to meet you, that's all."

"Thank you." Celeste composed herself with a deep breath. "I'm on sabbatical at the moment, but I'm happy to speak with any of you one on one, if you'd like a brief consult and possibly a referral." She looked at Erlea. "And I usually leave dietary advice to the sports nutritionists."

"There you go," Imane declared. "Now fill your plates before the stage crew hear the quiet and descend like locusts."

Erlea filed through the line, spotted an open chair by Maji and Celeste. "Sorry about them," she said, settling next to Celeste. "I guess you're a big deal in your field, huh?"

"A medium-sized fish in a very small pond," Celeste said without smiling.

"She's been very helpful to me," Maji said. "With a sleep issue, actually."

"Sleep?" *Well, her eyes are hypnotic. Like the ocean.* "That's part of your…"

"Performance coaching," Celeste filled in. "Yes. It can be. Any barriers to mental fitness."

"Then why not diet?" Erlea prodded. "Isn't that critical, too?"

"Yes, of course. And I am qualified up to a point. Safe muscle gain," Celeste nodded toward Maji's plate full of meat and vegetables, "and some tips for performance-oriented choices specific to concentration and mood. But not dieting as in weight loss."

Erlea looked at her unappetizing plate. "If I promise to listen, could I consult with you? Starving is kind of kicking my ass. Don't tell Imane I said so."

Celeste laughed softly, a sound Erlea longed to hear again. "Yes. I'd be happy to." Her smile evaporated. "However, I will have opinions on smoking and drinking also. Normally I refer those to a behavioral medicine specialist, but I doubt you want to seek one out right now. So you can hear my advice and follow it or not, as you choose. Fair?"

"Bossy suits you." Erlea spoke before she thought, then felt herself color. "I mean, yes. Do I have to come to your office? I'd rather not be seen there, no offense."

Celeste blinked. "Of course. Confidentiality is vital to my practice. The only clients you hear about have given unsolicited testimonials. I never ask for them."

"How about her suite?" Maji suggested. "Do you mind working over dinner?"

Celeste looked uncomfortable.

"That's okay," Erlea jumped in. "I mean, you don't have to. I can figure something—"

"No," Celeste interrupted. "It's no bother. I do business wherever my clients are. And it is better to talk in a relaxed setting."

Erlea wasn't sure how relaxed she would ever be around Celeste.

"I can't believe I let you talk me into this." Erlea plucked yesterday's clothes off the couch and tossed them into her bedroom. She should take better care of the suite. It was her home for now, like it or not.

"Into what?"

Erlea's head began to throb. "Into a house call. Like I am some kind of diva."

"I don't think Celeste is thinking of it like that. It's more an excuse to hang out with us."

"Hang out with me? She doesn't even like me."

Maji shrugged. "You know people get funny about celebrities. She's actually a fan of yours."

"Not of me. My music maybe. She thinks I'm some drunk who can't take care of herself."

"How do you know what she thinks?" Maji's voice hardened. "Give her a chance."

Erlea sighed. "Sorry." Some of the lounge conversation came back to her. "Oh, shit. I think I hit on her." She bounced to her feet, heading for the bar. "I need a drink. Dammit. When I really want one, it's never a good idea."

"Have you ever tried pretend drinking?" Maji asked.

"What, like pouring your glass of wine into a planter when a guy's not looking?" Erlea frowned. "No. That's stupid. Either I want the drink or I don't."

"Well, I do it all the time." Maji looked annoyed at Erlea's look of disbelief. "Because…sometimes I want to seem more relaxed than I really am, less like I really feel and more like I want to—or am expected to." She held up her glass of mineral water with lime. "Who's to say this isn't vodka, or gin?"

Erlea poured a single shot into a tall glass of mineral water. "Just enough to take the edge off." Enough to chill out around Celeste, but not enough to act like a jerk.

"Whatever gets you through."

Erlea grabbed her acoustic guitar and headed for the balcony. She rolled a cigarette, a ritual that never failed to calm her. Maji appeared as she was about to light it. "Want one? It's just tobacco."

"No thanks, I never smoked that."

"You're smart. Quitting is a bitch." Erlea took a drag. "I do much better at home."

Maji nodded. "Gotta be hard there, too, the way everybody smokes outdoors. Can't sit at a café without smelling smoke from the next table."

"I suppose. Doesn't bother me either way. I stay quit until the stress kicks in. Being on the road is the worst."

"Also makes it very clear where you are out here, even in the dark," Maji noted. "Not to scare you."

Erlea remembered the gun pointing at her, thinking it was real. And now she had to worry about someone she couldn't even see watching her? "Fuck scared. I can't hide all my life."

"Not that long, no." Maji sounded so reasonable, especially given she was a target herself, playing her double. "I wish we could rule out the ETA thing. We don't even know if your father's really trying to reach you."

"Oh, he definitely is. I just didn't want to tell those government assholes. They won't care that he was set up for that bombing. But he would never have done such a thing."

"How can you be so sure?"

"He was my father. I knew him, what he was like. I may have been little, but a kid can tell. He hated the violence."

"I believe you. He sounds a lot like my dad, taking on immigration and street thugs both, back in New York." Maji paused. "What I actually meant was, why are you sure he's alive? If you don't mind telling me."

Erlea picked out a few signature chords. With a touch of whiskey, a little nicotine, and most of all the feel of the strings against her fingers, she could talk about it. "First of all, the little hand-drawn bee. My logo is based on it. Papa's wasn't good enough for Nigel, not polished enough."

"And how many people know your father drew the original?"

"Two. Nigel and the artist he hired." Maji probably didn't trust Nigel. Couldn't blame her. "But only I know what the poem means." She looked to gauge Maji's reaction.

"Heaven and forgiveness, et cetera? Seems kind of generic."

"Not to me. To my father it means sunrise at Our Lady of the Angels."

Maji seemed surprised. "Here on the island?"

"Yes. A few kilometers away, in Pollensa. Have you visited?"

Maji tilted her head. "Nobody put churches on your public appearances list."

"No, it wouldn't fit the image Nigel works so hard to craft for me. But this place is very dear to me. Not long before he disappeared, we vacationed near here on the Bay of Pollensa. He took me to the parish church that Sunday. That was later in the morning, of course, but the stained glass on the east side was still very beautiful. And I remember him telling me that in the first light of day it was like a peek at heaven."

"What about the rest?" Maji prodded. "Tears, sin, waves. Another conversation?"

Erlea shook her head. "No. I think it is a metaphor and maybe a joke." She sighed. "My mother finds the big Catholic churches a little much, along with other aspects of Catholicism. This one has a giant shell above the main altar, and she offended my father by joking about Mary on the half shell. They had a big fight, and I think maybe he regrets that in the last months they had together, things were very tense at home."

"I'm sorry." Maji let the silence rest a moment. "You've had a lot of time to look back and wonder, huh?"

"He's been gone nearly two-thirds of my life. Every big thing since I was eight he has missed." Tears threatened for the first time since they handed her that card. Erlea sniffed them back and took another drag on the cigarette. "I'm not sure I'm ready to see him."

Celeste knocked, and the door to Erlea's suite opened, but it was Maji who stood there with a welcoming smile. "You're punctual."

"I try not to keep clients waiting," Celeste said. "Is Imane here, too?"

"Uh, no," Maji said. "You want me to go?"

"God, no." She wasn't ready to be alone with Erlea. "I mean, not right this instant. Supper smells wonderful."

They touched cheeks and Celeste heard the strains of a guitar, with that unmistakable voice singing softly. "Erlea?"

"Herself. Live in concert." Maji pointed toward the balcony and led her to the gap in the curtain.

Under the night sky Erlea's face was obscured. "I've never heard this song," Celeste whispered. "It sounds old." Then she sneezed.

Erlea stopped playing. "It's a folk tune from my grandparents."

"Beautiful." Celeste sneezed again. "Sorry to disturb you. I'm allergic to cigarettes."

Erlea popped up. "So sorry. I'll come in, close the door. I only ever smoke out there." She joined them inside, tossing her jacket into the bedroom and shutting that door as well. "Our American friend is probably fainting from hunger."

Maji snorted softly. "Just because you Europeans like dinner in the middle of the night, that's no reason to pick on sensible people."

"With sensible shoes?" Erlea replied. "Celeste, look at her shoes. Do they look sensible?"

Celeste found herself momentarily tongue-tied. This wasn't shy Erlea or drunk Erlea. This Erlea was trying to make her laugh, and it was sweet. "Well, they look athletic. I think we should feed them. Do you have suitable food for high-performance footwear?"

"Maji ordered it," Erlea replied. Celeste laughed with her at Maji's perplexed look.

Celeste helped herself to the fish and roasted vegetables. It was nice to dine with friends, not in a restaurant or on the boat alone. But when Erlea held the bottle of cava in her direction, a wordless invitation, she hesitated.

"No shots," Erlea promised, her always expressive voice full of remorse. "Sorry about the other night. I had too many and I wasn't thinking straight. No pun intended."

"Are you sorry?" Celeste resisted the urge to capitulate. "Because a real apology includes steps to make sure a harmful behavior is not repeated."

Erlea looked at the ceiling a few seconds, then met her gaze. "You mean the press? The supposed string of men from clubs? That's overblown. And nobody gets hurt."

"Perhaps they don't, but you could." Celeste took the bottle and poured herself a glass.

"Women get raped sober, too." Erlea watched Celeste process that, then added, "But I do practice safe sex, and for the record, I get tested regularly. And Imane's way ahead of you on lectures."

"Well, she is your best friend," Maji noted. "Mine gives me endless grief. And I can't argue, 'cause she loves me."

Celeste nodded in agreement. "A true friend is priceless. Imane's concern comes from love, I am sure."

Erlea laughed. "That's never been in doubt. She says she loves me, right out loud regardless of who's around. Used to embarrass the shit out of me. In high school we got bullied for it. When they ran out of other excuses."

"I'm sorry," Celeste said. "I preferred books to teenagers, myself. Adolescents can be such assholes."

Erlea stifled a laugh, and Celeste wondered if she was buzzed or just relaxed. She wished she knew her well enough to tell the difference. "Well, as I said back then, I'm flattered you'd think I could get so lucky."

"I think you would both be lucky," Celeste said. *And I would be jealous.*

Erlea blushed but also look skeptical. "I already get the better deal in our friendship. She has her shit together. As you've noticed, I don't."

"I wouldn't say that," Celeste replied. "I admire your work and your professionalism. If you think drinking is a barrier to your success, then I will do what I can to help."

And there was the shy Erlea again. "Thanks. When I figure out how to stop screwing up, I'll apologize again, for real."

"We all have areas to improve," Celeste conceded. "A good diet—for health, not appearances—helps in all areas. Including the physical craving for alcohol."

"I don't really have that at home. I mean, a beer at lunch or a glass of cava with tapas, but I don't go out clubbing. Bars aren't my scene anymore." Erlea's husky voice held no regret.

"I'll let you two talk shop in private," Maji said, rising. "Thanks for supper."

Alone at the table with Erlea, Celeste searched for something to say. Something appropriate for a professional meeting, not a date. "Since we are talking shop, let me get my notepad."

"Right, yeah," Erlea said. "You want some tea? We could move in there."

Celeste looked at the cozy sitting area. This little suite was comfortable and functional, but not lavish like Nigel's. Not long ago that would have surprised her; now it seemed to fit the Erlea she was coming to appreciate more and more. "Yes. By all means, let's get comfortable."

Erlea busied herself in the kitchenette. Celeste grabbed her notepad and took a corner of the couch. She wondered if Erlea would share it. Being that close would not help her concentration.

When she returned with the tea mugs, Erlea took the overstuffed armchair, tucking her bare feet up. "Where do we start?"

Kissing. I would start with kissing that adorable mouth of yours. Celeste gave herself a mental kick. "With your goals. What does success look like to you? In terms of energy, mood, strength, comfort in your body."

Erlea frowned, fiddling with the teabag in her mug. "Well, for that of course I need to lose some weight."

"Really? According to whom?"

Erlea blinked back at Celeste. "Everyone."

"Everyone does not count. What counts is what you think. And how you feel. Which is?"

"Fat." Erlea stripped off her pullover and stood up, turning around. "See? Compared to Maji, I am—"

"Womanly. Curvaceous." Celeste longed to trace those curves. She cleared her throat. "Are you weak?"

Erlea frowned. "No. But don't you think she looks like a better version of me than I do?"

"Definitely not."

Erlea looked over the rim of her mug, a sly smile starting. "Is that your opinion as a physician?"

Dangerous territory. Celeste needed them both back on track. "Your shape is perfectly you. If you want to burn fat and add muscle, of course you can. And with the changes in catering that Alejandro is making and the amount of dancing you are doing, that is likely to happen."

Erlea sighed. "That sounds very clinical. Look, I'll follow whatever plan you prescribe, but my shape will never be perfect." When Celeste didn't try to mask her irritation at that attitude, she pressed on. "Trust me. When I was twenty kilos lighter, the tabloids still called me fat. They want a Barbie doll that sings."

Celeste didn't stop to think. "Screw them. Skinny is not what makes you sexy. If you feel good, it shows. That's what makes you sexy."

"You think I'm sexy?" Erlea stared at her like Celeste had just suggested she give up singing to become an astronaut.

The room was much too warm now. "My opinion is not important. And neither is Nigel's, or some troll's on the internet." Celeste hopped up and opened the balcony door a crack, sucking in the cool night air. And sneezed. Dammit. "Let's get back to your goals. What do *you* want, for yourself?"

Erlea leaned back, crossing her arms. She looked up at Celeste with a challenge in her eyes. "I want to feel sexy. Even when I'm sober. I don't want to starve myself, or weigh everything I eat, or keep a fucking food journal with calories. You got a plan like that?"

"Yes, of course." Celeste perched back on the couch. She'd love to see Erlea feel about herself what Celeste felt all too much. "I will even write down the key pieces for you. They are: protein, vegetables, healthy fats. Lots of each. On the less side: alcohol, sugar and simple carbs, nicotine. And stress. Also you must have some fun each day, do something quiet just for you, and sleep eight hours. See? A very simple plan."

Erlea's challenge shifted to astonishment. "You want me to pretend I'm at home."

"This is your normal regimen at home? Tell me more."

Erlea picked at the upholstery by her tucked-in feet. "I'm pretty boring, I guess. I shop at the market, I cook, I read, and of course I play with the cat. She demands it. I work on songs, and when they won't come, I go for long walks. Sometimes I meet friends for tapas or a coffee, or go to see someone I know play. Oh, and Aikido. Three, maybe four times a week."

"That sounds like a lovely life." *One I would enjoy.* "Which market? Not the Boqueria?"

"God, no. My neighborhood has one just as good, without the tourists. But here I can't do any of that." She paused and smiled. "Except the Aikido. Maji's going to train with me before call each morning."

"Excellent." Celeste set her notebook aside and asked more about life in Barcelona. They exchanged notes on parks, museums, favorite restaurants. Celeste didn't need more information for the consult, but she loved seeing Erlea animated and at ease. Plus, Barcelona was her own favorite place to visit.

Erlea seemed impressed by how well Celeste knew her city. "Why don't you live there?"

"I meant to after I got through med school. But you know, life and family. I visit friends as often as I can."

"Well, let me know when you're in town." Erlea frowned. "Assuming I'm ever home again."

When Celeste shivered a short while later, Erlea noticed and got up. "You want me to close the door? Or I could bring you a blanket."

Celeste stretched. "I should probably go. You have an early morning, and we ran out of shoptalk ages ago."

"Yeah. It's easy to lose track of time with you. Thanks." She gestured for Celeste to stay put and popped out to the balcony. Returning seconds later with her guitar in hand, she said, "Can I play you something? I need an unbiased opinion."

Celeste doubted she had any opinions about Erlea in that category. "I don't know if I can help, but I'm happy to listen."

"Perfect. Just let me run through it once, then tell me what you like and don't like."

Celeste watched Erlea play, finding her eyes drawn to her hands. Erlea's fingers were so dexterous and sure between the frets and on the strings. The room grew too warm again, but Celeste no longer wanted to cool off.

It was a beautiful song, lyrical but compelling. Hearing Erlea's husky alto with just the acoustic guitar made Celeste's scalp tingle. And when she met her gaze as the last chord faded out, the rest of Celeste tingled as well.

"So, tell me what didn't work, first." Erlea looked surprisingly vulnerable. "Too sappy?"

"Not at all," Celeste said. "But I am not sure I trust my Spanish. Are you singing about a cat?"

"Yes." Erlea's warm brown eyes shone. "My Athena. How she is like a tiny jaguar, prowling the rooftops of Barcelona. Fierce and independent, but she knows where her home is." She spoke one of the verses, then translated, "She will not be controlled. I love her as she is, free to come and go." She snorted. "Nigel loved the sound until I told him what it was about. Then he sniffed like he does. You know." When Celeste shook her head, Erlea imitated his imperious tone. "No children's songs on your next album. Or any album I produce."

"Pardon my bluntness, but your manager is a jerk. And not so smart." Celeste bit a lip, pulling her thoughts together. She wanted to reward Erlea's openness with more than just praise. "Perhaps he doesn't like the metaphor. Or can't see it."

"What do you think it is?" Erlea sounded genuinely curious.

Celeste blinked at the question. "Women and self-determination. I could see your fans at marches, linking arms and singing it in unison. Wearing those pink hats with the cat ears."

"I like the way you think." Erlea glowed, and Celeste basked in her happiness. Then Erlea dropped her head. "But Nigel would say that we are too late to ride the wave of that movement. He's all about the next big thing."

"Women will always want someone to love them that way. That will never go out of style. And they will always fight against bad lawmakers and bad lovers who want to control them." Celeste wanted to confess how deeply the song touched her, but she had gotten much too personal for a professional consultation already. Still, Erlea was hanging on her words. "It is like a love song and a fight song, both. There is nothing sappy about those claws," she added, playfully showing her nails.

Erlea stared at Celeste's fingers, then closed her eyes. "If you don't want to get scratched, don't hunt me like a dog." She smiled and met Celeste's gaze across the little room. "You're right. It is a love song to strong women." She stood and laid her guitar aside, stretching.

Celeste glanced at her phone. "Oh, my. I really must get going."

"Thanks for working late," Erlea said. "For everything, really."

"It was a pleasure," Celeste replied. Too much so.

Erlea followed her to the door and they touched cheeks good-bye, friends now. "Can we do this again sometime?" Erlea asked softly, her face close enough to kiss.

Celeste backed into the open door. "I don't think that—"

"Oh, shit, I've made you uncomfortable again." Erlea withdrew her warm hands and crossed them over her heart. "I wish I had a time machine, so I could go back and stop myself from doing that."

Celeste held herself back, resisting the urge to take Erlea's sweet face in her hands. "It's not the past that worries me. Right now, you are my client. And I like you very much, but I must keep clear lines. You understand?"

"Can you be friends with your clients?" Erlea asked. "Or is that too much?"

Erlea sounded sincere, not bitter. Celeste sighed. "No, not too much at all." *But so much less than I want.* "Thank you. For everything." Celeste slipped away before she could betray herself.

CHAPTER TWELVE

Maji sat quietly on the hard wooden pew, enjoying the solitude and the patterns of color from the early morning light through the stained glass windows.

"Company approaching on the plaza side," came Dave's voice through her earpiece. "Two photogs and a camera van."

"Want me to stay put?"

"They can't get in. What do you see in there?"

Looking around at all the frescoes, the stations of the cross, the stained glass, and the gilt work, Maji could almost imagine being here in the 1700s. Well, minus the sneakers and jeans. She'd probably be in rags, a peasant. "Just a really nice church. Soaring ceilings, aroma of incense and candles, the usual."

"Way to sell it. You must have grown up with serious Catholic bling if that place doesn't impress you. No sign of him?"

"Not everybody with a Spanish surname goes to mass, Brown. But, yeah, it's pretty cool." Looking at the emblems of the cockerel on the floor tiles, Maji wondered if Arturo Echeverra had discussed those with his daughter as well. It was pretty funny, roosters all over the floor of an otherwise grand and cathedral-like church. Her own Catholic father would have made it seem hilarious. "And spooky quiet. How long do we give him to show?"

"Until staff arrive to open the place to the public. Keep checking out the interior. We'll make sure the press stay out."

So Maji wandered to the side chapels, checking out the smaller altars of the saints. None of it spoke to her of a higher power the way the ocean did, or the mountains or desert, for that matter. But the deep silence was soothing.

The massive front door rattled. "The press seem pretty sure Erlea's in here."

"Roger that. One of them is going around the side of the building."

Maji heard movement and faded back into the shadows. A man in work clothes emerged from the sacristy and headed for the rattling door. "Staff's here already." Paid off by a news outlet to provide access? "The sexton may be letting them in."

"Stay out of sight."

"Roger. Rios out."

Maji slipped into a shadowed nook. Not a great spot to run from, but…

"We're closed!" the sexton yelled through the slot in the front door, first in Catalan and then in Spanish. For good measure he did so one more time, in thickly accented English. Maji couldn't make out the voices on the other side, but the sexton sounded resolute when he replied, "Come back at ten," and stomped away. Bless his cranky heart.

"Still out front. Setting up video," Dave said, updating her. "Stay put. Any sign of Echeverra?"

The sexton stopped in the dead center of the church, sweeping his eyes over the side chapels in Maji's vicinity. "Please tell me you didn't leave," he said in a low voice, his Spanish more cultivated than what he'd yelled at the reporters. "It should be safe to talk now."

Daddy in the house. Maji waited to hear if Dave had caught Echeverra's entreaty.

"Proceed with caution," Dave instructed.

Maji stepped out of the shadows. "I'm here."

"Beatriz." Echeverra crossed himself and headed toward her, stopping short when he was a few feet away. "No. Who are you?"

"A friend of your daughter. Hired to protect her. We needed to make sure it was safe for her to meet the person claiming to be her father."

"I know my face is different, but I swear to you, I am Ar—"

Maji acted alarmed. "No. I haven't swept this place for bugs. We should go somewhere more secure. The press already thinks"—she mouthed *Erlea*—"is in here."

"I never dreamed the whole world would call her by my pet name," Echeverra said. "How do I know you are really her friend?"

Maji gestured toward the flower-petaled stained glass. "She told me about the peek at heaven and"—she pointed to the wall over the altar—"Mary on the half shell."

Echeverra laughed. "Oh, what a fool I was. To be angry about such trifles, so pious and self-righteous. What can I do to assure you, and her, that I am me? And that she should see me."

Maji was convinced. But she had instructions. "We'll set up a meeting in a secure location when we've verified your identity and what it is you want from her." He flinched when she reached inside her jacket pocket. "Relax. I'm unarmed. I have a DNA swab. And I promise we'll keep the testing a secret."

"Oh," he said, taking the vial. "What do I do?"

"Just scrape the swab inside your cheek and seal it back in the tube." Maji took a seat on the nearest pew and motioned for him to join her. He sat, perched near the end, still wary.

"Tell my daughter that I still make sure no one eats the roosters. She'll understand." He used the swab and handed the vial back. "Technology. Keeps making it harder for a man to disappear."

"Especially one who wants his life back. Do you?"

"I can never get back the years stolen from my family, the pain of losing me. But I am still committed to peace, and I would help if it did not endanger them."

"I'm told the government will wait to prosecute you until after the talks, if you attend."

Echeverra gave a bitter laugh. "It was the government who set me up. The National Police infiltrated my group, and the two men who orchestrated the bombing were rewarded with promotions. They are quite high up in government today."

Oh, crap. If Romero was with GEO, he was clean. But GEO was under the National Police. How classified was his mission briefing, and who had access to it? Would they hear this? "Stop," she said. "Don't say their names out loud. Don't tell me them at all."

"Of course. I should not endanger you for helping. But I have evidence. And if I can get it to...my daughter, she can give it to the press. They pay attention to her. Once it is out, I will be safe and so will my family."

Was Romero listening on the comms? The whispering voice of intuition said to get Echeverra out of there. "Sir, it may not be that simple. Who helped you to disappear? Got you papers, changed your face?"

"Some bad men of a different sort. Criminals. They would sell me out in a minute."

Yes, the Nuvoletta would indeed. Intel trading was one of the many rackets that put them on Delta's hit list. And a corrupt official in the National Police might already have bought whatever they had to sell on Echeverra. "I think we should move this conversation, sir. Now."

Romero's words, "Keep him there," rang in Maji's ear. In response, the little voice in her head switched from whisper to scream. Get Echeverra out now, let Dave sort out whether Romero was compromised or not. *Get out now.*

Maji pressed a finger to her lips and motioned Echeverra to get up and run with her. He clearly knew this place well, so she followed him toward the sacristy, across the church from the side door Maji had used to enter.

"No one uses the emergency exit but workers," Echeverra said, starting to suck wind after only a short jog down the back hall.

"Stop," Romero commanded as they rounded the next corner.

Echeverra smacked into him and flailed backward, panic on his face.

Maji caught him and stepped between the two men, keeping both within reach. "Stay calm," she urged.

"Yes, please." Romero stood with his hands out in a placating gesture, his suit tidy as always. "Ms. Rios, I am on your side."

"Maybe you are," Maji said, "but consider who you work for." She avoided the words National Police. Echeverra already looked close enough to a heart attack.

"I understand your concern," Romero said with a tiny nod. "But my unit is very much like your unit," he said, using the name Delta used for itself, with emphasis. "If you had a general under suspicion of corruption, wouldn't you investigate? Independently."

So she was getting her operator-to-operator talk after all. Maji had pictured chatting over beers, but this would do. "You may be clean. But are you sure your team isn't compromised? Because this man is under my protection now. So I need to be sure, too."

"Downshift, Rios," Dave's voice said. "Our team will escort them both. Hand him over at the back entrance. Play nice."

Romero heard that, too, Maji realized as he flashed her a brief, hopeful smile. But he spoke to Echeverra. "We have had Aguilar under watch for years, Mr. Echeverra. He's on the brink of retirement and likely to disappear if we don't get him soon. We haven't confirmed the second man's identity, but if you have proof, we'll gladly take him down, too." He met Maji's watchful gaze again. "I'm going to reach inside my jacket for my ID. Okay?"

Maji nodded.

Echeverra read the ID to himself. "Internal Affairs, eh? You don't think I'm a terrorist, then?"

"That will depend on the evidence you provide," Romero admitted. "But I hope not. My wife is Basque. I understand that peace is long overdue."

"Sounds like you have a lot to talk about," Maji said. "Mr. Echeverra, will you go with him?"

Echeverra nodded. "You will keep Beatriz safe?"

"Yes, sir." Maji shook his hand and walked back through the church. "Dave, you got another exit in mind for me?"

"Out the way you came. Keep the paparazzi focused on you," he instructed. "Put on a show if you have to. Anything but singing."

"Roger that. Listen for the side door."

The minute Maji appeared in the alley, a voice rang out, "Erlea. Over here. Hey, I've got her."

Maji turned quickly, as if startled, and headed for the main plaza. "One guy in the alley, behind me," she told Dave. At the corner she paused and peeked out to check on the video crew. A local constable was gesticulating at them while giving a lecture on parking in the pedestrian plaza. She started across it at a slow jog, watching her footing on the uneven paving.

Hearing a shout behind her, Maji glanced back and saw a guy with the video camera on his shoulder leave his fellow journalist to deal with parking enforcement. Fortunately, he couldn't gain much speed while looking through a viewfinder and running over the treacherous stone surface.

She could be out of range in seconds, if she didn't prolong the diversion. "What do you need from me?"

"Just take your time," Dave replied. "Clear the plaza, duck into that café with the green awning. A white van's waiting by the back door."

"Roger that."

Behind her, there was a thud and crunch followed by a keening laced with curses. Maji glanced back and saw the videographer on the ground, clutching his knee. With all eyes on her, his colleagues didn't seem to notice. She sprinted back to him and knelt by his side.

"Medic," he gasped, all the color drained from his face.

Maji stood and pointed at the constable by the camera van. "You. Call a medic," she yelled at him in Catalan.

He looked at her, hesitant. Was her Catalan that bad?

"Call a medic, right now," she yelled in full command voice, this time in Spanish.

He lifted the radio mic to his mouth as the telephoto lenses on the other reporters' cameras whirred and clicked. "Good luck," she said to the fallen journalist, then pivoted and ran.

"Good show," Dave said.

Erlea stopped stretching and greeted Maji as she arrived on stage. "Good morning. I can't believe I beat you here."

"Went running first," Maji said. "Over to this beautiful old church in—"

Nigel stormed onto the stage, spotted them, and didn't even ask who was who. "You two. A word." His nostrils pinched in that way that showed he was livid. "Do you know what's all over the internet? Erlea *helping* the paparazzi."

"What happened?" Erlea asked.

Maji lifted one shoulder in a half shrug. "One of the journalists fell and twisted his knee. I stopped to see if he was okay. No big deal."

"So it was you," Nigel said. "I thought as much." He turned to Erlea. "She went back to him, heedless of the cameras closing in, and called out for the policeman to get him a doctor."

"Did they get close enough to tell it wasn't me?" Erlea asked.

He looked appalled. "No. But it was very out of character. They are calling you a hero."

"Well, that's a little like calling me a decent human being." Erlea threw one arm dramatically over her forehead. "How dreadful."

Maji just smiled softly and kept her mouth shut.

Erlea did not wait for more from her manager. "If you think all good publicity is the diva melting down or blowing up, perhaps it's not too late for me to talk with Claudia Sandoval."

"Break your contract and I'll ruin you," Nigel said in a low, dangerous tone. He stalked off.

Erlea turned to Maji. "You've already had a workout. Want breakfast instead?"

"Nope. He makes me want to puke. I need a dose of the energy harmonizing way before I can think about food. And I can't wait to see what your style of Aikido looks like."

Erlea laughed. "It looks like flying lessons. You up for that?"

"Hell, yeah."

❖

Maji sat silently at the skirted table, glad for the big sunglasses. All the lights and camera flashes were trying to give her a migraine.

"Just another minute," Dave spoke to her via the earpiece.

She gave Alejandro a nod.

"Mr. Winterbottom is nearly here. We will begin in a moment," he told the assembled press.

"All clear, good to go," Dave's voice announced.

Nigel stepped from behind the curtain and raised at hand. "Thank you all for coming today," he said. "We understand your interest in current politics, but please limit your questions to those pertaining to music." He managed to sound haughty even in Spanish.

"Ready to swap out," Dave said, and on cue Maji began coughing, softly at first, then harder. Red faced, she took a drink of water and held up one hand. "Momento."

She ducked behind the curtain, handing Erlea the glass with a smile. "Room's secured. Knock 'em out."

Erlea, dressed and styled identically, gave her a wink and went out to face the media.

Maji pulled baggy coveralls on over her outfit, tugged the knit cap over her hair, and settled in to listen to Erlea talk like a rock star.

Nigel called on a reporter from *Entre* magazine first.

"Erlea, what were you doing at a church at sunrise?" the pretty blonde asked. What was her name again?

"Giving first aid to one of us, Julia," a voice called out. "Can I get some CPR?" Laughter followed. Friendly laugher, Erlea noted with relief.

Julia looked annoyed but pressed on. "Were you meeting with your father? Is he alive?"

Erlea smiled and removed the sunglasses. "Julia," she began, ignoring Nigel's warning look. "I don't know for sure. I would like to think so. From time to time I visit Our Lady of the Angels, which holds good memories for me. It makes me feel closer to him."

"But what about the bombing? The murder charges?" a man a few rows back called out.

Nigel stood. "If you continue in this vein—"

"Then we might clear a few things up," Erlea interjected. "The man I knew as a child was truly devoted to peace for Spain, as well as cultural autonomy for his people. The bombing was a crime, a tragedy, and I find it hard to believe my father could have done such a thing. If he is alive, I hope we all will finally learn the truth."

"When you say his people, what do you mean? Aren't you Basque, too?"

That's the part you heard? Erlea gave him a smile anyway. "I feel a misquote coming on, but let me try and explain. All my life, some people have told me that I am too Basque, and others that I am not Basque enough."

"And now on to music," Nigel interrupted.

"When we are done," Erlea said. She took a moment to look at the men and women with their recorders and video cameras running, to see them as people, and to breathe down into her center. "I am, before all else, an artist. And art belongs to everyone. I have Basque blood, yes. But also Catalan. And I am Spanish from both sides. All of my grandparents remind me of what Spain was like under Franco, the repression even my mother grew up with. As a musician, I have a responsibility to reach for freedom, to honor all cultures, and to support the self-determination of all people. Spain's diversity is its greatest wealth. If you find my music reflects this, then I am doing my job as an artist."

"Which brings us back to the show," Nigel said, pretending with his tone and expression to defer to her. "Yes?"

"By all means," Erlea replied. "This show will slay you, I swear."

❖

Erlea sounded hoarse by the time Nigel finally called time on the press conference.

Maji offered her a high five as Erlea followed Nigel and Alejandro back through the curtain. Erlea slapped her palm and collapsed into a chair. "Why can't you learn to talk like me? We could have taken turns."

"You don't want me talking music or politics for you," Maji assured her.

"Shut up," Nigel hissed. "Are they gone yet?"

Maji got Dave's confirmation. "The room is clear. Awaiting clearance for transport."

Nigel turned on Alejandro. "Did you know she was going to pull this...this..."

"Having opinions on things that matter?" Erlea suggested. "Or being nice to the press for once?"

"They loved it," Alejandro said. "But no," he hastened to add, "I had no idea."

"Well, you'd better hope it plays well," Nigel said. "Watch all the outlets and give me a report every four hours."

Alejandro swallowed hard. "Yes, sir."

CHAPTER THIRTEEN

Maji and Erlea hung their gis in the dressing room, a postworkout ritual after only a few days practicing Aikido together. Maji hoped Erlea found the workouts as grounding as she did.

"What sights am I seeing today?" Erlea asked.

Maji shrugged. "I guess after the press conference, I get to lie low awhile."

"You deserve a break," Erlea said. "But...never mind."

"No. What?"

"It's just, it seems like an opportunity to send my father a message back." Erlea shook her head. "But that is selfish. Every time you go out as me, I worry someone will try to hurt you."

When were Romero and Dave going to approve the meeting? "I thought you weren't sure if you wanted to see your dad."

"I'm a grown woman. It's time to know the truth." Erlea gave her a cynical look. "Without telling Nigel about it. He's hoping the VIP reception will make the press forget about politics for a bit. Should I invite Celeste?"

Maji had watched the attraction between them bloom. "I bet she'd appreciate that. Don't you?"

Erlea shook her head. "Celeste might hate these things as much as I do. Just rich people trying to be seen and tabloid press there to help them. There's not enough whiskey in the world. Not that she needs it—but I know I will." She looked at the ceiling. "And I already made an ass of myself with her once."

Maji quirked an eyebrow. "You think Nigel is hoping you'll get drunk and act out?"

"Probably. But you know what? He's going to be disappointed. I'm going to invite Celeste, and I'm going to behave myself." Erlea glanced at her phone. "Shit. I'm almost late for morning call."

As Erlea rushed off, Maji followed, wondering at Nigel. What good would it do him if Erlea imploded? Surely a show with great reviews would sell more albums than a few scandalous headlines. She caught angry voices coming from the theater and hurried to catch up.

"Not even English?" Nico's voice echoed to the rafters. "Useless Russians. I should have known."

Must be the aerialists, finally. Maji saw a man and woman, their huge rolling trunks beside them, flinching as Nico yelled.

Erlea plugged one ear, grimacing. "Tranquilo. It's not the end of the world."

"Really? Do you speak Russian? They lied about their Spanish, who knows what else?"

"Couldn't we just hire a translator?"

"You going to pay for that from your pocket?" He didn't wait for her to respond. "I didn't think so. And Nigel's already impossible on the budget."

"Hey, Nico," Maji called from the wings. "Can I help?"

He sneered at her. "Do you speak Russian?"

"*Da*." Maji continued in Russian, addressing the anxious couple. "Welcome to the show. Don't worry, we'll work something out. And please say hello to your real boss, Erlea."

They followed her head tilt toward the star.

"*Hola*, Erlea," the man said with a strong Russian accent to his Spanish. "I am Dimitri, and this is Tania."

"Welcome," Erlea said with a smile, shaking their hands. "Maji, can you tell them that I admire their work and am sorry the visa process was so difficult? Oh, and that Nico can't fire them, so they should relax."

The message, along with Erlea's warmth, visibly assured them. Nico fumed, but at least he did it quietly.

"Mind if I get them checked in and set up?" Maji asked.

"Please," Erlea answered.

"You can't babysit them every day," Nico said. "You have your hands full babysitting Her Highness."

"No worries," Maji replied. "I'll have them flying solo in no time. Get it—flying solo?"

Nico didn't laugh.

❖

From her seat next to Alejandro in Row L, Celeste observed Maji up on the lift with Dimitri, taking notes as he pointed up into the rigging and gestured descriptively.

"Thank God she speaks Russian," Alejandro said. "We need to start incorporating the aerials as soon as possible. I know Imane has some ideas, but Erlea must agree, too."

"Will Erlea be performing with them?"

"Oh no," Alejandro responded. "She refuses. Erlea can dance like a dervish, but she'll keep her feet on the ground."

"Damn right," Erlea said as she slid into the seat next to Celeste. "Where's Imane?"

"In the wings," he said, handing her a headset.

Celeste began to cough, just a tickle in her throat.

"Are you okay?" Erlea asked. "Do you need some water? Alejandro—"

He was up and off before Celeste could protest. "I'm fine," she told Erlea.

"Oh, shit, I must have smoked in this." Erlea pulled off her sweatshirt and threw it down a few rows. Her T-shirt clung to her, damp with sweat. "I should send all my clothes to the cleaners. Sorry."

"Oh no—I should go and let you work," Celeste said. "Besides, you'll get chilled."

"I'll live. And you shouldn't suffer just because I can never stay quit."

Celeste gave her a stern look. "There is no call to beat yourself up. Nicotine is an insidious addiction. If you want to be free of it, I will help any way I can."

"Really? I don't even like the smoking part of smoking, you know. It's the ritual I like. I roll my own, and I think about things." She mimed the action.

Celeste watched those nimble fingers dance in the air, as they had on the strings, and her mind slipped again to a vision of those hands in motion on her. *Be professional.* "Do you do that at home?"

"No. Instead I play with the cat or fiddle with the plants."

"Excellent," Celeste said. "Let's schedule a time to talk, and I will teach you some mindfulness exercises." She remembered her original excuse to visit. "Oh, and here are my notes on diet, as promised. I wasn't sure where to deliver them."

Erlea took the folder. "Thanks. You're always welcome to stop by my room, if I'm not here."

"No, I shouldn't make a habit of that."

"Right. Wouldn't want to ruin your reputation."

Celeste frowned at her. "That's not funny. We may be friends, but the media would make it look like I date my clients. Image matters in my field, too."

"Of course it does. I didn't mean to imply that my career is more important than yours. If anything, what you do matters more, I mean..." Erlea caught herself. "I should just shut up."

Celeste smiled at her. "Let's just agree that art and health are both important. Call me for an appointment, yes?"

Erlea reached out for her. "No, stay. I mean, if you want." She flushed adorably. "It's just, the aerials are really cool."

"Ready when you are, boss." Alejandro plunked back down, handing Celeste a bottle of water.

Hemmed in, Celeste hesitated.

"You are a perfect test audience," Erlea assured her, pulling on her headset. "I'll tell you what they're doing. You tell me what moves you, makes you feel something...visceral."

Being so close to Erlea did that. With the sweater gone, Celeste could smell a spiciness on her skin. "I'll be happy to tell you what I can."

Alejandro got on the headset and started conferring, with Maji as translator.

Dimitri stood by a thick braided rope that fell in a straight line from its trestle and carabiner on the crossbeam over the stage to the floor, over forty feet in total. He wrapped a length around one foot, reached above his head, and lifted himself both vertically and horizontally, smiling.

"The corde lisse is a classic art," Erlea said. "Over twenty moves can be executed with just one rope." She narrated as he flipped and turned his body, working his way higher. "Arabesque. Leg wrap. Horizontal flip. Crucifixion."

A few feet from the girder Dimitri paused and smiled. Though he made the moves look easy, Celeste could see him breathing hard. Then he descended halfway, repeating some moves in reverse. Celeste held her breath and grabbed Erlea's hand. Erlea gave it a gentle squeeze and held on.

Tania approached the rope and began ascending.

"Some pairs work is quite nice on the corde lisse," Erlea commented. "Watch how they move between the two." She pointed with their joined hands, but didn't let go.

After the corde lisse, the couple used a remote to make a large metal hoop descend to knee height. Tania climbed inside it, her feet curled around the bottom of the metal rim and her hands near the top. Dimitri held the remote, smoothly sending her about twenty feet up as she performed a graceful routine. At two points, she fully extended her body down, dangling by her hands from the bottom rim before sliding up and back through the center.

"Wow," Celeste said. "The upper body strength, the agility."

Erlea leaned close. "Admit it. That's sexy."

The rasp in Erlea's voice begged Celeste to flirt back. *Unprofessional.* "Because she's skinny?" Celeste challenged, instead.

"No. Because she owns that space. She's…" Erlea looked sideways at her. "Okay, I get it. Point taken."

As the hoop ascended into the girders, two long swaths of cloth descended. Tania and Dimitri each took hold of one, which they revealed to be two very long loops of a silky-looking fabric about four feet wide. Then each lay in one as if it was a cocoon.

Celeste watched entranced as the couple emerged and used their silks like the corde lisse, pulling the whole width into one large handful, twisting the length around one limb or another, turning, flipping. "Marvelous."

Back in their cocoons, the partners reached out to one another, pulled themselves together, and kissed.

"Aw," Celeste sighed.

Erlea chuckled and caressed Celeste's hand with her thumb. "Mark that down," she instructed Alejandro.

Finally, Dimitri sent the silks back up to the girder and lowered a harness on a thick black rope. Tania stepped into it and snugged it on. Dimitri took the slack out of the rope attached to her low back, almost to the point where it looked like it would lift her off the ground. Tania walked in a small circle.

"Here is one of my favorites," Erlea said. "The dance bungee is very playful."

Tania leaped forward, catching herself with her hands, her feet up in the air. She pushed off from the ground with no apparent effort, and the bungee carried her backward onto her feet again.

"That does look like fun," Celeste whispered.

Tania reached up with her right arm, grabbed the rope and leaned forward, starting a counterclockwise circle. At first she appeared to be walking, in long, tilting steps. Then she flipped herself into an upside-down split, continuing the walk on her hands before scissoring her legs and righting herself. Celeste clapped.

"Yes, agreed. Those have to be in the show," Erlea said into her headset. "No, just them. Not a chance in hell, Imane. End of discussion." She pulled off her headset.

Celeste reached over and touched her arm. She wished they were still holding hands. "Are you afraid of heights? I could help with that. If you wanted."

"No," Erlea replied, scowling. "You're helping enough already." She swallowed. "And I appreciate it. You did like the aerials, didn't you?"

"It was very exciting," Celeste replied. *Especially with you touching me.*

❖

Maji opened the door of her hotel room to Celeste. "Hey, thanks for the house call."

"Of course," Celeste said, touching the red hair. "I think I would hate being famous, always worrying who saw me doing what. I am too much the introvert."

"That makes three of us," Maji said, ushering Celeste in. "We're lucky to have you." Maji pulled a chair out and sat facing its back.

She lifted her right arm and rotated it until a pain shot down her bicep. "There."

"Okay. Give me dead weight while I move it through the full range. Call out at the first twinge."

Maji let her manipulate the arm and made a conscious effort to be compliant, describing what hurt, how, and when. She couldn't afford to be stoic now—she had to stay in the game. "Rotator cuff?"

"Sounds like you've been here before. You remember the exercises, stretches, rest, and ice regimen?" When Maji nodded, Celeste continued. "If it does not improve, I'll refer you for an MRI." She paused. "Dare I ask what you did? Was it the Aikido?"

"No. Erlea is a great partner. I got carried away trying out the aerials."

"Really? Are you going to stand in onstage?"

"No. They're just fun and—" A knock at the connecting door stopped her. "Hello?"

"Dinner's nearly ready," Imane called.

Maji hopped up and opened her side. "Great. Got enough for one more?"

"Sure," Imane said. She eyeballed Celeste. "Erlea won't touch the pizza or the liquor. And she's stopped smoking. That's some spell you've put her under."

Looking past Imane to Erlea's suite, Celeste frowned. "I should get back to the office."

"Oh no, really," Imane protested. "I'm grateful. Please stay for supper."

"I don't want to impose."

Maji exchanged a knowing look with Imane. "Just supper with friends. You've already worked a full day."

"Fine. If a guest needs me, I suppose they can call or page me."

Erlea didn't trust that glint in Imane's eyes. "What?"

"Set another place. Dr. Sexy Eyes is making a house call."

"Don't call her that," Erlea said. "She's next door? Keep your voice down."

"Hey, stop sweating." Imane squeezed her arm affectionately. "I haven't seen you like this in years. Not since…"

"Stop it. I don't need reminding." Or a calendar to know the date of Laura's death.

"Fine. But I'm rooting for you. And she would, too, you know."

"Don't pull that shit on me."

"It's not shit," Imane replied, her voice rising. "Laura loved you."

"And look how that worked out for her."

"It's not your fault and you know it," Imane insisted. "We were kids. And two of us got to grow up."

"What's that mean?"

"It means, stop wasting yourself on assholes you don't even like. If you were the one who died, would you want Laura to be miserable ten years later?" Imane didn't wait for a reply. "Of course not. You'd want her to grow the fuck up and move on."

As Imane stomped off to the bedroom, Erlea opened the cabinet with the whiskey. She eyed the bottle, growled in frustration, and slammed the door.

"Hello?" Maji called from the living area. "We let ourselves in. Door was open."

Erlea put on a brave face and greeted them, pulled dinner from the oven, and offered Celeste some wine. Seeing her hesitation, she said, "It won't bother me. Imane might as well have some company. As well as all the pizza."

"Oh no, I'm taking my share," Maji joked.

Erlea served them and sat, feigning interest in her healthy plate. Imane emerged a few minutes later, looking composed again. Why must she keep poking old wounds?

Celeste dabbed salad dressing from her lips. "You did a marvelous job at that press conference."

"Thanks. For a reward, now Nigel has a party that I have to make an appearance at. More nosy strangers, but with mingling."

"Oh God," Imane said. "That VIP thing the celebrity doctor is hosting? I hear he gives out free Botox shots."

"Is he licensed for that?" Celeste asked.

Erlea nodded. "Lyttleton is a plastic surgeon."

"And a starfucker," Imane added. "A lot of rich expats here are.

They'll all attend, of course, and make sure the gossip columnists spell their names right."

"I have a favor to ask, when you talk to Lyttleton," Maji said. "I need an appointment for him to look at my shoulder." To Celeste she added, "The left one."

Imane lit up. "Brilliant. Erlea gets an appointment, then you go to it." She looked thoughtful. "Let me guess—tattoo removal?"

"Scar. It's been reduced, but I keloid, so it's hard to get rid of completely." Maji kept her face blank, and Celeste held very still.

Erlea remembered how touchy Maji had been when Roger suggested tattooing over the scar. She sensed an unhappy story there. "Consider it done. It's high time I did something for you for a change."

After dinner they all moved to the balcony. Celeste noted that Erlea skipped the cigarette rolling ritual and went right for her guitar. "Good substitute?"

"Works at home," Erlea said and began strumming a slow tune.

Celeste removed Maji's ice pack and worked on her pressure points. Maji made no sound, stoic again. "You know," she said, "regular massage would help. And Reimi misses you."

"Who's Reimi?" Imane asked. Now that they'd cleared the air, Celeste decided she liked this exuberant woman, even her touchy ways and teasing. It came with love, after all.

"A blackjack dealer here," Maji told her. "Who I can't see, looking like this."

Celeste dug a thumb in under Maji's shoulder blade. "Too bad. You made an impression. She came to my office asking how to reach you. And I hate to lie, even for a good reason."

"Can't you just swear her to secrecy?" Imane asked. "It's just the press you're fooling." Maji stiffened under Celeste's touch, and Erlea's sure fingers faltered. Imane took it all in. "What? Are you in danger?"

"Just the usual threats," Erlea said. "Look, I'll talk to Dave, okay? Maybe he'll clear it. Celibacy's a lot to ask, on top of everything else."

"Dave who?" Imane asked, making Celeste both curious and

regretful for having started this. "Beatriz Echeverra Carreras, you tell me what's going on, this instant."

"Dave Brown," Maji answered. "My manager at Paragon. Nigel hired us to find out who's sending some particular threats and to keep Erlea out of view in the meantime. That's it."

"So this has nothing to do with your father?" Imane persisted.

Good question, Celeste thought. The press was certainly interested. "Yes. Is the ETA dangerous? To you"—she looked from Erlea to Maji—"and you, too, if you're out there in public, fooling everyone."

"That's above my pay grade," Maji said. Her face gave nothing away, but then it didn't when she was in pain, either. "But Brown has contacts with the National Police, and a support team watching my back. Nobody's getting hurt on my watch—including me."

"She's a professional," Erlea assured Imane. "And you know I would never ask anyone to put themselves in real danger for me."

"There's nothing dangerous about the bungee," Imane said.

Erlea frowned. "And yet here is the doctor, tending to her shoulder."

"Nobody asked me to," Maji said. "I was just playing around and overdid it."

"It would be a perfect number, with you in it," Imane said to Erlea. "A great finale."

Maji nodded. "It's the easiest aerial to learn. Not that different than a flying roll."

Ah, the Aikido practice. Yes, Celeste thought. Not a bad analogy.

"The hell it's not. On the mat, I'm in control every second."

"Sure, now that you're a black belt. But how were rolls when you started?"

Erlea gave a short laugh, almost a huff. "I would lean forward and just start to cry."

"But at some point you tried anyway. Right?"

"Yes. My friend Laura had started at the dojo a few months before me. She talked me through the fear and showed me what worked for her."

"There you go. Everything is learnable," Maji reminded her. "Once you get the hang of this it's really fun."

"Maybe. But it took me months to execute a decent roll. I don't have that luxury here. We have barely three weeks."

Celeste couldn't resist. "If you want to accelerate the process, I am happy to help."

"So you said." Erlea shook her head. "You're doing too much for me already."

Imane set her glass down hard on the table. "Seriously? The best performance coach in Europe is offering you help and you're turning her down?"

"You overstate my standing," Celeste said. "But still. I may be offended if you refuse. My shoes may even think you don't like lesbians. If they tell your fans, you're in trouble."

"Blackmail." Erlea pointed at Maji. "And don't look confused. I still blame you."

"Yeah, yeah. What's this with the talking shoe thing?"

Erlea gave Celeste a mischievous look. "Inside joke. Sensible shoes and all that."

Celeste felt herself color, not from the subject but from the way Erlea was looking at her, the teasing edge in that damn sexy voice.

"Settled," Imane declared. "Next order of business—the party. What are we all wearing?"

❖

Erlea felt sheepish, using the promise of another consult to spend more time with Celeste. The looks Imane and Maji had exchanged as they headed out said she wasn't fooling them.

"I think we should talk about heights down at the theater," Celeste said, "where I can see what is physically involved."

"Sure." Erlea's hopes rose. Then Celeste had stayed just to hang out with her. As Erlea reached for her guitar she saw Celeste shiver. "You want a blanket? Or to go inside?"

"I love it out here, with the view of the harbor. But a blanket would be nice, thank you." Celeste's profile against the sunset's backdrop was so exquisite Erlea wished she could take a photograph to hold the memory of the moment.

When she returned, Celeste was at the rail, watching the last pinks turn to darkness. So Erlea draped the blanket around her shoulders. She wanted to wrap her arms around her as well, but Celeste had been clear. If they were hanging out, even alone, it was as friends.

"It's the little things," Celeste murmured. She turned and faced Erlea. "Sorry. I was miles away. Ha. So much for mindfulness. Shall we begin?"

Of course. Celeste had stayed to work on another of her endless issues. "Ah, the smoking. You know, I'm doing fine with that." If Celeste couldn't be around smoke, Erlea would simply never light a cigarette again. "You're doing so much for me as it is. And you haven't even charged me yet."

"Tell you what, if I get you flying onstage, I will bill you properly. But for the rest, consider it an old debt settled." Celeste didn't smile, and her eyes still had a faraway look. Like the ocean on a cloudy day, still beautiful but poignant.

Erlea stepped back, needing something to do with her hands. Rolling more unsmokable tobacco? No. She plucked up her guitar and sat with it across her lap. "You don't owe me anything." Dinners and parties didn't count between friends.

"You don't remember, but I do," Celeste said, leaning back on the balcony railing and pulling the blanket snug. "Almost a year ago now. You told Adrienne to treat me better. And then you intervened when she hurt me, right in the middle of a crowded club in front of her teammates and everyone."

The soccer player? Erlea racked her memory, but the whole evening was hazy. "That woman assaulted you? That's why I went after her?"

Celeste half smiled, but her eyes held pain. "Yes. A perfect stranger. And yet you stood up for me. At the time I thought it was the alcohol making you brave. Now I know better."

Erlea couldn't imagine anyone hurting Celeste. Not on purpose. "She was your girlfriend?"

Celeste nodded. "It was the beginning of the end for us. For that I owe you more than you will ever know." Celeste winced and looked away. "But at that moment, I was so ashamed. I didn't stay to tell the police what happened, just fled. I thought surely someone would speak up. If I had realized she was going to sue you, well...I'm so sorry."

Erlea shrugged. "Don't worry about me. Nigel settled it." She hung her head. "If I hadn't been wasted, I would have made sure you were okay." She set the guitar aside, prepared to get up and embrace Celeste, comfort her. "And I would have made her pay for hurting you."

"More violence would help no one. And only land you in jail," Celeste said, her voice cracking. She looked to the night sky and blinked hard.

Erlea was by her side in a flash, reaching out to hug her. She stopped short. "May I?"

Celeste shook her head, and Erlea stepped back.

"See? The little things." Celeste gave her a weak smile. "You are a better person than you give yourself credit for. And I didn't want you putting me on some pedestal, taking my advice about your life, thinking I am so strong and together."

Not holding Celeste was killing Erlea. But it was good Celeste said no. If she touched her now, she wouldn't stop until she had kissed all the pain away. "I think you are a survivor. And they are the strongest kind of people."

"Thank you." Celeste unwrapped the blanket and handed it to Erlea. "I need to go and be alone now."

"Whatever you want," Erlea agreed. "But soon you will come to rehearsals and help me tackle my demons?"

Celeste gave her a real smile, a little light back in her eyes. "Count on it."

Chapter Fourteen

Celeste handed her invitation to the man at the door. He looked so familiar, despite the change in clothing. "You must be Dave Brown," she said.

"At your service," he replied with a smile. "Enjoy the party until the press arrive."

"Thank you. I will appreciate knowing when to disappear. Like the buffet." The crew were working diligently on the sumptuous spread.

"Always come early if you're hungry," Dave said with a smile, then pressed a finger to the earpiece attached to the wire that disappeared under his collar. Like Secret Service. "Speaking of which, please take a plateful into the control booth back there for Ms. Rios."

The booth was dim, set up for a DJ but occupied only by a security guard in uniform. "Hey, I'm glad you made it. Thanks for the food. I'm kind of stuck in here."

"Maji?"

"Call me Tomás."

"Incredible." Only her voice gave Maji away. "I never would have recognized you."

"I know. I helped Erlea haul you up onto the stage a couple weeks back."

"No wonder you didn't talk." Celeste laughed. "We thought you were a starstruck fan."

"Speaking of herself, there she is with full entourage. You should go save her."

Celeste looked down at her dress. "Do I look like I fit in here?"

"No, you look too classy." Maji smiled and the little mustache lifted. It reminded Celeste so much of Santxo that she had to laugh.

Erlea spotted Celeste emerging from the dark-windowed booth and smoothing down the short skirt on her jewel-toned blue dress. She looked at home in heels and makeup, like she belonged on the glossy pages of a magazine. Couldn't blame her for insisting on leaving before the press arrived, but…wow. Erlea made a beeline toward her.

"You look like a rock star tonight," Celeste said as they touched cheeks. She caressed the soft leather of Erlea's tailored leather jacket.

Erlea felt the touch through her sleeve and was glad she'd let Imane talk her into the jacket, extra zippers and buckles and all. She melted a little under Celeste's attention, the sound of her voice, her touch, her scent. "Is that gardenia?"

"That and lily of the valley, jasmine, some other flowers. White Shoulders. I know it's old-fashioned, but I like it for special occasions."

"It goes with the look." Erlea resisted saying just how hot that look was. "Kind of Taylor Swift, but more mature, of course. In a good way." Oops. "Hey, did you see Maji's getup? So not like me, for a change."

"Good thing—if she looked like you tonight it would be like a time-travel novel, where two versions of the same person appear and one has to hide."

"Exactly. That's what I thought the first time I saw her made up like me. Like, no wonder you're not allowed to meet yourself." *Stop rambling and breathe.* "It was really unsettling."

"I love time-travel novels," Celeste said.

"You do?" Erlea grinned with surprise. "Like *The Time Traveler's Wife*?"

Celeste considered. "Yes, but also *Kindred*, *The Redemption of Christopher Columbus*, *Doomsday Book*…"

"Heavy stories. Serious. Hmm, what about *To Say Nothing of the Dog*?"

"Sure. I love Willis when she's funny."

"Funny? Hilarious." Erlea knew she should probably dial it back, but really. "She'd totally get the lesbian shoe thing."

"I hate to interrupt your geeking out," Imane said, slipping an arm around Erlea's waist, "but Lyttleton is here. Go ask him for an appointment."

"Oh, right. I did promise." Erlea looked Lyttleton over. "But he looks like a twit. Are he and Nigel related?"

Imane laughed. "Shh. You haven't even hit the bar yet."

"And I'm not going to," Erlea insisted, before Imane could pull her away from Celeste. "Maji taught me a trick. Will you get me something clear, soda or seltzer, with a wedge of lime?"

"Sure," Celeste said with a wink.

Erlea looked back as Imane dragged her away. "Thanks."

"You can canoodle on the dance floor later," Imane said. "Now act like a celebrity."

"We were talking about books," Erlea said. "And I'm only getting fake drunk later."

By the time she made it back to Celeste, the room was getting crowded and the music only added to the muddle of sound. Celeste handed her a tall glass.

"Most of the ice melted, sorry," she said. To the man next to her, she asked, "Could you get me another?"

"Uh, sure." He took her wineglass and headed for the long bar line.

"Do you know who that is?" Erlea watched him go, impressed.

Celeste shook her head. "Tony. No last name offered. Did I blow it?"

"No, you're perfect." *Stupid. Why not just tell her she's hot, too?* "I mean, he needs that sometimes. Owning the biggest label in Europe goes to his head."

Celeste covered her mouth. Was she giggling?

"Are you buzzed?"

"No," Celeste replied, flushing. "A little tipsy, maybe. And I have good news." She pulled Erlea close to speak right next to her ear. "I'm going to Barcelona on the weekend. I reached out to friends with a practice there, and they want to meet."

"That's great." Erlea pulled back so Celeste could share her smile. "Your dress doesn't match your eyes at all."

"That's what Roger said. But it fit. Well, a little tight, but who cares?" Celeste leaned back in. "Nobody knows me here."

That sounded ridiculously sexy. Erlea just nodded. The music changed to a slow number, and she slid an arm around Celeste's waist.

"Are we dancing?" Celeste asked.

"Unless you mind."

Celeste draped her arms lightly over Erlea's shoulders. "Just one. I love this song."

"It's my new favorite," Erlea whispered into her hair. She put her hands on Celeste's hips, wanting to slide one around and pull her close. But no.

To her delight, Celeste took the lead, dropping one hand and nudging Erlea's arm back, then slipping her hand under the back of her jacket. The feel of Celeste's palm through her shirt, the softness of her cheek against her own, the gentle press of breasts and hips, stole all the words from Erlea's mind. She closed her eyes and just moved her feet in tiny steps, blissful.

"You are perfect as you are," Celeste murmured.

Erlea smiled and leaned her temple against Celeste's. "Feels true right now." Her whole body thrummed. She had no liquid courage pushing her to try for a kiss, probably for the best. If she drank too much to remember this moment, that would be a tragedy.

As the music shifted tempo, they broke apart, Celeste looking bashful. "Here comes Tomás."

"First reporters being let in to play now," Maji said, her voice shielded by the noise level. "I'll walk you out."

"Good night," Erlea told them. "Thanks for coming."

Celeste leaned in and yelled, "Tell Tony he made quite an impression. He never brought me my wine back."

Erlea laughed until they were out of sight.

"It's great to see you happy," Imane said, slipping an arm through hers.

"She has the quirkiest sense of humor." Erlea looked sideways at her. "Don't say it."

"Say what?"

Erlea's chest squeezed tight. "Laura would have liked her."

"I didn't say it." Imane turned them toward the bar. "Come on, let's get you another fake drink. You've got rich assholes to offend and the night is young."

❖

Maji saw Celeste into a taxi out front. When she spotted Reimi, just off shift and still in her uniform, she hurried back through the lobby. *No time for games tonight.* She let out a sigh as the elevator doors began to close. A hand with long dark nails swept between them, the sensor worked properly, and the doors slid open.

Reimi walked in, eyes flashing. "I thought Celeste didn't know where you were. Yet here you are together." The elevator began its ascent to the party floor.

"I'm here on a job again," Maji said. "Right now, actually. I can't talk."

"But we're alone," Reimi said. She punched the stop button and the elevator shuddered to a halt. "And you're so perfect."

Maybe not angry, Maji thought as Reimi pressed her against the wall of the elevator. And gave her the kind of let's-make-up-by-fucking kiss that left Maji gasping. When Reimi tugged the zipper of her trousers down and started fiddling with the belt, Maji's common sense returned.

"Wait." She clutched Reimi's wrist, hyperaware of the nails lightly brushing her skin. "I really can't right now. Not 'cause I don't want to. Really want to."

Reimi grinned at her. "Keep wanting me. I'm going to change and get a drink. When do you get off?"

"Not sure," Maji said. "Big party. Might be hours." Her breathing was coming back under control now. "We should talk."

"If that's what you want to call it, Tomás," Reimi said with a satisfied look as she let herself out on the next floor. "Until then."

On the ascent, Maji wiped Reimi's lipstick off and tried to reach Dave. All she heard was static.

Romero grabbed her as she stepped out. "Take the stairs, we're searching this floor."

"Sorry, what? My comm was out."

"Erlea's missing. Check the stairwell," he barked at her. "Go, go."

"Gone." She ran for the Exit sign and through the door, then paused to listen.

"*Crackle...squeal...*elevators." It sounded like Dave in her earbud.

Below her, a muffled curse and a thump. "Movement on the stairs," she said, hoping Dave or somebody on the comms had decent reception.

And then she flew, using the handrails to propel herself down half a flight at a time, then around the corner, down again, around again. She landed as softly as she could, pausing on the third landing to listen.

"Get the fuck off," Erlea's voice slurred.

"Shh, I'm helping you," a man's voice responded. "You're drunk. You need air."

Maji said, "Between floors six and four, with at least one male." Then she flew again.

Rounding the fourth corner, she spotted them. "Hey," she yelled.

One man looked up and let go of Erlea, who appeared to be deadweight now. The other guy grunted, pulling her toward the exit door with her feet dragging over the landing. The door burst open and Dave grabbed for him.

Maji took off after the runner, leaping over Erlea's sprawled form as Dave bit out commands for medical backup.

Despite his head start, the runner only knew how to pound down the stairs two at a time. Maji closed in, watching for him to stumble. Just before the next landing, he twisted with a yelp and went down flailing. She assisted him by pinning one arm behind his back, his face pressed to the steps.

"Rios to Brown, over."

"Go for Brown." Dave's voice came through loud and clear.

"Third floor landing, accomplice in custody." Why didn't the uniform come with handcuffs? "Escort available?"

"On their way. Out."

She handed him over and headed to the medical office to check on Erlea. In the corridor, Santxo and one of his real security staff kept a small clump of guests and reporters from getting any closer.

Santxo spotted her. "Tomás. What took you so long? Are you hurt?"

Maji started to shake her head, then realized he was giving her a reason to go in. She clutched one arm for the benefit of the rubberneckers. Once alongside him, she murmured, "Thanks. Anyone call Celeste yet?"

"No. The medics were here already. Should I?"

She shook her head gingerly, amazed her wig and cap had stayed put this long. Before she stepped back into public view, they would need resecuring. "Let me check."

Three faces turned toward her as she entered Celeste's office. Then two went back to working on Erlea, monitoring vital signs and adjusting an IV. Erlea didn't stir—but at least she was breathing.

"Nice catch," Dave said. "We thought she went to the restroom. Next thing you know—"

"Our comms cut out," Maji said. As if jammed. By whom? "Debrief?"

"Later," Dave said. "Romero's got one perp upstairs, I've got the other in there." He nodded toward the back room. "They got Erlea puked dry and stabilized, but somebody should stay with her tonight. Where's the doctor?"

"On my boat. I'll call her." Maji started dialing. Within two minutes, Celeste was climbing into a taxi.

Dave handed Maji's phone back. "You hurt? You don't look great."

"No, I'm good." Maji put both hands behind her, embarrassed they shook slightly as the adrenaline wore off.

"Rios. Go back to your room and get some rest, order some food." He smiled. "Call that woman from the elevator to share it with you. If you can keep your hat on."

"Really, Dave?" Maji shook her head. "When did the comms stop working, exactly?"

"Not sure. Did she say anything after *until then*?" He added an eyebrow waggle to his terrible Reimi imitation.

"You seriously want me off the clock right now?"

He nodded gravely. "Take a break. And if you have company tonight, turn your comm off. Seriously."

Maji rode the elevator up to her floor, wishing she'd sent Reimi an apology rather than an invitation. Not that sex didn't appeal, now that she knew she could handle herself in the heat of the moment. For that she should thank Reimi, but was gratitude enough reason to keep play-acting?

Reimi moved toward her the moment the doors opened. "Are you hurt? Look, your uniform is torn."

"I'm okay," Maji assured her, trying to gently redirect Reimi to the waiting elevator car. "But things got a little crazy, and I'm starting to crash. I'm sorry."

Reimi took Maji's face in both hands. "Baby, of course you are. You chased the bad guys down. That's so hot. Let me take care of you." She kissed Maji with tenderness.

"Word's out, huh?" Maji let them into her room, pressing Reimi against the closed door. Reimi held her close but didn't push her to pull off clothes or rush the heat. Desire built slowly, on its own, with an intimacy lacking the previous night. Maji nearly forgot her question.

"It's on TV already," Reimi answered as Maji kissed her neck, working down toward the swell of breasts peeking from the unbuttoned shirt. Maji stiffened and Reimi rushed to elaborate. "Not your heroic rescue. The press says she took drugs and is in the hospital. No word of a kidnapping attempt. Or Tomás."

Maji pulled back. "I'd really like to ditch Tomás tonight. I need a shower and some sleep."

"Let me run you a bath and kiss your bumps and bruises away. Then I will put you to bed and be on my way, I promise."

Maji let Reimi undress her and tut over an assortment of scrapes and contusions before she stepped into the steaming tub. When Reimi reached to take off her hat, Maji stopped her, remembering the red hair hidden under the black wig.

"It's okay," Reimi assured her. "Santxo told me about your other job here. Let's get this hot thing off and wash your rock star hair out."

Maji sighed with relief and nodded, letting Reimi pull out the clips and free her hair. "I hope he swore you to secrecy, at least."

Reimi chuckled as she lathered up a washcloth. "All of your secrets are safe with me." She eyed the large tub. "Is there room in there for two? I want to rub your back."

Maji nodded, reclining in the delicious heat, soaking her sore muscles. "Please."

"I do like when you say that," Reimi purred, stripping off her shirt and slacks as Maji watched. She added a sensuous sway to her removal of the lacy bra and panties, then kissed Maji deeply before carefully slipping into place behind her.

Maji leaned back against Reimi, cradled by her soft belly and breasts and the silky legs draped around her hips. She sighed as Reimi slipped her arms under Maji's and began kneading her pecs while sucking a low spot on her neck. "This is so nice."

Reimi pushed her gently forward, moving her hands to Maji's shoulders. "I could be a very good girlfriend for you. We could take care of each other, the way we both like."

Maji moaned as Reimi's fingers found and released the knots in her muscles. "Um…" She really needed to say something, not lead her on.

"Oh yes. Look how strong you are. Most women are not built like this. And you would look so hot with short hair. You are such a stud." Reimi reached one arm around again, finding a nipple.

Maji's body cried out for more touch, to be driven to release by the luscious woman pressed up against her. But she couldn't let her under false pretenses. "Stop," she gasped.

"Are you all right?" Reimi asked.

Maji turned as far as she could within the close space and tight embrace. She leaned her forehead into the side of Reimi's head. "You are a wonderful woman, and you deserve to have exactly what you want in a partner. But what you want, that's just not me. Not full-time, not all the way, not like you want."

"No one is exactly right. Believe me, I have looked. The internet brings many interesting women to my doorstep. All are nice in their own way. But you cannot expect to live on an island, with family obligations, and reel in exactly the right fish."

Maji nearly laughed. "She's out there. Try being more specific about what you want. You deserve someone who is heart and soul what you are looking for. Help her find you." She gave Reimi a sideways kiss. "I may be strong, but I'm not a stud at heart. We wouldn't work for long."

"You didn't have a good time the other night?" Reimi's lower lip trembled.

"Oh yes, ma'am, I did." More than Maji could explain. "It was wonderful, just not who I am every day. You understand?"

Reimi nodded and unwound herself. She silently helped Maji out of the tub, wrapping her in a fluffy towel. "Tomorrow you go back to playing the role Erlea pays you for. But tonight you are my hero. And I want to make you feel good, the way you like. One night, and then we are even, as friends should be."

That was hard to argue with. Reimi's hands and mouth were persuasive, too. Maji gave up the battle and surrendered. When Reimi pushed her down onto the bed's soft comforter and sank to the floor before her, pulling Maji's hips to her, Maji just closed her eyes and let go. Reimi took her on a slow ride, building gradually like their kisses earlier, until Maji felt like she was floating and then dissolving.

Reimi climbed up and pulled her up to the pillows, then held her as she drifted into sleep.

"No," Maji said, trying to break out of the dream. She felt a hand stroke her cheek and opened her eyes. "Oh, fuck. You okay?"

Reimi stretched languorously and pressed her lips to Maji's clavicle. "I feel marvelous. But I should go soon. I must be home when Mama wakes. And you should sleep in."

Maji turned toward her, tipping Reimi onto her back and claiming her mouth. Reimi returned the kiss with hunger and Maji slid one hand along her arm, her shoulder, down her torso and belly. She stopped with her fingertips in the tiny curls over her mons, resisting the urge to continue. "May I?"

Reimi responded by pressing her hips up, her legs falling open wider. She wove the fingers of one hand into the hair at the back of Maji's head and used the other to hold Maji close.

Maji curled her hand down and inside Reimi, shifting her top leg to capture both of Reimi's, pulling them tight around the hand caught between them. Then she kissed Reimi hard, thrumming her fingers against the soft pad inside and rolling Reimi's nipple between her fingertips at the same time.

Reimi sucked Maji's tongue deep into her mouth, moving her pinned hips in rhythm with Maji's fingers. Then she released Maji from the kiss abruptly, throwing her head back and arching up against her. Maji kept the rhythm up, pressing her hips down to intensify the connection. Reimi's ragged breathing hitched and she let out a guttural cry, clinging to Maji as her whole body undulated.

Maji kissed her softly as Reimi relaxed, slowly stroking Maji's face and back and humming in satisfaction. "Thank you," Maji whispered.

❖

Erlea woke with an arm draped over someone. Someone who smelled like pretty flowers. She opened her eyes a crack, and there Celeste was, as beautiful asleep as awake. On top of the covers and clothed.

What happened? This was not her room. Erlea turned her head and a wave of nausea hit. She thrashed at the covers, wanting to bolt for the bathroom.

"Trash can," Celeste said.

Erlea spotted it, held it under her face, and spewed a stream of bitter liquid. Her stomach cramped, her abs aching. She must have retched a lot already. In front of Celeste?

"Slow breaths," Celeste said a moment later, crouching nearby and wiping Erlea's face with a warm, damp cloth. "Let's try a little water."

Erlea sat up with help, the sheet sliding off her bare skin. Why was she topless?

"Here," Celeste said, tugging the sheet up. "Can you sip this?"

Erlea reached for the glass, missed, and let Celeste steady her until she gripped it properly. She took a cautious sip. It tasted wonderful, so cool and fresh.

"Slow down." Celeste gently took the cup from her. "Or it will just come back up."

Erlea swatted her hand away. "Stop being so nice to me. You were right."

"About?"

"All of it." Erlea groaned and put her head in her hands, pulling her knees up. "How can I say I'm sorry to you and then do this again? But I was sorry, and I tried fake drinking like Maji, and it was going great, and...Oh God, I can't even remember. How many shots did I do?"

"Shh," Celeste said. "You did zero shots. You left your soda unattended and a man put a drug in it."

"Oh my God." She was pantsless, too. "Did he…?"

"No. Maji and her people caught them quite quickly." Celeste paused. "Your clothes needed washing. Your body reacted violently to the drug."

"Oh God." *Did you wash me?* Erlea was afraid to ask. "Wait… them?"

"Yes. Two men. But I should let you talk to Mr. Brown. And if you can't keep something down soon, I want you to go to the hospital."

"No." Erlea squeezed her eyes shut. "No hospital. No press."

"Shh. I'll call the medics, see about another IV for now." Celeste stroked her hair gently while talking on the phone. "Brown? She's awake. Send me the female medic. Yes, only her."

❖

Erlea jerked awake, frightened and gasping, when her arm stung.

Celeste shushed her, squeezing her hand. "You're going to be fine. Try to lie still."

"Want me to spell you?" another woman's voice said.

Erlea turned her head quickly, then swallowed against a wave of nausea. A uniformed medic stripped off her gloves, eyeing them both from across the room.

"No," Celeste responded. "I'm not leaving her."

Too tired to speak, Erlea managed to squeeze her hand back before the room went dark.

❖

Celeste stepped into the hallway and quietly shut the door.

"Where is she?" Imane demanded. "I thought she ducked out last night—she hates big parties—and then she didn't show for call, and Nico said she was sick, but then Roger said—"

"Shh. She's sleeping," Celeste cautioned.

"Fuck." Imane looked to the ceiling. "So it's true, then? We swore to each other, when Laura died, we'd never do drugs again. Not that the drinking is great, but still. What did she take?"

Celeste wished she could reassure Imane. "You know I cannot discuss my patients. Even this one, even with you."

"At least you respect her privacy. But it's too late. Nigel's already released a statement."

"Really? Saying what?"

"Nigel told them Erlea's seeing a doctor for her addictions, trying to handle things before the show opens." Imane scowled. "That this has been a time of great pressure, with the new show and the uncertainty about her father."

Celeste wanted to hit something. "How could he do that to her?"

"He's a publicity whore," Imane said. "And lying, isn't he? Of course, Mr. Bait and Switch. I'm right, aren't I?"

Celeste couldn't answer one way or another without Erlea's permission. "Let me see if she is up to a short conversation. Short, you understand?" Imane nodded eagerly. Was it better to upset Erlea now or have this sprung on her later?

"Let her in," Erlea called out as soon as Celeste cracked the door.

Imane's face lit up and she squeezed Celeste's arm. "I'll be gentle. Promise."

"It's not what you think," Erlea told her before Imane could ask. "You know I would never. Tell her about Laura." Erlea nodded toward Celeste, then closed her eyes.

"Laura was our friend, the third in our terrific trio. We never came up with a better name, we were all such nerds. And they already called us the ménage à trois," Imane explained. "High school is the worst."

"It can be rough, especially if one is out. Or outed."

"Laura wasn't. I pretended to be with Erlea, since that was what they all thought anyway. Not like I wanted to go out with any of those losers." Imane pulled her focus back. "Sorry, tangent. No one knew they were dating until Laura's dad caught her with Erlea and threw her out."

"He threw his own daughter out?"

"Yeah." Imane squeezed Erlea's hand, and Celeste saw tears leak out from her closed eyes. "Then Laura dropped out of school, moved into a squat, started using. It went very bad very fast."

"I'm so sorry. Laura died?"

"She OD'd, ten years ago almost to this day. The cops called it suicide. But who knows? We failed her, either way."

"No. You were kids. What resources did you have to help?"

Imane nodded. "I know that now. I grew up, lived a little, gained perspective. But then, I was not in love with her."

Erlea opened her eyes and looked at Celeste. "And every year I do something stupid, right on schedule."

"This was not your fault," Celeste insisted. "And I cannot tell anyone the truth, but you can. You should know, Nigel told the press you are an addict."

Erlea gave a ragged laugh. "He probably thinks that's less embarrassing." She looked at Imane. "Some guy drugged me. Like a nobody in a bar. How *dreadfully common.*"

"Holy shit. Tell me he's in jail. And you're okay."

Erlea smiled weakly. "Maji and Celeste to the rescue. Getting no credit, as usual."

"You could tell the media the truth," Imane suggested. "There is a tox screen and a police report, right? You are lucky, really."

"Lucky?"

"Yes, very. This happens to so many women and the men are almost never caught. You could do some good by talking about it publicly, bringing attention to the issue."

Celeste agreed, but this was not the time to push. "Today the only thing she must do is rest."

Imane kept her promise, heading for the door after a quick, tearful good-bye. She pulled Celeste into a grateful hug and whispered, "No wonder she is crazy about you."

Maji woke feeling hungover and went next door to check in with Dave. "Got coffee?"

"Only if you eat, too." He waved her toward the dining table that smelled like heaven. While she sat and dug in, he filled her in on the team's follow-up at the party. "Everybody there was either a great actor or they really think she got smashed and waltzed out with the latest boy toy."

"Convenient for Nigel. I saw his press statement. Asshat. Sorry, go on."

Dave nodded. "The accomplice must have been waiting in the

stairwell. We pulled all the video feeds, but they were interrupted as well."

"Are they pros?"

"Just a couple of scared fuckwits, from what I can tell. Said they were paid to play a prank, don't even know what they put in her drink."

And I'm just a sweet short guy named Tomás. "How's Erlea?"

"Sleeping. We got her to a room, and Dr. G stayed up to watch over her. Medics helped," Dave said. "At least one did. The other one sounds sketchy."

"Okay. So who fucked with the comms and the video, just at the right moment?"

Dave stood and rolled his neck. "Let's go chat with Romero about that."

Maji followed Dave to Romero's room and let him do the talking. Given her suspicions, she wanted to stand back and observe.

"I beg your pardon?" Romero asked Dave. "You want me to do what?"

"Account for every member of your team," Dave repeated. "Who's GEO, who's on loan to you. When they came on board, how much they knew."

And who was in on last night's debacle, Maji thought. She didn't need to say it.

"You think the sabotage came from my team," Romero said. Thoughtful rather than offended, Maji noted. Sincere, or a good actor?

"Okay, let's explore that theory." Romero described each of the people on his team, including a female medic.

"I didn't realize she was GEO," Maji commented. Even female operators could overlook each other. When Romero smiled, she added, "Yes, I get the irony. What about the other medic?"

"The male medic is not GEO. We borrowed him from the National Police, just to cover the party. So many notables in one place, we wanted to have enough personnel for immediate response."

Maji bought that. If there had been a shooter, or a bomb, casualties would have been high. "Well, that explains the aftermath. But not the audio and visual interference."

"What aftermath?" Romero asked. "I thought Erlea was recovering fully."

"She is now," Dave said. "But Dr. Guillot raised some concerns.

The first IV bag seemed to do Erlea a lot of good. But when the guy took second shift, he switched them out. Erlea started twitching, shallow respirations, thready pulse. And your loaner kept giving Dr. Guillot excuses, I guess not realizing she'd worked trauma and would know better. She kicked him out, unhooked Erlea right away, and stayed with her the rest of the night."

Romero winced. "I will find out who assigned him to us. And see if the trail leads us to either of the two men Echeverra named."

"When your team's medic responded to Dr. Guillot's call this morning, she was surprised at the shape Erlea was in," Dave reported. "Put her on another drip and she improved again. When she went to look for the loaner guy, he was gone. Left a note about getting called to another scene."

Romero nodded. "Okay. I'll talk to her, see what she thinks the loaner gave Erlea."

"And why," Maji added. "To keep her sick, send her to the hospital with kidney damage or respiratory failure? Or to kill her?"

"I can't see how her death would draw Echeverra out. But I'll let you know everything I learn." Romero pulled out his phone and dialed. "Where is Diaz right now? No, leave him be. Don't tell him I was checking, either."

"Another loaner from the National Police?"

"Yes. I already grilled him at debrief about all the comm system problems we had. He had explanations ready, and they sounded plausible."

Dave looked as skeptical as Maji felt.

"Since he hasn't done a runner like the medic, let's keep him in place under surveillance," Dave said. "And keep him occupied while we sweep everything for bugs and trackers."

Romero nodded. "I'll let you know what we find."

"When I said we," Dave clarified, "I was including me doing that sweep."

Fortunately, Romero agreed. Maji's gut said they could trust him. But she still trusted Dave more.

CHAPTER FIFTEEN

"Welcome to Villa Perfecta," said the man in the security booth. "How may I help you?"

Maji flipped up the windscreen on the full-face helmet. "I have an appointment with Dr. Lyttleton. Beatriz Echeverra," she rasped.

"Take off your helmet, please."

Maji rolled her eyes as if exasperated and pulled the helmet off, revealing the red hair and makeup. "Satisfied?"

"Thank you, Ms. Echeverra. Down the road to the main house. You may park the moto anywhere you please."

She gave him a wicked grin. "I always do."

The cliffside compound overlooking the Mediterranean looked more like a resort than a medical facility. But Maji supposed if you paid for both Lyttleton's services and complete privacy you might expect a spa experience for your recovery. Just what had Echeverra had to do for the Nuvoletta to afford a full facial reconstruction?

A woman in a lab coat came out to greet her as she parked Reimi's motor scooter in the shade. "Aren't you clever? And brave. I hope those horrible paparazzi didn't chase you today."

Maji kept the hoarseness in her voice. "I was as anonymous as any moto on the streets of Barcelona." She cleared her throat. "Sorry. Too much rehearsal."

"Ooh. Well, we have a lovely little café with a view of the ocean. Let's get you something hot to drink. I am Carolina." As Maji walked with her through the main house she added, "I watched your interview on TV last night. I wanted to say thank you. I have a friend who got drugged at a bar, and the hospital didn't even have a rape kit available."

"I'm so sorry," Maji whispered. She'd listened to the surveillance feed taken from Erlea's room. But who knew what the magazine edited out and what it left in.

"Maybe your act of courage will help." Carolina offered the coffee machine and a seat with a sweep of her hand. "What can I get you?"

Maji craved a cortado, but that wasn't what Erlea would drink while nursing sore vocal cords. "Tea with honey, please." Maji found the interview on her phone and streamed it while sipping the boring drink. Erlea was very forthcoming with the reporter she'd selected for the exclusive.

Maji skimmed through the part about Erlea being drugged, the data on how many women this happened to, the unreported cases, and the difficulty in prosecuting rape. All good. Then she reached the part about Celeste.

"The woman you danced with that night, our sources have identified her as Dr. Celeste Guillot. She's been linked with a number of famous athletes previously. Care to comment on your relationship?"

"If you've researched Dr. Guillot," Erlea replied, "you know she's a performance expert, the kind Olympians credit with overcoming their personal obstacles to winning the gold. She would never talk about a client, of course, but I'm not embarrassed to admit that I have a terrible fear of heights. And everyone wants me in the air for this spectacular aerial number. So why not hire the best?"

"And is dancing with clients part of the service?"

"Hey, everyone's allowed a little fun in their off time. But it's not like that."

"So it's true what they say, you're just an ally for LGBTs, straight but not narrow?"

"I wouldn't make that assumption. I know I've been photographed with a string of guys, but if they get called out for fucking around, everybody thinks they're studs, right? Like it or not, women get judged by a different standard. So if I was dating one, I wouldn't kiss and tell. Not for lack of pride, but out of respect for her. Get it?"

Not so bad. Maji admired Erlea, back to rehearsals after two days in bed and refusing Celeste's offer to delay her visit to Barcelona.

"Ms. Echeverra? The doctor will see you now." Carolina held a CD and pen, looking bashful. "Would you mind very much…"

Maji stood and smiled. "Not at all." She scribbled Erlea's signature, glad she'd practiced until it became as automatic as writing her own.

❖

"Do you have to film every damn thing I do?" Erlea winced at her own tone. "Sorry. Could you maybe just not capture the part where I freeze up and flail around?"

Alejandro set the video camera down. "Of course. But conquering your fear would be great behind-the-scenes stuff."

Erlea groaned. "Only if I get to approve the final cut. No matter what Nigel tells you."

"You're the boss," he replied in his usual agreeable manner.

At least someone thought so. "Okay, let's go again. Show me the move again?"

Tania, in the harness on the cord next to her, leaped up and forward. Instead of tucking her feet up and trying to roll as Erlea had, she kept her legs stiff and her core taut, letting the momentum of the harness lever her lower half into the air. Then the elasticized rope pulled back against Tania's waist, and in a heartbeat she was back on her feet, giving a little at the knees to stick the landing. She looked expectantly at Erlea.

"Sure. You make it look easy," Erlea muttered. She pantomimed her tight core, stiff legs, and the little push-up from the stage floor by her hands. Tania nodded her encouragement.

Erlea took a deep breath and dove forward, thinking *plank* while resisting the urge to curl into a wheel for a forward roll. Determined to not let the cord pull her back onto her ass again, she held the right body mechanics. Not as gracefully as Tania—but it worked. On her feet again, she laughed out loud.

Tania beamed at her and demonstrated a new move, holding the cord up high and walking in a circle in the opposite direction. As she gained speed and bounce, her feet came off the ground at controlled intervals.

Erlea had to admit it looked like fun. She made her own less ambitious circle around the stage. Small hops. Not so bad.

"That's a start," Imane said as she approached from the wings.

"Have you seen Maji? Celeste is all wound up and trying to track her down."

"Maji's out for a few hours," Erlea replied, not wanting to say where. The cast and crew didn't need to know about Maji's doctor's appointment any more than the media did. "Celeste is back? I could really use her about now."

"I bet you could," Imane said with a wink. "But seriously, I don't think this is a good time."

Erlea spotted Celeste in the wings, pacing. "Is it the interview? Did I fuck up? Please say no."

Imane shrugged. "She just said it was personal." She waved Celeste over. "Maji's out doing double duty. Can you consult for a few minutes?"

Celeste strode out to join them onstage. "Show me the piece as you intend it." Erlea noticed she spoke only to Imane, not looking her way. *She hates me. Did they misquote me?*

"We're still working out the ground moves, but here's the kicker," Imane told Celeste. She put on the headphones, spoke to the control booth, and gestured to Tania to run for the wall.

The music came on near the end of the song, and Tania moved to it, getting into the rhythm and position. Erlea held her breath as Tania heard the cue and started running for the wall, lifting off the ground with her arms outstretched. Just as she reached the second story window, the wall tilted away and the bungee pulled her back. She landed safely on her feet and crumpled to the stage, just as she'd done in the earlier demos.

Celeste nodded. "I see. And how are the nonflying parts coming?"

Imane looked to Erlea to answer. "Okay. I'm getting my feet off the ground for short periods."

"Good. Keep doing that," Celeste said, looking at her briefly. "Develop some confidence with the basic moves first." She switched her attention back to Imane. "Call me when she hits a sticking point."

"Okay. Thanks," Imane said to Celeste's retreating form. She turned back to Erlea. "What are you waiting for? Get out of that rig and go apologize."

"For what?" Erlea said.

Imane stared at her. "I don't know. I'm not the one she's pissed at. Just go."

❖

Celeste opened her office door to find Erlea, shifting from foot to foot but not speaking. "Are you ill? Was it too soon to send you back to rehearsals?" Now on top of everything else, she was failing as doctor to her only patient. Erlea deserved better. "I shouldn't have run off. I'm sorry."

"No, I'm sorry," Erlea said. "I feel fine thanks to you. And now I've pissed you off."

Celeste motioned Erlea to come in. "It's not you I'm mad at." She turned away, not able to meet her gaze.

"The reporter then," Erlea ventured. "I thought she was a safe choice, even read her notes. But after they edited, I can see it sounds like we're involved. I'm so sorry."

Celeste had pushed that worry back, but now it leaped onto the pile of her anxiety. She looked at Erlea, willing herself to not cry. "I was so close to starting over. Now I won't be surprised if they rescind the job offer."

"You got a job in Barcelona? That's great." Erlea looked cautiously happy for her. "If it would help, I'll tell them you've been nothing but professional with me. I'll do a press conference, whatever it takes."

"No. I don't need you to speak for me," Celeste said, her voice rising. "I don't need my name splashed across the tabloids. I just want my life back." She burst into tears, covering her face and turning away again to hide her shame.

Erlea placed a warm hand on her back. "I'm here. And I believe in you."

Celeste spun back and buried her face in Erlea's shoulder, comforted by her embrace. "Tissue," she managed after catching her breath. She took the tissue and blew, accepted another, and used it up, too. What a mess. "I can't do this anymore. I'm sick to death of being scared, of running away and hiding." Anger surged through her again, but not turned inward for a change. She pushed Erlea away. "She's still fucking controlling me."

"I can't tell you what to do," Erlea said. "But I'll help in any way I can. Do you need a place to stay?"

Celeste could see she meant that. But it was time to stand on her own two feet. "I can afford a hotel while I get settled. Just for a week or two."

"My apartment is empty, except for the cat, who would love you. You could stay as long as you like," Erlea said. "It's very secure. And I made Alejandro show me the settlement terms. If she comes near there, the deal is off. I can talk about what really happened that night, even release the whole video."

"The whole video?"

"Yeah. Some guy was stalking me with his phone. He got the whole evening. Most of it's really boring, until you come in." Erlea looked sheepish. "Nigel never told me about it. Alejandro showed me."

Celeste's stomach turned at the thought of Erlea watching Adrienne screaming at her, hurting her. "I'm on tape, too? That part never made the news."

"Only the little bit that makes me look like a drunken brawler," Erlea said. "If only I'd been sober, I would have handled things better, made sure you were okay. I missed a whole year of knowing you." She cradled Celeste's face in her palm and caressed her cheek with her thumb.

Celeste ached so much to kiss her, she stiffened up and pulled back. "No, don't be silly. I'd have thanked you and we'd have parted ways. You were very busy touring."

"I'll never be too busy to care about you," Erlea said, reaching for the door. "But I can't seem to stop overstepping. Think about the apartment, let me know, okay?"

"Yes," Celeste said. Yes to all this sweet, funny, achingly sexy woman offered. "I'll think about it. Thank you."

Erlea smiled and slipped out the office door. Celeste dropped into her desk chair and stared after her, still feeling the warmth of Erlea's touch on her face.

❖

"Someone's going to come fetch the moto," Maji told Carolina as she prepared to leave Villa Perfecta. "Apparently there's a reporter waiting outside your gates to catch me leaving."

"Oh no," Carolina said. "We can get you out of here in a van. We do it all the time."

"No need. I've got a car meeting me behind the Cuevas del Drach." Maji put on her curious face. "They said there's a path along the cliff top. Show me?" Should match the satellite images she'd gone over with Dave.

"Of course." Carolina beamed, delighted with the intrigue.

Maji changed from her moto-riding leathers into a sundress and sporty sandals, her hair under a wide-brimmed hat and her face half hidden by large sunglasses. She followed Carolina until the woods that shielded the compound from view gave way to hard-packed earth. As the trail opened out to look down into one of Majorca's many little coves, Maji reveled in the sound of the waves and the feel of the sun. And having a few minutes alone and unwatched, not making her throat raw with a fake voice or minding her every mannerism. She paused to admire the stone wall at the edge of the tourist attraction's property, the way the Majorcans remade the old into the new, refitting ancient stones into new walls. Life was rebuilt that way at the edges of farms, vineyards, and fincas all over the island.

A middle-aged couple in capris and sandals walked toward her, talking and pointing to the ocean. She smiled politely at them. They smiled back and even said, "Bon dia."

Entering the site's grounds, Maji coasted past families waiting to enter the caves, discussing the dragons in the attraction's name. More tourists thronged the shops and café by the ticket area and parking lot. Maji wound through them, listening for any buzz about Erlea, looking for any sign of paparazzi. She got in line for gelato and phoned Dave.

"I'm ready in the harbor," he said.

"Hi, Dave. I'm fine," Maji said, refusing to hurry. "How are you? Want a gelato?"

"I'd love one. But you better keep one hand free at least. My guy on overwatch says a camera van just pulled into the parking area."

"Almost showtime." Maji hung up and bought a two scoop cone, chocolate and coconut. She strolled away from the café, licking the cone like getting a little of each flavor in every bite was the most important task of the day. When she spotted the van and a group of tourists speculating on whether Erlea was really going to make an appearance, she looked for Dave's spotter. He stood up and waved his yellow ball cap at her.

Maji stopped to say hi and ask him for a thirty-second start.

Halfway to the road she took off her hat and heard him yell, "There she is—heading for the Majorica shop."

Maji started jogging lightly toward the shop, dodging a group of cyclists as she crossed the road. At the corner, the store's doors slid open for her and she stepped into the cool dry elegance of the famous pearl jewelry boutique.

"Welcome, how may I assist—oh," said the clerk in an incongruously Scottish accent. She switched to Spanish. "We're honored to have you visit. What can I show you today?"

"Just the back way out, I'm afraid," Maji whispered. "The paparazzi are at it again."

"Of course," the clerk said as if famous people being chased by the media was a daily occurrence there. "Right this way." She showed Maji the stairs down to the harbor.

Maji scanned the boats docked below, spotted Dave's yellow speedboat, and smiled. "Thank you so much. Selfie?"

"Why, yes. Please." They snapped two shots together just before a disruption at the entrance upstairs signaled the media's arrival.

Maji bolted, taking the stairs at a good clip but not so fast they couldn't keep sight of her. At the promenade at the bottom she stopped and looked up, saw the camera van parked on the road above, and waved. As she reached the dock with Dave's boat, she heard a voice calling out for her to wait. She turned and saw a lone photographer jogging doggedly to catch up with her. She shrugged and untied the bowline, hopping on board with a hand from Dave for good show.

"This could get interesting," Dave said, nodding back down the dock.

Maji couldn't make out what the photographer was saying, but his wad of cash and gesticulating toward her were clear enough. One little runabout's owner took the cash and ushered the reporter on board.

"We'll outrun him in a hot minute," Dave said. The engine engaged with a throaty rumble. "Want to go below?"

"No," Maji replied. "I want to drive."

Dave backed them out and handed the wheel over to her. Maji took the speedboat past the other pleasure boats at a reasonable speed, trailed closely by the runabout. A few boaters looked up and waved, did a double take, reached for their phones. As the harbor opened up, she gauged the channel's breadth and the locations of other vessels.

Nothing small enough to be endangered by a little hotdogging. "Hang on."

She opened the throttle and took off toward the ocean, then eased off just short of the harbor's outlet and swung the agile motorboat into a wide arc, making a circle around the runabout. She smiled and waved at the photographer as he tried to capture her in motion.

Dave laughed and took the wheel back, piloting them safely out to the coast. Once in open water, he set a moderate speed and gave her half his attention. "Romero says your uplink worked. His team is sifting through Lyttleton's records as we speak."

"Then the trip was worth something. I don't think I can stomach letting him work on me."

"What? He's good enough for Arturo Echeverra but not for you? Wait, he didn't brag about her daddy's face to Erlea, did he?"

"No. He's not stupid. Just a racist asshat who takes dirty money and gets off on celebrities."

"Point taken. What's the big deal, anyway? I thought they cleaned you up at Landstuhl."

Maji pulled up the cap sleeve on the sundress, exposing her left shoulder and the keloid scar. "They did what they could."

"Eh. That's a distinguishing mark all right. But it's not Mashriki's mark. What's Colonel Wyatt say?"

"I haven't asked him. I need to take care of it myself. My body, my life."

Dave nodded. "I get that. But fixing your skin won't get Fallujah out of your brain."

"Might make it easier to look at myself in the mirror."

Dave turned his eyes to the ocean ahead of them. "I had a hard time with that after my first kill, too. It was your first, right?"

"First, second, third, fourth. Shit, I don't even know how many." Maji held on to the top of the windscreen, looking ahead with the wind whipping her hair behind her. *I should at least know their names.*

"Look. You hit one kid by accident—or 'cause he's got an IED and you have no choice," Dave began. "You miss your shot at a van and watch a whole mosque go up. You run to a burning car and drag a woman out, only to watch her die while you hold her, waiting for the medics to arrive." He spared her a glance. "It all sucks, Rios. Whether you pulled the trigger or not."

"It's not the same, Dave. I mean, yes, there've been times I had to stay in cover, had to let somebody get hurt. I've had the nightmares, I've seen the shrinks." Never Ava before. "They got me back on my feet and back in the field. But this...I did this. I lost control. That's on me."

"You made it three years with no body count, Rios. You know how unheard of that is? Why do you think they call you Magic?"

"Well, now they can stop. I don't deserve the fucking pedestal you want to put me on."

"I never said you were perfect. Maybe you thought you could be, but seriously, no amount of training will ever get you there."

Maji used every swear word she knew in Spanish, then threw in a few Arabic phrases as well. It didn't help enough. "Then how do I know I won't do it again?"

"Just like this," Dave said. He gave her a quick sideways hug and let her go. "Work your way back to where you trust yourself again."

Maji stared out at the glistening ocean, wanting to dismiss his words as too pat, too simplistic. But after a few weeks on assignment, she felt worlds better about her abilities than she had after passing all her field recertification tests. "You haven't issued me a sidearm."

"Did you want one?"

"No. Not yet."

"Good. It'd be a lot to sell to the press if Erlea whipped out a pistol and suddenly became an expert shot."

"Dave. You've really got no qualms about working with me right now?"

"Not a one." He gave her a small smile. "But take it from somebody who's been there. It's better to keep talking with someone you trust than to try and gut it out alone. That will bite you in the ass."

"Hooah."

Chapter Sixteen

"Nice dress," Romero said as Maji walked into her room to change. She stopped, catching the door before it closed behind her and scanning the room. The connector to Dave's was open. That at least was reassuring. "Thanks. Am I late for a meeting?"

"I have news for both of you. But I wanted to ask you a question first."

"Ask away."

"Echeverra says the evidence against Aguilar and Perez is hidden here on the island. But he will only tell his daughter where it is."

"Well, she wants to meet him." Maji anticipated his question. "Yes, I trust her."

Romero nodded and went to Dave's room, closing her connector door most of the way behind him.

Maji changed into jeans and joined them. "What do Lyttleton's files tell us?"

"First, that he keeps meticulous records," Romero said. "Second, that Echeverra came to him with cash and an assumed identity."

"Provided by the Nuvoletta," Dave reminded her. "But Lyttleton doesn't appear to have given any proof of the work he did to anyone after Echeverra healed up and left his place."

"So the Nuvoletta don't know what he looks like," Maji said. "That's great. Safer for him to provide intel on the guys he worked for, right?"

Dave nodded. "Sure. They know his name, but we could get him a new one and a backstory to go with it. Except…" He looked to Romero.

"Echeverra must attend the peace talks as himself. Otherwise, no credibility."

"Oh, hell." Maji considered that. "Another new face wouldn't help, would it?"

"Nope," Dave confirmed. "He's going to have to choose between playing peacemaker and having Aguilar and Perez target him or helping us with the Nuvoletta and having to go into hiding again."

"We still hope to bring Aguilar and Perez in before the talks," Romero said. "In which case, he may not be a willing witness for you. I'm sorry."

"Any more good news?"

"Yes and no," Romero said. "Echeverra confirmed our suspicions about Ramon Perez being the second man involved in the bombing. Police archives show that he infiltrated the Batasuna and befriended Echeverra. And that he reported to Miguel Aguilar. Both remained in the National Police and rose through the ranks."

"There's a thank-you," Maji said.

Romero lifted a brow. "The dirty war was condoned by the government. Reopening this case will not be popular, but it is necessary. Today Perez is a chief inspector and Aguilar is a commissioner."

"And let me guess—one of them assigned the bad medic to us."

Dave nodded. "And the AV guy who screwed up our comms and video feeds, too."

"Diaz. But he thinks I bought his excuses," Romero added.

Maji blinked at him. "He's still here?"

"Where we can keep an eye on him. And monitor his communications," Romero said. "Speaking of which, we have also ruled Lyttleton out as a suspect in the party incident."

The guy had been obsessed with Erlea, trying to get close to her at every opportunity. And he worked with organized crime. But still. "He was a suspect?"

"Yes. We picked up some calls from Perez to a man with excellent Spanish but a British accent and a very entitled manner. At first we suspected Lyttleton was the accomplice."

"But now you've ruled him out, you're looking in house, right?" The description fit Nigel too well to ignore. "As much of a pretentious ass as Nigel is, I can't see him helping anyone sabotage his show. Even for a bundle of insurance."

"He's only worried about the show if the star is injured," Dave said. "If she's dead, he gets cancellation insurance plus that proven posthumous sales boost for all her prior work."

Maji ground her teeth. If she opened her mouth, only swearing would come out.

Romero nodded. "We tapped his phone after the paintball incident. Nothing of note for weeks, except some considerable financial stress. We're digging into that now. And we assume he is using a burner phone, with care about where he can be heard."

"Smart fucking weasel," Maji said. "But why would the National Police want Erlea dead?"

"Aguilar wanted her in danger, maybe in the hospital with barbiturate poisoning," Romero explained. "Enough to bring Echeverra rushing to her bedside. Initially he tried to extort Nigel to gain his cooperation—use Erlea as bait for her father or they would disable her. Which of course would interfere with the show."

"Mr. Bottom Line," Dave said. "Vulnerable to economic blackmail."

Maji shook her head. "Imane calls him Mr. Bait and Switch."

"She wins," Romero said. "After the party he was furious. Turned the tables on Aguilar, made his own demands. Said if they were going to hurt Erlea, they should do it right."

"So Nigel's been telling Aguilar where Erlea is and what she's up to," Dave said. "Trying to get them to do what he can't. We think Aguilar reached out as soon as the peace talks were announced. Nigel might not have been thinking murder that early. But he's an opportunist."

"That explains Nigel's foot dragging on locking in tour dates and venues. And why he wants a ton of video of her getting ready for this show," Maji noted. "Very merchandisable after a star's death. Like that other guy he represented."

"Santiago, yes." Romero sniffed. "Still making him money after all these years. And now you see why I am unsure how much to tell Erlea."

"Does Arturo Echeverra know?" Maji asked. "About the collusion."

"No," Romero said.

Maji gave that some thought. "Erlea's a great singer, but that doesn't mean she can act. If she knew Nigel was literally stabbing her in the back, she couldn't hide that."

"So we increase her protection, but don't tell her," Dave said. "Agreed."

Maji hated taking all of Erlea's choices away. "Meeting her father, keeping his secrets, that's different. I think we should give her a chance. Besides, who knows what he'll tell her that he won't tell you two."

"With their meeting bugged, of course," Romero said.

Erlea opened the door of her suite to find Celeste, looking agitated. "Maji hasn't come back yet?" she asked. She hoped nothing had gone wrong with the visit to Lyttleton.

"No." Celeste poked her phone, glaring at it. "Where is she? She's not answering her phone or her door."

"Why don't you come in?" Erlea suggested. "I can usually hear when she's next door."

"I don't want to impose."

"Nonsense. We're friends, right? I could use the company," Erlea assured her. "Let me get you something. Water? Wine?"

"You have wine?"

"For Imane." Erlea hoped Celeste trusted her to have a glass now and then, too. But this was the wrong time to ask. "And for you."

"Thank you. I could use some." Celeste swept in and headed straight for the fridge.

Erlea pulled a wineglass off the shelf and grabbed the almonds while she was at it. "There's cheese in there, too, and olives. It's not much…"

Celeste took the glass and sighed. "Thank you. Actually, I am starving. I forgot lunch."

"A well-respected doctor told me not to skip meals," Erlea ventured, offering her all the packages on hand.

Celeste swallowed half a glass of cava and started on the cheese before answering. "That's sound advice." She swallowed and breathed slowly, eyes closed. When she opened them, the seas were calm again. "How is the flying?"

"Better without a bungee." At Celeste's quizzical look, Erlea explained, "Maji and I talk about the rolls in Aikido as flying."

"Maybe I should come watch one morning."

Was that humor in those beautiful blue-green eyes? Erlea hoped so. But the idea of Celeste watching her was equal parts thrilling and terrifying. "Sure. If you want to."

Celeste turned her head toward a noise from Maji's room. She banged on the connector door. "Hello?"

"Well, open up," Maji's voice replied. "My side is open now."

Celeste turned the lock and opened the door, then threw herself into Maji's arms.

"Order dinner?" Maji said to Erlea, looking not surprised at all as she held Celeste.

Erlea tried to ignore the sting of jealousy. *Suck it up, princess. She wants Maji, not you.* She wished it was her place, her business to help Celeste with whatever she needed. But it wasn't. "Sure."

Erlea called an order in quickly, keeping one ear open. She shouldn't eavesdrop, but Celeste seemed so upset. She tiptoed over to the open doorway and stood out of sight.

"Adrienne is playing in Germany right now," Maji said. "Even if she wanted to, she couldn't get here."

"You checked? That makes me more scared, not less," Celeste responded. "Adrienne is so unpredictable. She might punch a ref just to get suspended. And blame it on me, somehow. Merde, merde, merde."

"Don't panic," Maji said. "We have time to set up security measures. Can I listen to the messages? It would help me assess the situation."

"The situation is, she still won't take no for an answer." Celeste sounded more angry than scared. That was good, right? "How dare she call my work number and act penitent, like we had some misunderstanding? If she comes here, I will have her arrested."

Yes, Erlea thought. *Do it.*

"But what if she finds me in Barcelona? I have to go to work. I don't want to hide. But the things she said on the second message, after she'd been drinking. She called me a bitch, but she called Erlea worse. I can't believe I've dragged her into my drama. God, it's embarrassing."

"All you've done is what you needed to stay safe. I'm proud of you. You will get your life back. Though I'll need you to call and speak with my boss yourself. Sorry about that."

"Don't be sorry. You've been such a friend all along, never judging me. Erlea, too."

Erlea tiptoed back to the kitchen. Eavesdropping was no way to pay Celeste back for her trust. When dinner arrived and they were still in Maji's room, she put it in the oven to stay warm and took her guitar to the balcony.

Only when they clapped did Erlea realize she had an audience. "Please tell me Maji hasn't eaten all my supper while I've been giving a private concert."

"Dinner is on the table," Celeste said. "You have sung for your supper. Come, I have news to share."

Erlea helped herself to a bit of everything, anxious but not willing to press. She looked up when Celeste cleared her throat and found her holding the bottle of cava by a wineglass, a silent question on her face. "Just one glass, thanks," Erlea said. "I don't want to miss anything important tonight."

Celeste poured and raised her glass to toast. "To friends. And new beginnings." She sipped. "I talked to my new partners in Barcelona. They still want me. I start in a few days."

A few days? "That's wonderful." Erlea did her best to smile.

"Yes. And I would like to say yes to your generous offer," Celeste said. "Maji has a few questions about security."

"Sure. Anything. It's good, but we can add alarms, or monitors, or whatever you want," Erlea said, feeling herself ramble. "There's even room for a bodyguard. I mean, if you take my room. When I'm not there. I mean…I'm shutting up now. Just happy. Yes."

Celeste laughed and raised her glass. "To just happy. But no bodyguards. Maji's firm will hook me up with less intrusive protection. And I have a plan to deal with Adrienne. If you'll let me have the video."

"Of course. But are you sure you want to watch it? It made me want to hurt her. I mean, I'm against violence, obviously, but for you I'd make an exception. And she can't come after you if I break her kneecaps." Erlea tried to keep some lightness in her voice, to let Celeste take it as a joke. It scared her how much she wanted to hurt Adrienne, to make her suffer.

"Thank you for the sentiment," Celeste said, a frown warring with her half smile. "But I have to get my own self out of this mess."

"Why should you have to do anything?" Erlea said. "That's not fair. Did you do anything wrong? I've met you. I don't think so."

"I appreciate your faith in me. But I did make mistakes. I saw beneath her facade but still trusted that she could change—until it was too late to leave. And even then I protected her, as if her well-being was more important than mine. But no more."

Maji's face gave no hints, so Erlea asked, "Are you going to give the video to the press?" That seemed fair.

Celeste shook her head. "I thought about it. But the media would have a field day. And you know how they treat women who accuse famous men of abuse. Plus my own community would hate me for making a lesbian look bad."

"It's an ugly truth," Maji said. "And it would only shine a spotlight on Celeste, not make her safer."

"Like my interview," Erlea said in a moment of recognition. She looked to Celeste. "I'm so sorry about that. I should have been more careful, thought about it from your perspective." First Laura, now Celeste. At least when she got drunk with strangers, she only hurt herself.

Celeste reached across and took her hand. "Stop beating yourself up. You are one of the most caring people I know. No one needs to be protected from you." She pulled back and crossed her arms. "But someone must act to protect the next woman from Adrienne."

"Now I am proud of you, but also kind of scared," Erlea confessed. "What are you going to do?"

"I am sending the video to Adrienne's team manager. And demanding they send her to therapy. I know she had a rough childhood and all of that, but it's not my fault. And she won't change without help. When she understands what she has done, then I'll accept an apology."

"What if she refuses help?"

Celeste shrugged. "Soccer is everything to her. She would never go see someone for me, but this way she will go for herself."

"Same with anything," Maji said. "Smoking, drinking, whatever. You can't change for someone else. You've got to want it for yourself."

If Celeste never wanted more than friendship, Erlea wondered, would she go back to smoking? Maybe. To getting wasted at clubs? No.

She never wanted to miss her own chance at happiness again, to not be present for her own life. "I get it. Good plan."

Celeste let herself into the little boat and waved good night to Maji. As she watched her friend ride off on the borrowed scooter, she reflected on how lucky all three of them were to have each other as friends. Now that she had the details, Erlea's apartment in Barcelona sounded perfect, so close to work and the market as well as private and secure. Weeks ago she would never have dreamed of getting to see where the famous rock star Erlea lived. Today she looked forward to learning more about sweet and sexy Beatriz by sharing her safe haven in the city. Well, not sharing exactly. She'd have her own place by the time her friend came home. Being under the same roof, without the buffer of friends like Maji and Imane, would be too tempting. And no matter what she said about being friends, Celeste still couldn't stop that feeling she got when their eyes met, or she watched those talented fingers on the strings, or…

Stop already. Celeste went below to call Hannah and begin making arrangements. But first, she would fulfill the favor Maji asked of her. Celeste didn't understand why Maji couldn't talk to Ava herself, but there must be a reason and it was not her business anyway.

The phone only rang once. Celeste asked the woman who answered if she was Bubbles.

"Who wants to know?"

"My name is Celeste. I am a friend of Maji." The silence stretched. "Hello?"

"Is she hurt? Just tell me what happened."

"No, no—she is well. But she cannot speak with Ava herself, and she asked me to send a message through you. Can you help?"

Bubbles chuckled. "Brat. She would find a way. But hold on, I can do one better."

"Hello?" Apparently Bubbles had put her on hold. Celeste waited.

"This is Ava. Dr. Guillot?" The melodic voice sounded tired. Celeste remembered that Ava was not only the godmother-therapist but also the friend with cancer.

"So sorry to disturb you. Maji wanted you to know that she is doing well, sleeping better. Oh, and that work is going well—no, great. And she may not use the plastic surgeon after all."

"Thank you for being there for her. And for letting her help you. She needs that, as you probably guessed."

How well this woman understood Maji. "Yes. Being a helper is key to her sense of self. She has been brave and kind for everyone here. Including me."

"Ah, yes. Are you safe?" Ava paused. "Not to intrude, but Hannah has been expecting your call."

Celeste blinked. "Right after I let you go. Which I should do."

"Don't run off yet. We might not get another chance like this." Ava coughed. "Tell me about the sleep. You didn't prescribe drugs, did you?"

"No," Celeste said, opting not to mention the one bad night on the boat. "Some relaxation techniques and your mint soap."

"My what?"

"The liquid soap. She says it smells like you. So she washed her pillowcase with it."

Celeste heard sniffling.

"Hey," Bubbles said, back on the line. "Why is Ava crying? Oh, hell, she wants you back. Keep it short."

"Hello?" Celeste said. Things were clearly not okay there. "Are you all right?"

"All good," Ava replied, sounding like she had pulled herself together. "Now listen. Don't let Maji off the hook about that scar. It represents much more than the physical to her."

"I understand," Celeste said.

"No matter how this assignment goes, she will need you." Ava stopped and sipped something. "Understand? I need to know that someone is there for her."

"Are you not going to recover?" Celeste ventured. "Should I try and help her prepare?"

"No. I mean, yes, I am fighting of course. I'm not ready yet to leave my brave and kind helpers—any of them." Ava sniffed. "But don't you dare worry her. Distractions at a time like this can be fatal. Tell her I sounded well. Strong. Understand?"

"If you think that is best." Celeste hated to lie to Maji. But she understood. "Yes, I will keep her focused. I am here for her."

"Good. And Dr. Guillot? You will be a better coach to your clients for having weathered your own storm."

"Thank you. I believe you are right. Please rest now."

Ava chuckled. "Another helper, eh? One last thing, then. She knows I love her. But make sure she also knows that I am proud of her. Au revoir."

❖

Nigel's nostrils flared. "How can you know it's him if you don't even know where he is? What if it's an impersonator trying to lure Erlea away from the safety of the hotel?"

"We're ninety-nine percent certain that it's really Echeverra," Dave said. "We'll have the meet set up in the next few days. We need the lead time to secure the site he's proposing." Dave paused, looking to Romero.

Romero raised a brow as if he wished Dave had stopped sooner. "He wants us to bring her to the Real Cartuja in Valldemossa."

"Out of the question," Nigel said.

Erlea couldn't take it anymore. "That's not your decision."

"Send the double, then," Nigel insisted. "You don't need to stick your neck out for these people."

"My father is not going to hurt me. And I care about peace for my country. And keeping my word."

Nigel sighed dramatically. "You've become so politicized. First the Basque business, then women's lib, what's next? Oh, right. Waving the rainbow banner. If you start writing heroic ballads, you'll lose your following."

"People who don't like who I am don't need to buy my music," Erlea replied with more equanimity than she felt.

Nigel acted as if she hadn't even spoken. He addressed the men in the room. "I want a bodyguard with her. And Alejandro. This is a historic moment—at least we can get some footage."

"No, this is a private moment," Erlea protested.

Nigel deigned to recognize her. "For a public figure of your stature, there are no private moments."

CHAPTER SEVENTEEN

Celeste slipped into the back of the theater, finally coming to observe an Aikido practice as promised. Down on the stage, two red-haired figures in white gis moved in an odd dance of tosses and rolls. No music, no voices, just the occasional whump on the marley or the shushing of a cotton uniform.

Halfway down the aisle stairs, she spotted Alejandro with his video camera. She crept closer and sat a few seats from him.

"Good morning," she whispered. "I meant to see this show sooner, but I kept oversleeping." Anxiety and anticipation about the move to Barcelona kept her awake, tossing fretfully at bedtime. Turning her thoughts to Erlea helped but left her feeling hypocritical about insisting they were just friends.

Alejandro set the camera down and blinked, looking over at Celeste with a smile. "Me, too. I wish I had filmed them sooner. See how it looks like Erlea is battling with herself? It's great, such a lively metaphor."

"Are you sure Erlea is okay with you filming this?"

He shrugged, looking guilty. "Nigel said to. I'm to shadow her every minute today."

"Why?"

"Don't know. He won't say, but we're going somewhere and I'm not to tell anyone. Oh."

She smiled at his chagrin, his youthful enthusiasm, his good intentions. "Don't worry. I'm still in the dark. I was expecting to consult on the bungee number today." No one had mentioned a day off from rehearsals to her.

"Yeah, I don't know. I guess they'll call when she's back?"

"Tell you what. You make sure she calls me later, and this conversation never happened. Deal?"

An hour later, Celeste was packing up her few personal items when the office phone rang. "Dr. Guillot speaking."

"Hey, I thought you were coming to rehearsal today," Erlea said. "I really need you. Unless you're too busy."

"On my way," Celeste said with a smile. Alejandro must have been mistaken.

Celeste found the stage crowded with people trying to be helpful. Erlea and Maji wore bungee harnesses, while Imane and Tania and Dimitri took turns giving advice and instruction. The backup dancers loitered nearby while Alejandro stood in the wings filming.

"Stop," Erlea demanded, putting her hands to her ears. "Let me breathe."

"Yes," Celeste concurred as she approached. "Give us a minute, please."

Imane looked to Celeste, back at a pale and sweaty Erlea, and then at the crowd. "Everybody take fifteen."

As they cleared the area, Maji struggled to unbuckle herself.

"You can stay," Erlea told Maji, then looked to Celeste for confirmation. "Right?"

"If you like," Celeste replied. "It seems you have hit a wall. And here I thought it was designed to fall away."

Erlea looked puzzled, then smiled. "Oh, you're being funny. Got it."

"Sorry. I'm rusty at humor," Celeste said. "I got tired of being put down for that along with everything else."

"Well, some people just aren't smart enough to appreciate your quirky side. I think you're great." Erlea blushed but didn't take it back. "And just in time. I've got the hang of going up, but every time the damn cord tugs me back, I flail around."

"Can you demonstrate?"

Erlea looked to Maji. "Would you?"

"I'll try." Maji looked at the wall as if gauging it, then walked away before running at it. She lifted off and stretched forward, then pedaled in the air as the cord and gravity brought her back. "Sorry," she said.

"It's okay," Erlea said. "You're not a flailer. I don't know why I am."

"Will you get hurt if you try again?" Celeste asked.

"Only my pride." Erlea closed her eyes and spoke softly. "Fall down seven times, get up eight." She opened them and said, "Here goes. Don't laugh."

Celeste didn't find Erlea's attempt comical, but the comparison was helpful. "You seem to be anticipating the return, trying to see the ground."

"Yeah, you twisted to look," Maji added.

"I did?" Erlea considered. "Maybe that's where the flail comes in."

"When you fall backward in Aikido, you don't look," Celeste said.

Erlea eyes grew wide. "Alejandro and his damn camera. Did he show you the video from this morning?"

"No," Celeste confessed. "I stopped in briefly. I didn't want to disturb you, but it was wonderful to observe. You are both very graceful."

"Oh. Thanks. Twelve years of practice will do that for you." Erlea looked thoughtful. "I don't need to look back in the dojo. I just know where the ground is."

They played with this premise for a while, Maji demonstrating and Erlea observing.

"Now you know you can, because you have seen yourself do it," Celeste said when Erlea's expression finally showed not just comprehension but enthusiasm. "Like Harry Potter casting the Patronus across the lake."

Erlea gaped at her. "Time travel—he met himself."

"And saved his own life," Celeste said, grinning.

I love how she gets me. Erlea turned to Maji. "Can we have a couple minutes in private?"

"Course," Maji said. Removing her gear, she added, "The caterers are due in ten. Just don't hold up lunch."

Erlea exchanged a look with Celeste, and they both laughed.

"I wouldn't dare keep you from a meal," Celeste joked.

Maji didn't laugh. "Don't be late." She left without elaborating.

Seeing Celeste's puzzlement, Erlea explained, "We're going out this afternoon. I'm meeting with my father."

"He's alive?" Celeste blinked. "That's wonderful. Right?"

"I guess. I mean, of course." Erlea fiddled with the bungee harness. "But it's been forever. And he never reached out, not once. What the hell do I say to him?"

Celeste put her arm on Erlea's shoulder. "May I?"

Erlea welcomed the hug. She tucked her head by Celeste's chin, drinking in her scent. "I don't want to be mad at him," she confessed. "But what if he doesn't have a good reason? What if he doesn't love us anymore? Mom got remarried. Maybe he gave up, too."

"Ah," Celeste said, "what if he stays out of reach, even now you've found him? I see."

Erlea pulled back and pointed up at the empty window in the prop wall. "Everybody thinks the song is about a lost love. Even Imane does—she assumes I wrote it for Laura. But it's not that. It's for whatever we can't get back." She shook her head. "I grew up without him. Without even knowing if he was alive. Or innocent, and dead."

"He lost all those years with you, too," Celeste said. "Did he love you when you were little?"

Erlea didn't have to think. "Yes. I felt very loved."

"Then he never stopped." Celeste made an arc with her arm, reaching toward the wall. "You reach for what is past, but you cannot grasp it, cannot change it." She smiled at Erlea. "Still you land back on your feet."

"God, you're smart," Erlea said, wrapping Celeste in a hug before she could stop to think. Celeste squeezed her back. "Sorry," Erlea said. "I didn't ask." She let Celeste go.

"No harm done," Celeste said, taking her hand. "Just promise to tell me all about it tonight."

"It's a date," Erlea declared. "I mean, yes, all the stories. For all three of you. And tomorrow I leap for that wall with no fear in my heart."

❖

Two black vans waited in the parking garage under the hotel. Romero stood by one, Dave and Echeverra by the other.

"Where are you going?" Erlea asked.

Maji looked her in the eye. "The Real Cartuja. You and your

father are going with Dave to a secure location until I get back safe and sound."

"He's in there?" Erlea pointed at the Dave's van. "It's really happening now."

Maji gave her a hug. "You'll be fine."

Erlea eyed Maji. "I will. But why is the Real Cartuja not safe? Are you putting yourself in danger?"

"I'll be fine. I've got training," Maji replied. "And other protection." Like Kevlar.

Erlea climbed into Dave's van. Maji watched it pull away before peering inside her ride to Valldemossa. "Hey, Alejandro. Sorry for the change in plans. We have a fake dad up there, too. Think you can get some touching footage without zooming in too much?"

He looked surprised. "Nigel may be pissed. But sure I can."

There should have been one more guy in the car. "Where's your backup?" Maji asked Romero.

"Running late. Upset stomach." He looked past her to the elevators. "Don't turn around. It's Diaz, the loaner from National Police."

"Does he know about the switch?"

"We thought it better not to tell him," Romero replied. "Let me handle him."

Maji leaned back into the van as if talking to Alejandro again. She put one finger to her lips and he nodded silently.

"Where is Garcia?" Romero asked as Diaz's footsteps approached.

"Puking up his guts," Diaz answered. "I volunteered to stand in."

"No need," Romero said. "I called a local asset while we waited. We'll pick her up on the way. Don't give me that look. She's a regional police officer with military experience. And cute. Everyone will think she's a groupie."

"Well, I'm here and ready to go."

"We've got it covered," Romero reiterated, giving Maji a little push. "And now we have time to make up."

Maji buckled up as Romero pulled away. She looked back through tinted windows at Diaz, standing in the lot with a phone to his ear. Wasn't hard to guess who he was calling.

❖

Erlea climbed into the back of the van, expecting to recognize her father. Was this man across the wide bench seat him? Only the eyes said yes, so familiar and also wet with tears.

"I never dreamed I would get to see you again," he said.

"Daddy." Erlea could barely catch her breath. The door's slam jolted her, and she laughed. But still, no words. She reached her hands out, and he took them in a strong grasp she remembered well. His hands seemed smaller now but just as warm.

"You are so grown up. Maybe you would rather call me Arturo? And we begin again, two adults with a shared history."

Erlea shook her head, "No. I want to have my daddy back." She couldn't stop the sobs, and she didn't care. She leaned into him and let him fold her into a comforting embrace.

When she finally sat up and looked around, the road was unfamiliar. "This is not the way to Valldemossa."

"No," her father confirmed. "I did spend some years there, and my things are there, but we will not retrieve them ourselves. Mr. Brown felt that would put you in too much danger."

Erlea thought of Maji. Fooling the media was one thing, but this… "Brown, are you sure Maji will be okay? And where are we going while she risks her neck?"

Brown turned in the front passenger seat to look her in the eye. "Rios is trained and has a full detail watching her back." He paused. "We're going up a very long and twisty road. You don't get carsick, do you?"

"Yes," her father said at the same time Erlea said, "No." They looked at each other and laughed. "I grew out of that," she added.

Romero pulled off the highway at the sign for Inca, a town barely a third of the way to Valldemossa. "Anyone need a pit stop?" he asked as they pulled up in front of the Guardia Civil's station house.

"Yes," Alejandro said, sounding grateful. He hopped out.

The front passenger door opened and a woman got in. Cute, and dressed like a groupie. "Military experience, huh?" Maji asked.

Romero shrugged. "Best to stay close to the truth. Ms. Rios, this is my old friend Amelia."

Maji leaned toward the front seat and shook their backup's hand. "*Con gusto.*"

"Likewise," Amelia replied. "Wow, you're convincing. Except your voice."

"And here's the last of our crew," Romero said as a Guardia Civil motorcycle cop pulled up alongside the van. "Thanks for outfitting him, Meli." He added, "That guy's one of my team, with borrowed gear. Speaking of which, reach into the back. There's a jacket for you."

Maji twisted herself over the back seat into the storage area and fished out a heavy leather jacket. Extra heavy. "Kevlar?"

"Please tell me it fits properly. I only have the one."

Maji shrugged it on and zipped it up, folding the flap over the zipper. No point wearing bulletproof clothes if you left a long section of your front unprotected. She patted the front down, checking the placement of the panels. "Feels right. Everybody else covered, too?"

"So far. We'll get vests on Alejandro and the docent at the Real Cartuja when we arrive."

Alejandro climbed back in, looking refreshed. "Thanks so much." As Romero pulled back onto the highway, the motorcycle cop just behind them, he asked, "So what's at the Cartuja Real? I mean, I know it's an old monastery and Chopin stayed there once, and Rubén Darío wrote a famous poem there, too, but why meet Erlea's father *there*?"

"To hear Chopin played in the Palace of King Sancho and see the monastery, of course," Romero answered, giving nothing away. "And apparently Echeverra was a docent for several years, knows all the nooks and crannies. We just have to take a VIP tour of the place and he will find us." There, Maji realized, was his grain of truth.

"Clever," Alejandro said. "Hope he won't mind when he figures out we brought the double. No offense," he added to Maji.

"None taken."

When Romero pulled off the main road to Valldemossa and began winding his way down little cobbled streets filled with pedestrians, Maji realized just how popular this site must be with tourists. She hoped they wouldn't be treasure-hunting for Echeverra's hidden evidence while also dealing with paparazzi and fans. Romero ignored a no-entry sign and tooted his horn at the tourists ambling along the tiny lane. He parked by a nondescript door in a stone wall, where a gray-haired man in a tweed jacket waited for them.

They all piled out and Romero went to greet the docent. Romero's teammate in the Guardia uniform parked the motorcycle behind the van and wrote a ticket out. As he placed it under the windshield wiper, Romero assured the docent, "Don't worry. He's with us. Now no one will tow the van."

Inside, Alejandro and the docent were shown how to properly adjust the vests before putting their shirts and jackets back on. Alejandro seemed to find the experience an adventure, but the older man did not. Maji noticed how similar his build was to Echeverra's and wondered how much Romero had told him about the purpose behind their tour.

"Ms. Echeverra, it is such a pleasure to have you here," he said after recovering his clothing and dignity. "I am Pedro Salazar y Muntaña, and I have given tours to heads of state, but never to a rock star."

Maji smiled and shook his hand, whispering, "Thank you, Don Pedro."

He beamed at her use of the honorific. "Ah, the laryngitis. Just the body's way of saying it is time to take a day off. I will not bother you to speak again, young lady."

They began in King Sancho's palace, a stately home of the island's signature sandy colored stone. Don Pedro insisted they take front row seats for the piano recital only a few minutes away. Maji silently admired the painted walls and ceiling, already feeling a bit too warm in the heavy jacket. After the pianist played Chopin for an appreciative crowd, they let the tourists exit before strolling through the walls hung with portraits, the little chapel, and the ornate dining and sitting rooms. In each section, Romero shooed the tourists ahead of them on to the next section while his uniformed teammate blocked anyone from coming in after them.

Don Pedro narrated the story of King Sancho, the decor, the art, and the role of the palace in the politics of the time. Maji did her best to look interested and nod at the appropriate pauses. Finally they reached Rubén Darío's writing room, with its glass-fronted bookcases, sedate artwork, and somewhat creepy manikin of Darío at work on his poem, "La Cartuja."

Maji faked a coughing fit and Don Pedro hurried off to get her a bottle of water from the staff area. While he was gone, Maji stepped over the red velveteen cords keeping the public away from Darío's desk and slipped the little metal key Echeverra had given her into the top drawer. Inside she found a computer disk, as promised. She tucked it inside her jacket and stepped back over the cord, resuming her coughing.

A moment later Don Pedro returned and Maji whispered her thanks. Hoarse from coughing and hot from sweating under the jacket, the water tasted delicious. She saved half the bottle for later, knowing she would be thirsty again soon.

To reach the monastery, there was no choice but to leave the palace and cross a large plaza to the entrance of the church. A few heads turned and voices murmured as tourists recognized Erlea in their midst. But before anyone could approach her, they passed through the tall heavy doors into the cavernous place of worship. Amelia kept up a show of helping Alejandro navigate safely while filming. But Maji could tell she saved some of her attention for their surroundings and potential threats. She made an effective, low-key bodyguard.

They exited the church into a long stone-floored hallway with whitewashed walls. The tourists taking photos of two twice-lifesize figures didn't seem to notice the quiet entourage led by a policeman. At the apothecary, he entered first and cleared the small room, taking the far doorway while Romero stood sentry at the entrance. Maji admired the row after row of ceramic and glass containers used to store medicines that the Carthusian monks used to treat the villagers centuries before. While Don Pedro provided his monologue, Maji gestured to Amelia and Alejandro to direct his attention to the giant pestle and the basin of holy water on the far wall. While the docent turned to tell them about the items' history and uses, Maji stretched up on her tiptoes for a specific blue-and-white china vessel. She took it down and reached a hand inside, hoping she had followed Echeverra's precise instructions correctly.

Maji sighed in relief as her fingers touched the thumb drive, then nearly dropped the ancient urn when Don Pedro called out to her.

"Stop. That's priceless. Hand it over, please. Carefully."

Maji couldn't close the thumb drive into her palm and still get her hand out, so she tilted the urn and let it slide into her hand. Then she turned and handed the urn over with a whispered apology.

Don Pedro seemed quite put out by her behavior and began to hurry them along, abbreviating his narration. It was a relief, really. Maji hoped they would reach the monks' library and obtain the final hidden item soon. Her T-shirt was sticking to her torso, her skin prickling from the heat. The damn jacket really needed some ventilation. She was tempted to unzip it and let some air in. Instead she drank the remainder of the water.

Fortunately Romero encouraged their guide to bypass the Chopin rooms and breeze through the artifact room and gallery. The paintings of landscapes and pastoral scenes were lovely, but Maji had no desire to stand for a long lecture about the mountain range and the art it inspired.

❖

Porto Cristo looked so small from their perch at the top of the hill holding the ruins of Castell de Santueri. Down there at the coast, only a few miles away across forests and farmland, happy families laughed by the protected harbor's clear blue waters. Up here, only crumbling walls of the old castle and its empty cistern offered protection from the wind and sun. "How desperate would you have to be to seek refuge up here?" Erlea wondered aloud.

"Well, a sanctuary isn't meant for living in long-term," her father replied. "Still, there is beauty even here." He pointed to the little yellow flowers poking from the dusty brown earth and the rocks.

They walked the rugged trail around the top of the hill together, arm in arm. Erlea held on as if he might disappear if she let go. They talked mostly of the missing years, trying to catch each other up on too much, in too little time.

Stopping to rest and drink in the shade of a cave-like room dug into one hillside, Erlea's father took her face in his hands. "I am so proud of you. Such talent, and so much hard work. I am glad for your success." He squinted, as if trying to see inside her. "Are you happy?"

Erlea pulled back, overcome by conflicting emotions and the intimacy after so much distance. She uncapped her drink, keeping her hands busy and her eyes averted.

"I'm sorry," he said. "I've lost the right to say such things, to ask such things."

"No," Erlea said, looking at him again, this man who could be her father. *Was. Is.* "It's okay. Just a lot to take in. And life's more complicated than just yes or no." She gave him a smile meant to reassure. "But now we'll have time, right? After you clear your name and get done with the peace talks." When he looked down, the fear welled up again. "Daddy?"

He met her gaze, looking as serious as when he tried to explain the dirty war to her as a child. "I have choices to make. When you were a child, I had to make them alone. And I did what I did to protect you, your mother, my parents. I lost all of you, and all of you lost me. Every day I wanted to undo my choice, but you could not be safe that way. I am so sorry for your pain."

Erlea nodded. "Apology accepted."

"Don't forgive me just yet. I did bad things to stay alive and hidden. I had no resources when I ran, but that is no excuse. Soon I will be free from the false charges of murder, but I will still not be free. Not if I want to return to my real calling and help make peace a reality."

"Daddy, you have to," Erlea said. "Good people are risking their lives to clear you. They believe in peace. And I believe in you." She stared at him, bewildered. "Why wouldn't you go to the talks?"

"My life is paid for in sin," her father replied. "I paid for my new face, my new name and papers, with the suffering of others. I worked for the mafia, and I have much to atone for." She saw him struggle to hold back tears again. "If I go to the peace talks, everyone will know that I wear this face now. And then I must disappear again, to pay Mr. Brown back for restoring the safety of my family."

"He wants you to inform on the mafia?" Surely that was more dangerous even than taking on corrupt officials in the National Police.

"It is the right thing to do. Peace talks will save lives and let healing begin among Spaniards. But the criminals who helped me years ago will keep destroying lives if I do not help to stop them." He took Erlea's hands in his. "Now you are grown, I can ask your opinion."

How dare he do this to her? "You've already made your choice."

"Then your blessing, or at least forgiveness. Because this time when I go, you can understand why. And know how much I love you always."

When they finally reached the library, Maji scanned the three walls of ancient manuscripts. She hoped Romero knew just where to find the folder of photos and papers Echeverra had stashed among them. She listened politely to Don Pedro for a few minutes, then got the nod from Romero and fanned herself with one of the books for sale on the display table in the center of the room.

"She's not much interested in old books," Romero said. "Would you mind showing her the balcony?"

Don Pedro escorted Maji out to the expansive balcony planted with shrubs and trees, palms and a tropical-looking plant. "What is this one?" Maji whispered to him.

"Brugmansia," Don Pedro replied, "also known as angel's trumpet." He went into the horticultural and medicinal history of the plant, and Maji waved Alejandro over to get a close-up of the flower. Tired and hot, she wandered over to the low stone wall and looked out at the sweeping view of tiled roofs and terraced hillsides. Behind her, Amelia asked Don Pedro about farming in the rocky terrain, drawing him farther away from Romero's search of the library.

They stood together admiring the view and determined farming efforts until Romero called from the doorway, "Such a beautiful day. But we should get you back to the hotel."

Just as Don Pedro began to turn, he took a hit to the torso that spun and dropped him. Maji fell automatically to the ground, hearing the rifle's retort, three shots in quick succession, as she went down. Romero took cover, barking out orders into his comm, while Amelia scrambled low to reach Don Pedro. She checked on him and prevented his attempt to rise.

Shielded by the wall, Maji scanned the area inside the balcony. No one moved, thank God. No—there was Alejandro, scuttling in a crouch with his camera out, trying to film the events. Maji yelled for him to get down, but he ignored her, rising to look her way instead. She leaped over a shrub, knocking him back to the ground just as two more shots pinged nearby.

"Stay the fuck down," she told him.

In the distance, sirens sounded.

"Report," Romero called out.

"Don Pedro is stable but can't crawl out," Amelia called back.

"I'm fine," Maji called. "Alejandro? Can you crawl to the door?"

"Think so. My arm stings and it's bleeding, but I'll try."

"No. Stay there. I'll come to you." Maji combat-crawled over to him and checked the wound. "He got winged," she called to Romero. "Not deep. Wrapping it and sending him in."

As Alejandro crawled toward the door and safety, Maji made her way to Don Pedro and Amelia. "Can we carry him?"

Amelia shook her head. "The wall's too low for cover."

So they waited while the ambulance made its way to the monastery and the police on the hillside searched for the shooter. Finally Romero said, "They think he fled." After a pause, he announced, "Stay down. I'm going to come out."

"No," Maji barked. They couldn't send the EMTs out until they were sure the threat was over. And she was not going to let anyone else shoulder the risk of drawing fire. "I'll do it."

"Rios," he objected as she stood. "Oh, hell, move quick."

Maji took a deep breath, wondering as she looked into the gorgeous vista where the shooter had hidden. And where he'd run off to. "Okay, I'm coming in," she said. And then the bullet hit her in the chest.

CHAPTER EIGHTEEN

Celeste found the theater nearly empty with no dancers or musicians, only crew working on the sets. She spotted Nico checking some of their work. "Shouldn't Erlea be back by now?"

Nico frowned at her. "You obviously don't watch the news. Some idiot shot her."

"No," Celeste protested. "She can't be..." Her vision swam. *Gone?* No. Impossible.

He sneered even as he steadied her. "Oh, use your brain. Would I be here fussing with staging if she was dead?"

"You heartless son of a bitch." Celeste grabbed his sleeve. "Where is she?"

He shook her off. "Some hospital, probably giving an interview by now. Maybe she'll mention you again."

"Screw you." Celeste backed away, trying to dial Maji with shaking hands. "She deserves better."

"Oh, it's like that, is it?" Nico looked smug. "Her new champion, in a skirt for once. Well don't think that just because you're a woman she'll keep you any longer than that string of starfuckers she's hooked up with before."

Nico turned back to his task, dismissing her. Her hands, normally so calm and sure in a crisis, shook too hard to punch the buttons on her phone.

"There you are," Imane said from behind Celeste. When Celeste turned, Imane enveloped her in a hug. "Why aren't you in your office? I know she's in there, but they won't let me in."

"She's here?" Relief surged through her veins, making Celeste feel giddy. The injury must be minor. She led Imane down the back corridors, nearly at a run. "What the hell happened?"

"She went up to Valldemossa, to that old monastery. Someone shot the guide showing her around. They took him to the hospital. She must not be so bad if she's here instead."

"Yes. She must be okay." *She must be.* Celeste tried to open her office door, found it locked, and fished in her pockets for the key card.

"Hey, let us in. I brought the doctor," Imane said, banging on the door. Before Celeste could key it, Romero stood in the doorway.

"Let me see her," Celeste said, pushing past him.

"Right this way, Doctor," Romero replied. "Not you," he added to Imane.

"Give us a moment," Celeste said before she could protest. "But stay close."

Romero drew back the curtain to reveal Erlea reclining on the exam table. She huddled inside a blanket, eyes closed, no doubt chilled by the ice pack peeking out at her chest. And possibly shock.

"Get a hot pack and make her some tea," Celeste barked at Romero. "In there," she added, waving toward the adjoining room.

"Keep him busy," Erlea said. "He's a hoverer." Only it wasn't Erlea's husky voice.

"Maji?" Celeste said. "What is going on?"

Maji opened her eyes and gave a weak smile. "Surprise. I brought you a fabulous bruise, and I'm not going to pretend it doesn't hurt like hell. You can even X-ray it if you insist."

"That bad? You promised to be careful." Celeste wanted to hug her and throttle her at the same time. "What about Erlea? How is she?"

"Breathe, Doc." Maji stretched gingerly. "She had a quiet day out of sight. And my jacket caught the worst of it."

Romero handed her a steaming mug. "You said it needed ventilation. Be careful what you ask for."

"Why don't you go make Celeste some tea now?" Maji retorted.

He raised a brow and went back to the other room without comment, leaving the door open a crack. Neither he nor Maji seemed fazed by her state. Celeste wondered at the world they must work in.

Maji shrugged the blanket off her left shoulder with a wince. Her

T-shirt was cut away on that side, exposing her breast below the ice pack. "Little help here?"

"Yes, yes, of course," Celeste said, willing herself to focus. Erlea was fine. Maji needed her now. Celeste lifted the ice pack off and stared at the distinctive, ugly bruise. "Jesus, you've been shot. Thank God you were wearing a vest."

"Actually, a hot, heavy jacket. Looks great on me, but Romero won't let me keep it," she said, raising her voice. "Even though it's damaged."

"Still government property," Romero's voice replied from behind the door.

Celeste shook her head. How could they joke like this? "Can you move your left arm?"

Maji nodded. "Hurts, but yeah. Clavicle's intact, shoulder girdle's fine. I think it's just strain and swelling from the impact."

"Should I ask what happened?" Celeste began her exam, moving Maji's arm for her and palpating her neck and shoulder.

"I went out on the balcony at the Real Cartuja, and a sniper shot the docent next to me. Shortly after that, I stopped a bullet with my chest. Remind me to avoid that in the future."

Celeste frowned at her dark humor. "How is the docent?"

"Bruised, scraped, and grazed." Maji paused. "We think they mistook him for Arturo Echeverra. Have you seen the news yet?"

"Mr. Salazar has been publicly identified now," Romero called to her. "The press is asking Nigel about the Echeverra rumors, and he's only giving a no comment. Oh, and Erlea is officially stable, more details on tonight's news."

"Thanks," Maji called back. She looked to Celeste with genuine concern. "I can't tell if it hurts to breathe from the impact itself or if maybe I cracked a rib. Can you?"

Celeste palpated the area as well as she could without pressing on the worst of the deep red marks. "I would say no, but we should watch over the next few days. Limit movement, stretch gently, and keep icing at intervals."

"And call you if the nature of the pain changes or gets suddenly worse." Maji gave her a weak smile. "I've played this game before."

Celeste didn't smile back. "Risking your life is not a game."

"It's the one I get paid to play. But don't worry—I always beat the house."

❖

Erlea heard voices on the other side of the doors connecting her suite to Maji's room. "Is she back?"

"Sounds like it," Dave Brown said with a smile. "And that's my cue to head out. You okay here?"

"Yes. Thank you for the time with my father today."

Dave showed himself to the door. "Thanks for rolling with the change of plans."

Erlea opened her connecting door and knocked on Maji's. It flew open and Celeste reached for her.

"Beatriz Echeverra, don't you ever scare me like that again," she said into Erlea's hair, her arms squeezing tight.

"Okay, okay," Erlea said, hugging Celeste back. *She called me Beatriz.* "I promise. Where's Maji?"

"In bed," Celeste said, stepping aside so Erlea could see.

"Can I talk to her?" Maji didn't look up to a real conversation.

Maji waved listlessly. "Speak now, 'cause I'm going down for the count."

"Painkillers," Celeste explained. "Maybe we should talk next door."

Erlea gave Maji a kiss on the head and squeezed her hand. "Thank you." There would be time to dissect what had happened and what it meant for them both, later. "Rest well."

While Celeste made a final check on her patient, Erlea let Imane in. She took the hug and promised not to scare her best friend like that again. "You sound just like Celeste," she grumbled. "At least you didn't call me Beatriz."

"What can I say, Beatriz?" Imane countered. "Bossy women love you. Have you ordered dinner yet?"

"No. I wasn't expecting everyone here, not tonight."

"Where else would we be?" Imane said, already dialing room service.

Erlea pointed to Maji's room. "She's here for Maji."

"Yeah. Keep telling yourself that." Imane rolled her eyes. She placed the dinner order and fished a beer from the fridge. "Want one?"

Erlea really did. "After a day like today, I'd like a good stiff drink. But I don't want to disappoint Celeste."

"She's definitely got you motivated," Imane conceded.

Celeste poked her head into the kitchen. "Don't worry about me. Whether you choose to drink or not drink, it has to be what you want. For you."

Erlea met her gaze, recognized the smile in her eyes. Those lovely eyes. "I don't want to miss anything anymore. I nearly missed knowing you."

"Oh." Celeste's eyes glowed, and the blush spread from her neck to the ear she tucked her silky hair behind. "I'm on call, myself. But I think it would be safe if we each had one glass, yes?"

"And now everybody's happy," Imane said, opening the cava for them. "So—about today. We rehearsed without you, the band sounds great. Nico was a prick as usual, Tania left the stage crying, Dimitri went after her. The usual."

Erlea shook her head. "We can't afford anyone else quitting. I'll talk to Nigel again." She thought about what to tell them about her father, the evidence they had planned to collect, the unexpected switch. Too much. "I met with my father. We spent hours catching up. It was weird."

"I'll bet. Do you like him?" Imane said. "You always had him on such a pedestal."

"Well, he's an adult, I'm an adult. It's different now—as it should be." She sipped the crisp sparkling white.

Imane frowned. "I'm happy for you, really. But now that he's seen you, he can go. Aren't there peace talks he has to get to? Like, in a city nowhere near you."

"That's a little harsh," Erlea said. When Imane only crossed her arms and Celeste shrugged sympathetically, she asked them, "Where is this coming from?"

"Maji thinks the shooter mistook the man with her for your father," Celeste said. "And now the press thinks he is alive and on the island."

Erlea longed to tell them all, but she had promised. "Well, soon he will be in Bilbao, making headlines for good reasons. Happy?"

"I just want you to be safe," Imane said. She glanced toward Maji's room. "Both of you."

Celeste frowned. "Perhaps I should delay my move to Barcelona."

"No. You can't put your life on hold anymore," Erlea said. "We'll be fine here. No more risks. Except for that damn bungee number."

After dinner, Celeste checked in on Maji and came out to the balcony with her report. "Sleeping soundly. I'll stay with her tonight."

"Thank you," Erlea said. "I wish there was more I could do to thank her."

"I'm looking for a plastic surgeon for her in Barcelona. If I need star power to get her an appointment, I'll let you know."

It didn't sound like Celeste was kidding. "What's wrong with Lyttleton?"

"She doesn't like him. Among other things, he's racist."

"Surprise," Imane said. "Did he know it wasn't Erlea?"

"No," Celeste said. "Apparently, he saw the keloid scar and made a remark about having thought she was of too pure blood for that."

"Fuck him," Erlea said.

"Leave that to the Barbie doll trophy wife," Imane said. "I'm going to clean up." She nudged Erlea. "Play her the cat song. It's getting really good now."

When Erlea didn't pick the guitar up, Celeste gave her an expectant look. "Well? You said you wanted me to hear it."

"It's still pretty rough. I rewrote some parts, but it's not ready."

Celeste smiled at her. "You are so sweet, really. Not at all what I expected."

"What did you expect?" Erlea asked before she could chicken out.

"A hard-living, charismatic player," Celeste replied. "And you are charismatic. But also a homebody, often shy, a little geeky, very hardworking. And you care so much about your people. You're a good person, not just…"

"What?" *Please say hot. Or sexy. Or even cute.*

Celeste stood, that adorable blush creeping up to her face again. "I shouldn't ignore my own rules. You are still my client." She moved to the railing and looked out toward the harbor.

Imane was right. The realization emboldened Erlea. "No, I'm not," she told Celeste. "I'm practically flying on my own. Without you. So—you're fired."

"I've never been fired." Celeste sounded almost teasing. "Why would you do that?"

Erlea stepped close enough to see Celeste's eyes reflecting the harbor lights. "Because you don't date your clients." She rushed on before Celeste could rebuff her. "I know this is a bad time for you, with the move and all, and you probably don't want to think about—"

"Kiss me."

"I don't want to push you into anything you—"

Celeste pressed a finger to Erlea's lips. "Kiss me."

Erlea put two fingers under Celeste's chin and gently raised it, leaning in toward her. She stopped just shy of touching her mouth to Celeste's, still afraid the incredible pull she felt was one-sided. Celeste's fingers running through her hair at the base of her skull, pulling her in to make a perfect fit of their mouths and then their bodies, erased all doubt.

Erlea opened up to her, riding the high of Celeste's hunger. She slid a hand down Celeste's back to the curve of her hip and snugged her closer, sinking her weight so she wouldn't topple them both. Who was humming? Must be her—Celeste's little noises were more like moans, increasing in intensity as the kiss deepened. A harmony to her melody.

A clattering from the kitchen tugged at Erlea's awareness, an irritation. But Celeste stiffened in her arms, pulled Erlea's head back with a gentle tug on her hair that only felt erotic, not painful. "No," Celeste breathed.

Erlea searched her eyes, trying to see beyond the desire on the surface. "Are you okay?"

"No. I want so much more." Celeste shuddered. "And I'm not ready. I need to be me again. I can't do this—not now."

She looked so anguished that Erlea wanted to hold her, to make it better, to convince her to take a chance. But instead she stepped back, gently removing Celeste's hands from her hair and holding them in the space between them. "Okay. I'm not going anywhere."

"I'm sorry," Celeste said, rubbing her thumbs across Erlea's knuckles. "I really am so attracted to you. And I want to get to know you, to spend time with you. Not just in bed. But—"

"You're not ready. I get that. No need to apologize."

Celeste nodded, and Erlea still felt the pull between them. "I should go check on Maji," Celeste said, but she didn't move.

"Yeah," Erlea agreed. But if Celeste didn't stop looking at her with those eyes, they'd surely be kissing again any second. Erlea wrenched her gaze away, stepped back, and picked up her guitar. "I'll play for you soon."

She heard Celeste make her good-byes with Imane, then both doors clicking shut between the rooms.

Imane came out and took the seat near where Erlea sat, strumming without noticing the tune. "What did you do to her?"

"Kissed her."

Imane laughed. "Finally. Wait, should I leave?"

"No. She's not coming back." At least not tonight. "Could you stay with me awhile?"

"Uh-oh. Don't tell me you're sorry." Imane paused. "Was it bad?"

"No. It was perfect. Worth waiting for."

From her favorite box seat, Maji watched Erlea fly toward the wall, singing as she went, and come back to the stage in a soft landing that fit the music almost perfectly. When Dave slipped into the seat next to hers, she looked at him sideways. "I'm officially cleared to work again." Three days of sitting around was more than plenty. "You can stop checking on me."

"Great news," Dave said, keeping his eyes on the rehearsal. "But I came to check on this. Pretty cool."

Imane called lunch and the dancers began to disperse.

"That's it for a while," Maji said. "Any updates?"

"Yeah," Dave replied. "Hey, look—she's going again."

Maji watched as Erlea found her placement, ran for the wall, and moved through the air while singing a cappella. The wall didn't fall away as usual, and she bounced off it, flailing back to the stage.

While Imane rushed over to her, Dave raised both arms like the barrel of a rifle and sighted down them to the spot where Erlea had hit the wall. "Winterbottom's a criminal genius." He mimed firing a shot and laid his imaginary rifle down with a smile. "At least he thinks he is."

"No fucking way," Maji said.

"Yes fucking way," Dave replied as Erlea limped offstage with her arm over Imane's shoulders. "Romero fed the National Police the idea that Echeverra is staying on the island to see his daughter perform just once before he heads off to the peace talks. Aguilar wants to nab him on opening night, and Nigel suggested they shoot her down during the finale."

"And I suppose Romero wants to catch them all in the act?" Maji asked.

"Makes the case against Aguilar and Perez really solid," Dave acknowledged. "Plus, don't you want to see a solid case against Nigel?"

"Not if he kills Erlea in the process."

"We're working on that. Thinking some costume modifications, along the lines of that jacket you wore at Real Cartuja."

Maji glared at him. "No. What if the sniper takes a head shot? Or hits her in the vest, but she's injured. This is her career and her life, Dave. She's a civilian, for Chrissake."

"I hear you. What if we could sub their sniper for one of our best?"

That would help. But so many things could go wrong, using a civilian as a moving target. Erlea had enough trouble with the flying bungee without that kind of stress added. "That helps on our end. But Erlea is a wild card, and it's not fair to ask her. Use me instead."

Dave laughed at her. "What are going to do, lip-synch?" When her silence made it clear she wasn't joking, he added, "No, Rios. This is your first time back in the field, and you're banged up already. I'm not risking you."

"Dave, I respect that you are team lead on this op. But if you put Erlea in danger, I will go over your head. And Cohen will tell the colonel I'm ready." At least, Hannah had better.

"Look, I don't like risking a civilian any more than you do. I'll run it by Command myself, get clearance to use you." He frowned. "And please don't bother Cohen right now. I heard she lost her wife recently."

"No. Ava's sick. That's all." It had to be. "They've been through this before." Maji stood. She needed to call Hannah. No, that would get Hannah in trouble and if Ava was in the hospital again, she didn't need any more trouble. "I have to find Celeste." Before she caught her flight.

"Hey," Dave said, grabbing her arm. "Maybe I misunderstood."

Maji shook him off. "Damn right you did. And now I have to get my head clear on this."

"Rios," Dave said, starting to follow her. "Where you going?"

"Marina. I need to hear for myself." She looked back at him. "Just give me an hour."

Dave nodded. "An hour. Don't blow your cover."

Maji called Celeste from the car park as she climbed on Reimi's bike. "Call Bubbles right now. And stay there. I'm coming to you."

Celeste was waiting in the cockpit. When Maji flipped her face screen up, she told her, "Your friend Bubbles's number just keeps going to voicemail."

Maji swung herself over the rail and climbed down into the cabin, whacking the helmet on the low ceiling as she tugged it off her head. "Try Ava's line."

Celeste dialed and put her phone on speaker. An automated voice intoned, "This number is no longer operable. If you need a provider—"

Maji swayed and caught herself on the counter. *No.* Ava would never quit practice. Maji tried to dial, but her hands shook. She gave her phone to Celeste. "Try Bubbles again."

This time the phone rang twice before a man's voice answered. "Maji?"

"Yes," was all Maji could manage.

"Hey, it's Rey Martinez." Bubbles's husband. "La Bubbles is out cold. It's been like that all week. Losing Ava is crushing her. I'm doing what I can, but...Wait. You are off duty, right?"

"No," Maji said. And then it was all she could say, over and over. She felt Celeste against her, drawing her head to her chest.

Celeste kept speaking with Rey, her voice low. Maji couldn't make the words fall into order, make sense. Nothing made sense anymore. Maji closed her eyes and shut the world out.

❖

Celeste left Maji below deck to speak with Dave in the cockpit. "Thank you for coming. I didn't know who else to call."

He nodded. "I got her. Could have avoided this if I'd fucking known they were family."

"How did you not? Ava was very dear to her. How big is this company you two work for?"

"Big. Rios and I only met once before. And it's the kind of work where you don't want the guys thinking you got your job due to any kind of favoritism."

"I don't think I like security work," Celeste muttered. "Medicine has enough politics."

"Yeah, well. Is that your taxi?"

Celeste spotted the cab on the drive, heading for her dock. "I could stay here, delay my job start."

Dave shook his head. "I got her. And I'll tell the others. You go on."

"I'll call her when I get settled in." It felt like much too little to Celeste.

"Yeah," Dave said. "She'll want to know you're safe. Don't be surprised if she doesn't answer her phone for a few days. Just keeping leaving messages."

Chapter Nineteen

Maria handed the empty cookie tin across the balcony rail to Celeste. "Jordi devoured them. I did manage to get one myself. Delicious."

"I have a few left. Come for a cup of tea?" Celeste could see how these neighbors had become chosen family for Erlea. After only ten days of friendship, she wanted to adopt them.

"I would love to, but I'm getting the house ready for Jordi's colleagues." Athena hopped up and balanced on the rails. Such a natural athlete. "You are welcome to join us for dinner."

"Thank you, no. I am meeting friends tonight myself." Celeste loved being able to say that again. "Have you heard from Beatriz lately?" It felt odd to call Erlea by her given name, but Maria insisted.

"Not for a couple days. Why don't you call her? I'm sure she'd love that."

"Oh no, I don't want to intrude. I'm sure things are getting very tense so close to opening night."

"Well, at least send her a picture of Athena. That's how I remind her she has a home here even when she is on the road."

So Celeste took a short video of Athena racing around after the red dot. She added the message, *Why does she love chasing the dot when she never catches it?*

The phone rang moments later. "She loves the hunt," Erlea said, "and that you play with her. Thank you. Jordi says you are a natural with cats, that Athena only visits them now."

"I didn't mean to steal her," Celeste replied. "Or interrupt your rehearsal."

"A welcome break. Nico is on everyone's last nerve. Everything must be perfect, and we lost another crew member yesterday. How do you like my place?"

Celeste hesitated. She loved it. As Barcelona apartments went, it was large, with two bedrooms and an office. The light was good, the street noise low, the kitchen well-appointed. But best of all were the orderly shelves of books, the paintings by artists she'd never heard of, the array of instruments by the composition table. And the roof garden. Plus that lovely, peaceful bathroom full of plants. The only thing missing was Erlea. "It feels like you."

"Uh-oh. Did I leave a mess?"

"No, silly. It's wonderful and I love it." *Too much, Celeste.* "How is Maji doing?"

"I'm concerned. Can I call you after we wrap today?"

"Sure. Catch me before eight."

"You're going out?" Erlea sounded genuinely pleased. "Good for you."

Celeste went into Erlea's bedroom to change for her evening out. Her small wardrobe of dresses hung next to Erlea's clothes. She put her face to one of Erlea tops and inhaled, sneezed, and laughed at herself. The remnants of smoke clung to it, but also Erlea's scent.

Celeste kept the shower short, not letting her thoughts dwell on Erlea as they often did while she lathered and rinsed, thinking of her strong and graceful musician's hands. When she stepped out and toweled off, Athena waltzed into the large basin and started licking the drops of warm water.

"You are so strange," Celeste told her.

Athena only purred in response.

It was the first thing Celeste recounted on the phone to Erlea, who made a purring sound. "Maybe it tastes like you."

Even over the phone, Erlea's voice warmed her through. Celeste cleared her throat.

"Sorry," Erlea said. "I retract that. I want you to feel at home there. I won't do that again."

"I am not fragile, or so easily scared off," Celeste assured her. "And you have a good purr. Not as good as Athena's, but then, no one is petting you."

She heard Erlea sputter and Imane laughing in the background.

"Hey. I'm drinking here. Nearly sprayed beer out my nose. And it's the only one I get today."

Celeste chuckled. "Well, don't waste your ration. Is Maji there with you, too?"

"No, just Imane. And I am not putting her on speakerphone," Erlea replied, her voice climbing. A door swooshed and clicked. "There. I locked her out on the balcony. Where she is making very childish faces. I wish Maji was here, but she is all work since her friend died."

"How so?"

"Well, she spends hours in Dave's room and working out. I've never seen someone exercise so much. During our Aikido hour, she is very focused, no joking."

"I'm glad you're still doing that together. Initially I thought it would help with your stress, but now I think she needs it more. I'm glad you are there for her."

"Oh, and she's practicing my finale, the bungee number. But I don't need an understudy, especially one who can't sing."

Celeste pondered that. "She needs to feel that she is helping. Are you in any danger of panicking on opening night, not being able to perform the number yourself?"

"No. Every day it gets locked into muscle memory more. But I let her because, like you say, she needs to." Erlea took an audible sip. "And she is working daily with Santxo, too, upgrading security measures for concert nights."

"They haven't caught anyone yet?" By now the Spanish police should have made some progress. "Someone shot at you, for Christ's sake."

"Not yet. And they were trying to hit my father, not me. Still, I can't think too much about it or I feel caged in here. I wish I was home with you." The line went quiet, then Erlea asked, "How are you there? Do you feel safe?"

"In your building, with the security and Jordi and Maria next door, yes. When I am at work, yes. On the metro and walking alone, I look over my shoulder a lot." No point lying. "But I have a panic device and other measures Paragon helped me devise. Plus, my friends look out for me."

"I'm glad you have them. You deserve freedom and happiness."

Erlea paused again. "You really don't mind the cat? I know you didn't grow up with them."

"That's true, but I always wanted one. My mother is allergic, med school was too busy, and Adrienne didn't like them." Celeste heard a little growl at the mention of her ex. "Anyway, Athena is great. I had no idea cats were so funny."

"Funny?"

"Fascinating might be a better word. Such rituals, such a love of her routines. Sometimes Maria has to interpret, to tell me what cues I am supposed to pick up. Does she sit by the toy she wants to play with and just look at you?"

Erlea laughed. "And then you have to play with her, yes. For a reward, you can give her a massage."

"Oh, she tells me when it's time for that. I read half a novel the other night when she claimed my lap. And missed supper." Celeste waited for Erlea to stop laughing. "But some things she does scare me."

"Such as?"

"She climbs up to the roof."

"Well, she is a tiny jaguar. It is in her nature."

"It's dangerous. Aren't you worried she'll get hurt?"

"Of course. But keeping her locked indoors would be cruel. She may be domesticated, but she is wild at heart."

Celeste considered that. "Are we still talking about the cat?"

"Naturally. A cat is her own person. You want her to claim you, you must respect that."

"Do I want her to claim me? I mean, I am only here temporarily. This is still your home."

"It's yours as long as you want it." Through Erlea's words, Celeste heard a banging. "I better let Imane back in. She's going to grill me now."

Celeste smiled to herself. "Tell her we only talked about the cat."

"She won't believe that. She's too smart."

❖

Maji cleaned up after the morning Aikido session and stopped by Dave's room to check in. "I'm heading back to the theater. One more time through the finale."

"Don't hurt yourself overworking," Dave said with a frown. "And did you eat any breakfast?"

"I had a protein bar." His room, in contrast, smelled of bacon and coffee.

Dave waved her to the table. "Sit. Eat. You can rehearse when you've had something real." He set a full plate in front of her and went over to the coffeemaker.

"I'm not hungry," she grumbled, dutifully taking a bite. It tasted fine, but her body rebelled. Good food was like the gorgeous weather, wrong somehow.

"I know," Dave said. He'd been very open with her, sharing his own stories of grief.

"Two days to curtain," Maji said, full up on sharing the personal, even if it did make her feel less alone. Work was easier to focus on. At least she could do something about it. "How do we look?"

Dave sat and matched her bite for bite, talking around his food. "Nigel will be in the VIP seats, so no worries he'll know you're backstage. We'll tell him you went home for a funeral."

"Clever." Maji knew the cast and crew were aware that she was grieving. They'd been really sweet, especially Roger. She felt bad shutting Erlea and Imane out, but what could she really tell them? It was easier to keep to herself. "What about Nico, Erlea, Imane?"

"Erlea and Imane we tell tomorrow. Nico, well...we're thinking maybe a serious case of food poisoning from tomorrow's lunch."

"I wouldn't trust him to not tell Nigel either. Alejandro?"

"The kid knows the show as well or better than Nico. You trust him?"

"Yep. And Roger. All they really need to know is that I'm standing in for the finale, right? If Erlea's on board, everyone else will follow."

"How do you feel about getting her on board?"

Maji looked down at her plate, surprised to find it nearly empty. "Good. I think she'll want to nail the bastards who stole her father from her as much as I do."

Maji turned in to the alley to the loading dock and spotted Santxo chatting with one of his security force. Only after the shooting at the

Real Cartuja had they finally put someone back here. The closer to opening day, the tighter security got. Better late than never.

"Hey, Santxo. What brings the chief down?" Holding a giant flower arrangement.

He smiled at her, his mustache lifting at the corners. "Celebrities. A French women's football team sent Erlea these. I guess they are big fans of hers."

Odds on it was Adrienne's team. "Did they send a note?" Maji asked.

"Of course. Full of good wishes, no doubt." He held it out.

Maji plucked it from his fingers. "No doubt. Here, I'll take them to Erlea."

"Very well," Santxo said, his proud posture deflating a bit. "Give her my best."

Maji nodded. "I always do. And she's very grateful for your hard work. She says so regularly."

"Really?" He straightened up and touched his hat brim. "Well, no one gets hurt on my watch."

Maji set the arrangement down as soon as she was out of sight backstage. She dialed Dave and glanced at the note, confirming her suspicions. "Got flowers and a note from Adrienne at the theater. Don't know if it's a peace offering or a threat. You wanna come see?"

"I'll bring the kit," he replied.

Erlea read the card from Adrienne as Maji and Dave stood by in the empty wardrobe room. The disassembled flower arrangement lay on the counter. *Wish I could come see your show in person. They think I am mailing you an apology. But if you steal my girlfriend, I swear I will come find you.*

"Who does she think she is? You can't own a girlfriend. Is this supposed to frighten me?" It only made her want to tear the flowers to shreds. "How is Celeste?"

"We haven't told her yet," Maji said.

Erlea hated to worry Celeste, but…"I think you should. What if Adrienne shows up in Barcelona? I don't think counseling is doing the trick."

Nico banged through the door. "There you are. We open tomorrow and you are playing with flowers?" He glared at Maji and Dave. "You two get out. You've interfered enough with my show."

"Your show?" Erlea said. "Stop acting like you do all the work. It takes dozens of people, and they deserve the credit more than you."

"You would say that." Nico scowled, his inner ugliness ruining his handsome features. "You've got this *sudaca* doing your stunts for you. Too bad she can't sing."

Erlea moved toward him, her pulse beating loud in her ears at the racist epithet. "How dare—"

"Don't bother," Maji said, putting a hand on her shoulder. "I've been called worse things by better people."

"Nico," Erlea said, measuring her words. "Get out. Pack and leave. Nigel will send you severance papers."

"You can't fire me. Not now."

"No, I'm way overdue," Erlea said. "And if you don't go this instant, I will have you removed." She felt Maji give her shoulder a friendly squeeze as she stared Nico down.

"You'll hear from my lawyer." Nico spun on his heel and left.

Erlea blew out her breath. "At least I didn't hit him. I nearly lost it for real."

"So did he. He forgot to snap," Maji said.

Celeste's fingers trembled as she pulled up Adrienne's Skype ID. Lunch didn't want to stay down, even with the ginger tea she had sipped all afternoon while trying to keep her focus on her new clients. She took a deep breath, let it out slowly, and hit send.

Adrienne's face appeared after only three rings. "Celeste? Is that really you?"

"Yes. We need to talk."

"Damn right," Adrienne agreed. "Turn on your view. I can't see you."

Same tone. *You can't change her*, Celeste reminded herself. *Only yourself.* "One moment." She took another long breath and clicked the video button. "There. Now—"

"God, you look so beautiful," Adrienne cut in. "I've missed you so much. Don't tell me you're sleeping with her. She isn't right for you. If you just give me a chance—"

"Stop," Celeste said. "Just stop, and listen for once. You and I are over. Nothing in my life is your business. Do you understand?"

"Then why did you pull that crap with the video? Are you trying to get me kicked off the team? Therapy is bullshit, but I'm going for you. For us."

Celeste shook her head. "No. You are going for you." *And for the next woman who dares to love you,* she added silently. "You need help. Not just to keep your career. But to be happy. I do want that for you."

"Then give me another chance. I've changed."

"Really? You sent Erlea a threat."

Adrienne had the decency to look embarrassed. "I didn't mean it. It's the Ambien. I sent flowers to, like, a dozen people. And bought a lot shoes, too." She sat up straight. "You can't blame me for that. I wasn't myself."

Nothing had changed. "Doesn't matter what the excuse is," Celeste said. "You still aren't taking responsibility for your actions. I won't contact you again. And I expect the same from you."

"Or what?" Adrienne's tone and expression made Celeste swallow hard.

"Or I will press charges against you," Celeste said.

Adrienne laughed. "You out me, you out yourself."

"I can live with that. I am not ashamed anymore," Celeste said. "Good-bye." She ended the call before Adrienne could reply.

While she was making a fresh cup of tea, Celeste's phone buzzed. If that was Adrienne…no, she did not have the new number. She sat and blew on her mug, checking the texts.

Thinking of you. <3 Virtual hug, Erlea's message said.

Celeste called her, smiling. "Got your message. Thank you. What is <3?"

"It's a geeky heart," Imane called out.

"I'm taking this off speaker and making her go inside," Erlea said.

"No, it's okay," Celeste replied. "Are you on the balcony? Show me the view."

Erlea turned on the video call function and Celeste saw the bands of pink and orange clouds above the ocean. Then Erlea turned it to Imane, who waved, and to her own smiling face at last. "Hi. How are you?"

"I've been better," Celeste said. "I called Adrienne and told her off."

"Wow." Erlea's face in the little viewscreen scrunched with worry. "Are you safe? Do you want me to find Maji? How do you feel? I mean…shutting up now."

Celeste laughed. "I will update Maji when she calls me back. No rush. And I feel good. I'm sorry she dragged you into this, but I'm glad, too. It gave me the push to confront her at last."

"I'm proud of you," Erlea said.

"Me, too," Imane called out. "What for?"

Celeste smiled. "Please fill her in later." At Erlea's nod, she continued. "Right now, I want to hear about you. Are you ready for your big night?"

"I feel great. Oh, and I fired Nico today." Erlea laughed at Celeste's obvious astonishment. "I used my sensible shoes to give him the boot."

Celeste raised her tea mug in a toast. "To freedom and better days ahead."

"Did you get the tickets?" Erlea asked after clinking glasses with Imane.

"Yes. Maria and Jordi are so excited by the VIP seats. And the backstage passes." Celeste paused. "Me, too. Thanks. I can't wait."

Erlea beamed at her. "And your names are on the after-party list. I will see you there?"

"Count on it. I want to dance with you again."

"Look what happened this morning. There could have been a bomb in those flowers, yet you carried them directly to Erlea, didn't you? You can't even keep her safe from one crazy woman," Nigel said. "I want additional security on patrol tomorrow night. I will hire them myself."

"Fine," Romero replied. "As long as they don't keep us from apprehending Echeverra."

"You're sure you'll know it's him?" Nigel asked. "Not like last time."

Dave's calm facade flickered. "Mr. Winterbottom, we never thought the docent was Echeverra. We just hadn't reached the rendezvous yet when the shooting occurred. I expect that scared him off."

"And what will you be doing to protect Erlea while they hunt this terrorist at my show?" Nigel asked Maji.

Maji put on her contrite face. "I'm sorry, sir. I won't be there. I've been called home on family business."

"Oh, right. I heard some mention. My condolences, dear."

Maji bit her tongue, looking down at her shoes in lieu of a reply.

"Erlea shouldn't be in any danger," Dave said, "so long as we scoop up Echeverra and get him far from her."

"Well then, the sooner the better," Nigel said.

Romero nodded in agreement. "Let us know when your security contractors arrive, and we'll brief them on how to recognize Echeverra and when and how we plan to apprehend him."

Chapter Twenty

Maji watched Roger finalizing Erlea's makeup for the opening number. "Nervous?"

"Only about the finale," Erlea said.

Roger looked between them. "Well, that's why you've got an understudy, innit?"

"Yeah," Maji said. "I've got the moves down and nobody will guess it's not you." Roger didn't know about the anticipated shooting, so she added for good measure, "What with my flawless lip-synching."

Alejandro popped his head into the do shop. "Ten minutes to curtain." He spotted Maji. "And Nigel's coming to give his pep talk." He ducked back out, chatting on his headset as he went.

"Out of sight with you, then," Roger said to Maji with a wink. To Erlea he added, "Don't worry. You probably won't need her, and either way he'll never know."

"Thanks, Rog," Erlea said as Maji hid herself.

The door swung open again, and Nigel strode in. "Nearly ready then?"

"As I'm ever going to be," Erlea replied.

"You're a rock star, dear," Nigel said. "The crowd out there is wild for you already. Chanting your name. Just go out there and do what you always do. Knock 'em dead."

"Nigel," Erlea said. "Sod off."

"There's my girl," Nigel said with a wink. As he left he tossed back, "I'll be watching."

Maji waited a few minutes to come back out, got the all clear on the comm from Dave, and gave Erlea a hug.

"I just wish we could warn Celeste," Erlea whispered. "She's going to be furious with both of us."

"We'll all live through it," Maji promised. And hoped she was right.

❖

At intermission, Celeste waited in the line for a glass of wine with Maria and Jordi.

"I can't believe we've never seen her live," Maria gushed. "She's incredible. Nothing like the shy homebody we know."

"Now, how can you say that?" Jordi replied. "We saw her play clubs for years before she got famous. She had a stage presence even back then. Admittedly, the arrangements are more complex, the instrumentals more layered…"

"Sexy, you fool. She's on fire up there." Maria looked to Celeste for confirmation. "Am I wrong?"

"No," Celeste said. "Half the people in this theater want to go home with her, I'm sure." *Including me.*

Jordi squinted at her. "You're not jealous, are you? Despite her reputation, you have nothing to worry about."

"Oh no. I mean, we're not…that is, we're friends." The sight of Reimi with a date on her arm saved Celeste from having to defend that assertion. She waved at them.

Reimi introduced Celeste to the dapper butch who appeared thoroughly smitten with her, and Celeste introduced them to Maria and Jordi.

"You are neighbors?" Reimi exclaimed. "That must be so exciting. Think of the parties," she said to her date.

The lights blinked and the chimes tolled, calling them back to their seats.

As they walked back to the VIP section, Maria said, "I loved that woman's tuxedo."

"She has the build to carry it off," Jordi said. "I should have asked where she got it. It would look good on me, don't you think?"

"Almost as good," Maria replied.

Reimi seemed to think so, Celeste thought with satisfaction. She made a note to tell Maji. Hopefully she'd get to see her backstage after the show and introduce her to Jordi and Maria.

❖

Maji watched Celeste and Erlea's friends resettle into their seats. In the next box up, she spotted Dr. Lyttleton and his very young petite blond wife. Even if it meant waiting, or learning to live with an ugly souvenir on her shoulder, she was not giving him her money.

"Aguilar's guy is out, ours is in place," Dave said through her earpiece.

"I hope you got somebody really good," Maji said. "There's people at home who need me back in one piece."

"And ye shall be delivered, Rios," Dave said. "We got you Taylor. He volunteered."

Maji let out a sigh of relief. Tom had made it through Fallujah with barely a scratch. He was not only like a brother to her, but he was also the best sniper she'd ever known. If she had to get shot very precisely while in motion in the air, he was her top choice. "Hallelujah."

"Glad to bear some good news," Dave said with a smile in his voice. "Enjoy the show."

The crowd roared as the house lights went down for the second half of the concert. Erlea strutted onto the stage, belting out one of her top-grossing songs. Hands reached up toward her as she bounced down the catwalk, flinging sweat from her hair. Solo, she ruled the stage. And then the dancers came out and she shared the glory, syncing with them and the aerialists overhead.

Maji watched the second half from her spot in the wings, obscured from the crowd and dressed in Erlea's finale costume. During the song before the finale, she pulled the harness on and checked the calibration. If Tom missed his target on her back, she wouldn't be around to care. But it would gut him. And everyone at home had too much pain already. She double-checked everything before announcing into her comm, "Rigged up and ready to roll."

"If you need to sing along, don't worry, your mic's not live," Dave said. "But remember I can hear you, so take pity."

"Fuck you, Brown."

"Now I know you're ready," Dave replied. "Erlea's set on vocals."

And the rifle's in Tom's hands, Maji reassured herself. "Rios out."

When the big finale arrived, Erlea stepped out in the costume matching Maji's and danced and sang through the first three verses as planned. Then she left her backup dancers and stepped into the wings still singing, just long enough for Nigel to think she was harnessing up. She gave Maji a kiss on the cheek, looking worried.

Maji flashed her a grin and stepped out to the roar of the crowd and the glare of lights. As the final verse kicked in, she sang along. It helped keep her in sync, made her feel connected to Erlea as the crowd watched their idol. With a silent prayer, she lined up the run to the wall. *Just play a perfect game, Rios.*

As she ran through the air toward the outstretched arms in the window and the wall tilted away, Maji cleared her mind. Then she felt the bungee catch and took a breath just as the bullet slammed into her back. The shove from the impact met the backward pull of the bungee, and she dropped to the stage several feet short of the normally rehearsed landing point.

The dancers swarmed over to her, abandoning their elegant moves as the curtain fell prematurely. Maji struggled to breathe, aware of the band finishing the song without Erlea's vocals as several pairs of feet ran toward her. Dave scooped her up and carried her off the stage as Alejandro used the PA system to ask the audience to remain seated.

"Technical difficulties my ass," Maji gasped as the air finally returned to her lungs.

Celeste stood. Why had Erlea fallen like that? She had rehearsed so relentlessly. No, something was terribly wrong. "I have to go," she said, climbing over Jordi and Maria to reach the aisle. She pushed her way through the other concertgoers who were beginning to mill about, restless.

"Just a few more minutes, ladies and gentlemen," Alejandro announced, first in Spanish, then English, and finally in German.

Celeste reached the stage, where a line of security posted up to keep fans from rushing over the top. "I'm a doctor!" Celeste yelled, waving frantically. They ignored her. She spotted Santxo and called his name. He motioned the guard nearest her to help her up.

Celeste scrambled onto the stage with his help, then ran for the curtain. She batted her way frantically through the heavy velvet. And there, calmly tuning a guitar, was Erlea.

"I told her it would scare you," Erlea said quietly. "I'm so sorry."

"Oh my God," Celeste said, grabbing Erlea by the collar and kissing her face all over. "I thought they'd shot you for real this time."

Erlea hushed her with a kiss. She was most definitely alive, and unhurt. Salty with sweat, and very warm.

"Two minutes," Alejandro said. "Please come with me, Doctor, unless you want to be in the show."

Erlea let her go. "I'll explain everything later. Wait in the wings?"

Celeste let Alejandro lead her into the shadows and to a chair. He stood by her side, calling commands to the crew. The crowd grew quiet, then cheered and stomped as the curtain rose again. When Erlea, alone on a stool in the spotlight, began to play her acoustic guitar, the rowdy audience hushed.

Tears rolled down Celeste's face as she listened to the cat song in its entirety for the first time. It could be about Athena. But Celeste wondered how many women listening out there in the dark felt, like her, that Erlea was singing about them. And that someone special understood them so well, and loved them in all their wildness.

❖

"Sorry about the ribs," Tom said, holding Maji's hand as she lay in the hospital bed.

Damn it was good to see him. "Stop, *akhi*." He blushed when she called him brother. "They're only hairline fractures. I'll take it easy a few weeks, be good as new."

"You better, or those little girls will kick your ass," Dave said. He looked to Tom. "She's using her leave to teach teens self-defense at some summer camp."

"What do you know about that?" Maji asked. Only Hannah could have told him.

Dave smiled. "I'll let you know the minute you can call home. But I got clearance to tell you to stay put, take care of what you came here to do. Doctor's orders."

Ava? "Orders—or last wishes?"

"Same, same. Point is, you heal up right. We're almost done here, but there's plenty waiting for you when you're recouped."

"What are you wrapping up?" Tom asked. "I need to drop Echeverra in Bilbao and meet my team to round up our HVTs in the Nuvoletta." He smiled at Maji. "Then I'm taking an actual break like you. Visiting family in Philly, not teaching any little future operators. My sisters may kick my ass, though. They think I avoid going home. Course, they might be right."

Maji started to laugh, then stopped with a gasp when the pain hit her. "Don't do that."

Tom gave her a sorry-not-sorry look. "Back to you, Dave."

"You would have laughed if you'd heard Nigel on the phone with Aguilar. He was furious Erlea survived. Good thing he's in custody—for his own safety."

"Hilarious," Maji said. "I think the meds are kicking in. Why did they give me so much?"

"Face it, Rios," Tom said with affection. "You're just a lightweight."

❖

Maji woke herself yelling. She searched Tom's face in the half-light as he tried to calm her.

"Jesus, it hurts," she said.

He nodded. "Should I call a nurse?"

"No. I'm okay." Her back stopped spasming as she breathed shallowly. "Okay. I was dreaming. About Fallujah."

Tom looked worried, but he didn't interrupt.

"It was different than usual. This time I ran, and instead of picking up the AK, I started scooping up children. One after another, picking them up and carrying them, trying to get them out with me." She stared at him. "I'm rewriting the narrative. What I wish I'd done."

"Rios," he said, giving her hand a gentle squeeze, "that's not so far off. You saved a bunch of people by taking Mashriki down. Women, kids. Maybe your brain's letting you finally see the good side, take credit where credit's due."

"I don't want credit. I just want my life back. The one where I'm the good guy."

Tom took her hand. "What we went through, you're never the

same again. You just go forward, do a little good where you can. Only thing you can do. Right?"

That didn't seem like enough, but Maji didn't have the strength to argue. "How's Erlea?"

"Healthy and happy. She and that pretty Frenchwoman wanted to come see you."

"Maybe tomorrow."

"Well, I'm prepping to leave with Echeverra. Can he come in for a minute?"

"Sure."

Arturo Echeverra sat shyly by her bedside, hands in his lap. "You saved my daughter's life. I wanted to thank you, and to let you to know that I will testify against the Nuvoletta."

"Will you go back into hiding then?" Maji hated to think of Erlea losing him twice.

"No. Once the peace talks are concluded, if the Nuvoletta wants to get me they will know where I am. Hiding would only endanger my family, and I will not do that. But for the sins I committed to buy their help, I must atone. I spent many years in prayer, in a monastery not unlike the Real Cartuja. But repentance is not atonement. To restore harmony, I must take actions that help others. Even if I cannot undo the harm I did in the past."

Maji thought of the lives she'd destroyed in a few minutes of unbridled fury in Fallujah, and of the ones she had helped preserve here. "How do you know when it's safe to forgive yourself?"

"Myself, I don't seek absolution. I suppose the will to go forward is forgiveness enough."

"That was amazing," Maria said as she snagged a glass of champagne from a passing waiter's tray. "But why did the curtain stay down so long? What was the technical difficulty?"

Erlea saw that Roger was waiting to hear as well. And Celeste, who knew Maji was hospitalized, but not why. She took her hand. "The difficulty was that I didn't die. It seems Nigel was trying to kill me."

"Never trusted him," Roger said. "Not since Santiago."

"Maji," Celeste exclaimed. "Her double," she explained to Maria. "That was her up there, standing in."

Erlea nodded. "She and Dave knew about the plan, but they didn't tell me until a few hours ago. Maji risked her life standing in for me. Just a fractured rib, thank God."

"I missed all the excitement," Roger muttered. "And the chief asshat, as Maji calls him?"

Erlea smiled. "Arrested. They have all kinds of evidence that he planned to cash in on my death, like he did with Santiago. No wonder I couldn't get him to nail down the tour details." She shook her head. "I'm going to need a new manager."

"Is that why Claudia Sandoval is here?" Roger asked.

Erlea looked in the direction he pointed and saw Imane deep in conversation with the top woman in music management. "I think I need to go do some business." She felt Celeste squeeze her hand and let it go.

"I'll be here," Celeste assured her. "Go get your new life started. Ask for what you really want. If she's the right one, she'll say yes."

Erlea kissed her on the cheek and whispered, "Are we still talking about cats?"

Celeste just laughed and pushed her toward Imane and Claudia, who smiled at her from across the room.

❖

Celeste turned down Jordi's offer of another glass of champagne. "I'm drowsy already, thanks. And I told Erlea I would wait here."

"We're turning in, too," Roger said a few minutes after Jordi and Maria departed for their hotel room. "You all right with the dregs of the after-party?"

The crew, band, and dancers had almost all left, Celeste noted. "Who are all these people?"

"Glitterati and hangers-on," Roger replied. "And VIP journalists. Erlea won't want to chat any of them up, and now that Nigel's gone, she doesn't have to. Hold on," he said, pulling his phone out and texting someone. He read the reply silently and looked up grinning. "Imane'll get you into herself's room."

"I feel a conspiracy at work," Celeste said, knowing she was blushing. But she didn't argue.

Just as she was drowsing off, the balcony door slid open. "So that's where you are," Erlea said. "Sorry to keep you waiting. I have a great contract with my dream manager, but…I'm sorry I missed any time with you."

"I said I would wait." Celeste stood up and stretched.

"You could have taken my bed. You do in Barcelona," Erlea joked.

"Well, you're not sleeping there. So that's different."

Erlea came close and tucked Celeste's hair behind her ear, giving her a look that made her quiver. "I should hope so." She stepped away abruptly, looking toward the kitchenette. "Sorry. You probably came to talk. Tea?"

"No," Celeste said, wanting to reach out and draw Erlea close. "Not what I had in mind. But if you're worn-out, I can see you in the morning."

Erlea shook her head. "I want you to stay. But if we're making a leap together, we have to go to your room. Mine is bugged." She laughed. "According to my father, who may be paranoid after so many years in hiding. But I really don't want an audience anymore tonight."

That made it a little easier to resist touching Erlea. A little. "Oh. But I am on Maji's boat. And you can't go out in public, can you?"

Erlea shrugged. "I'd rather not have you splashed all over the tabloids. But I have an idea." She took a big breath and said loudly, "Tell Maji we took her friend's moto to the boat." She grinned at Celeste. "There. I feel like an idiot, but Maji and Dave won't worry now."

Celeste climbed off the back of the bike, unwrapping her arms and legs from around Erlea. No ride alone on the streets of Barcelona had even been such sweet torture. Erlea flipped the helmet's windscreen up. "It's so nice out. Could we walk on the beach?" Erlea waited while Celeste took off her helmet, looked around the quiet marina, and peered down the unlit beach. "Unless you don't want to. If you don't feel safe, never mind."

Celeste smiled at her. "No, I was thinking of your privacy. Is there a hat in there at least, to cover your hair?"

Erlea popped the seat open and rummaged through the compartment, pulling out a bag and handing it to Celeste. "Here." She pulled out the cap underneath. "This will do."

As Erlea tucked her hair under the casino cap, Celeste opened the bag and grinned. She pulled out two dildos, then dropped them back into the bag.

"Not mine," Erlea sputtered. "I wouldn't presume. I didn't know they were there, really."

Celeste cut her off with a wave of her hand, laughing. "Not first date material. But I know the moto's owner. And believe me, she's going to want these back."

Erlea offered her arm and they walked down off the pavement onto the cool damp sand. They left the last pool of light and sat shoulder to shoulder on a lounge chair in the dark to take off their shoes. "Will these be safe here?" Erlea asked.

"From the surf, at least. All these chairs and umbrellas get rented out to holidaymakers in the daylight."

Erlea rolled up her jeans and took Celeste's hand. "Then we'd better collect them before dawn." She felt herself blush, grateful for the darkness. "Not that we're staying out all night, or anything. Can we talk about that?"

"We can talk about anything you like," Celeste said, leading her by the hand to the edge of the water. "I love the sound and smell of the ocean," she added as they walked in the cool damp sand, cold water brushing their ankles.

Erlea breathed deeply, taking in the lights twinkling along the crescent edges of Alcúdia bay. With just the moon for light, it felt like they had the whole world to themselves. "So do I. And twice as much with you." She stroked the back of Celeste's hand with her thumb.

Celeste shivered.

"Are you cold?" Erlea asked.

"No," Celeste said, stopping and turning toward her. "It's your touch. I love your hands. Why aren't they touching me all over?"

Why wasn't she? Now she couldn't think of anything else. But... "I just don't want to do anything that you don't want me to. Ever. I don't want to hurt you."

"Oh, Beatriz," Celeste sighed, taking Erlea's face between her hands. "You are so sweet."

They kissed until standing became a frustration. Celeste led her up to the rows of empty lounge chairs and pushed her back toward one until she sat with a thump, pulling Celeste down on top of her. "I love kissing you," Erlea told her. "If that's all you wanted, it would be enough."

"It's not nearly all I want," Celeste said, facing Erlea, feet in the sand on either side of the chair. She leaned in and Erlea felt her undulate against her thigh as they explored each other's mouths and necks. Erlea slid the side zipper of Celeste's dress down, slipping a hand inside to caress her torso, fingertips just grazing the curve of one breast. "Is this all right?"

Celeste moaned and kissed her harder, pressing into her thigh with more urgency. Erlea slid her free hand under the hem of the skirt, reveling in the silkiness of Celeste's thigh.

"Yes," Celeste sighed. It was the sexiest sound ever. "We need to go back," Celeste whispered in her ear. "I need you naked and in private."

Erlea felt herself clench with need. "Anything you want. And nothing you don't."

Celeste slid off her, straightening her skirt and zipping back up. She offered Erlea a hand up and didn't let go when they were both standing again. "I promise to tell you what I do and don't like. I love that you care."

Erlea wanted to say *I love you*. But it was too soon. Instead she said, "I do. Care. But, also, nothing in the world is so sexy as hearing you say *yes* like you do. It melts me and lights me on fire at the same time."

"Come on," Celeste said and took her hand, starting to run down the dark beach.

Erlea pulled her to a halt as they reached the last lounge chairs. "Our shoes."

"Oh, right."

Erlea laughed and followed the sway of Celeste's hips back into the light of the boardwalk. She barely felt the hard pavement under her sandy toes.

CHAPTER TWENTY-ONE

Celeste lay on her side in the V-berth, her head propped on her hand. Beatriz looked so peaceful asleep, her lively brown eyes closed and her red hair splayed across the pillow. She wanted to make coffee, but her beautiful songwriter had to be exhausted. After the performance, and negotiating a new contract, and...making love for hours. That was the right word for it, too. What a different experience, to explore and play and let go with someone she trusted. Celeste sighed with pleasure.

"Morning?" Beatriz croaked, opening one eye a crack. At the sight of Celeste, she smiled luxuriantly. "The best morning ever."

"I was thinking it would be better with coffee, but I didn't want to wake you." Celeste brushed a swath of hair off Beatriz's face and got a purr in response. "You have another show tonight and so little rest to sustain you."

"I don't care. I want to stay here all day with you." Both eyes blinked open. "I mean, if you want to."

Celeste chuckled. "You are allowed to ask for what you want, you know. Turns out it's really fun." She warmed to the memory. "But I am going to feed you and send you back to the hotel for a few hours' sound sleep. Doctor's orders, Beatriz."

"Better move quick then, because I feel more kissing coming on," she replied. "And don't say my name like that if you expect me to leave your bed."

"Oh. Is it okay to call you Beatriz? Should I stop?"

"Never stop. Just know it gives me all kinds of kissy feelings to hear you say it."

Safely dressed and separated by the dinette table, Celeste told her, "I'm going to visit Maji while you rest. Tomorrow I have to fly back to Barcelona."

"See if you can get her to go with you. If you don't mind sharing my apartment."

"As long as I get to keep your bed," Celeste joked. "Thank you. Now that you are safe, I think she might need a friend even more. And perhaps she will let us in a little bit."

"Show me the balcony again," Erlea requested. These video chats with Celeste made her feel not so far from home after all, seeing her own things and the woman who had claimed her heart among them. But today she had an ulterior motive.

"What is this?" Celeste said as she reached the balcony and found Jordi and Maria waiting just over the railing with air tickets and VIP concert seats for two. "Ooh, Erlea—she's the hottest thing right now. All her shows are selling out. Thank you, Beatriz."

Celeste accepted the tickets, let Jordi and Maria say their hellos, and took the view back inside. "These are right before Maji flies out. How did you know?"

"I'm a rock star." Erlea shrugged. "I got myself an assistant to do research, book flights, order me healthy food…She's very nice, really. And I think she's sweet on Alejandro."

Celeste laughed her wonderful laugh. "Well, it's a very thoughtful surprise. Maji's doing so much better these past few weeks. Her rib is healed and her shoulder is spotless. She's gotten out to the beach and all the Modernismo sites, and she had a long talk with her friend Bubbles. I expect she'll enjoy a chance to make her good-byes before she heads home."

"It's not much, but how do you repay someone who saved your life?" Erlea soaked in the sight of Celeste on the little screen, tucking her hair behind her ear. "Also, I miss you. Can you take the time away? I didn't know when you had clients scheduled."

"For you, I will rearrange a few appointments. I miss you, too. Any word on Claudia's plan for your tour?"

"Actually, we're not scheduling one just yet. The show here is so popular, we're extending, with fewer shows per week. And I'll be home on the off days. We're going to record an album in Barcelona."

"That's wonderful." Celeste's expression shifted from joy to concern. "You'll need your place again. I should have started looking for an apartment."

"Could you wait a little bit?" Erlea asked. "I mean, I know you need your independence, but Athena is very attached to you already. I think she loves you."

Celeste laughed. "Are you sure we're talking about the cat?"

"Yes and no. I want to say I love you, but not just so you'll say it back," Erlea admitted. "I don't want either of us to do something just because we think the other expects it. I really mean it, but I want it to stay special, not so casual it loses all its oomph."

Celeste chuckled. "I feel the seeds of a new song. Okay then, ciao for now. And also, I love you so much it scares me a little. I didn't know I could feel so much joy and so much peace at the same time."

"I know just what you mean. All my new songs are terrible, sappy things that I have to totally rewrite." Erlea smiled. "And none of them are about cats. Or shoes."

❖

Maji watched Celeste throughout the acoustic encore, the cat song. The tears on her face were happy ones. She and Erlea were clearly in love, their relationship so new yet on very solid footing. "That song's not about Athena, is it?"

Celeste wiped her cheeks and smiled. "Of course it is. And about wild things like you, too."

"Alejandro's made a couple nice changes in the show," Maji commented. "Course, I like it much better from up here than down on stage."

"I can't wait to get down there, myself," Celeste said, then blushed.

Maji chuckled. "I've been meaning to talk to you about your Beatriz addiction." At Celeste's affronted look, she laughed outright. "Come on, let's go use our backstage passes."

In the wings, Celeste seemed surprised when Maji headed for the back corridor. "You will meet up with us as planned, won't you? One last visit for the four of us on the balcony."

"Half an hour, I promise. I won't make Imane track me down—and I know she would." She paused. "Besides, I need to make sure and thank each of you."

"For what?" Celeste asked.

"For being there when I needed you. For getting me to the other side in one piece."

Maji waltzed into the do shop without knocking and started to back out when she found Roger and Alvaro making out.

"Hold up," Roger said, breaking away from the burly drummer.

Maji gave him a hug and handed him the gift card.

"What's this, then?" Roger asked.

"Dinner for two at Cuina Mallorquina," Maji said. "You won the bet."

"And you saved herself's life, and all our jobs to boot," Roger said. "Why don't you take that luscious dealer who has the hots for you?"

"Reimi has somebody else now. A much better fit for her than I could ever be."

"Sorry, love," Roger said. "But maybe it's for the best."

"Definitely. I played her table tonight. Staked a hundred euros on one hand, got double aces, split, and doubled down."

"And you won, I hope?"

"I always beat the house," Maji said. "Thanks for everything, mate."

Roger looked so sad it was almost comical. "Don't go without some token. What about all those outfits you wore as Erlea's double? Now that Nico's gone, nobody here would begrudge you."

"No. Not my style. No offense to Erlea, but I'd rather be me."

"Seriously? Money, fame, the lovely doctor on your arm. Most people would trade with her in a blink," Roger said. "You must really like being you. Cheers."

"It's the hardest role I've ever played," Maji admitted. "But I'm starting to get the hang of it again."

About the Author

MB Austin, a mild-mannered civil servant by day, loves to play with real people in the dojo and imaginary ones in her stories. She also enjoys cooking, eating, reading, dancing, and laughing as much as possible.

Her Maji Rios novels are inspired by real people, in and out of uniform, who work to make their communities and the world safer for all. And by the people who feed them.

MB lives with her fabulous wife in Seattle, an excellent town for coffee-fueled writers who don't need too much sun.

Books Available From Bold Strokes Books

Blood of the Pack by Jenny Frame. When Alpha of the Scottish pack Kenrick Wulver visits the Wolfgangs, she falls for Zaria Lupa, a wolf on the run. (978-1-63555-431-1)

Cause of Death by Sheri Lewis Wohl. Medical student Vi Akiak and K9 Search and Rescue officer Kate Renard must work together to find a killer before they end up the next targets. In the race for survival, they discover that love may be the biggest risk of all. (978-1-63555-441-0)

Chasing Sunset by Missouri Vaun. Hijinks and mishaps ensue as Iris and Finn set off on a road trip adventure, chasing the sunset, and falling in love along the way. (978-1-63555-454-0)

Double Down by MB Austin. When an unlikely friendship with Spanish pop star Erlea turns deeper, Celeste, in-house physician for the hotel hosting Erlea's show, has a choice to make—run or double down on love. (978-1-63555-423-6)

Party of Three by Sandy Lowe. Three friends are in for a wild night at billionaire heiress Eleanor McGregor's twenty-fifth birthday party. Love, lust, and doing the right thing, even when it hurts, turn the evening into one that will change their lives forever. (978-1-63555-246-1)

Sit. Stay. Love. by Karis Walsh. City girl Alana Brendt and country vet Tegan Evans both know they don't belong together. Only problem is, they're falling in love. (978-1-63555-439-7)

Where the Lies Hide by Renee Roman. As P.I. Camdyn Stark gets closer to solving the case, will her dark secrets and the lies she's buried jeopardize her future with the quietly beautiful Sarah Peters? (978-1-63555-371-0)

Beautiful Dreamer by Melissa Brayden. With love on the line, can Devyn Winters find it in her heart to stay in the small town of Dreamer's Bay, the one place she swore she'd never remain? (978-1-63555-305-5)

Create a Life to Love by Erin Zak. When sixteen-year-old Beth shows up at her birth mother's door, three lives will change forever. (978-1-63555-425-0)